Fleeing from Danger
Jessica West

Joyful Books Press

Fleeing from Danger, Jessica West

Fleeing from Danger

PUBLISHER'S NOTE: This is a work of fiction. Names, characters, businesses, places, events, locales, and incidents are the products of the author's imagination or used in a fictitious manner. Any resemblance to actual persons, living or dead, or actual events is purely coincidental.

Copyright © 2024 by Joyful Books Press
All rights reserved. This book or any portion thereof may not be reproduced or used in any manner whatsoever without the express written permission of the publisher except for the use of brief quotations in a book review.

Printed in the United States of America

First Printing, 2024

ISBN- 978-1-7349363-7-7

Fleeing from Danger, Jessica West

Special Thanks:

God- I love You. Thank You for blessing me with the best family ever.

Robert- I love you. I'm thankful for the life we share.

Abby, Jojo, Samuel, Matthew, Timothy, Gideon, Enoch, and Judah- Y'all are awesome. I love y'all.

Mom- You're the best.

Teresa Kirkpatrick- Thanks for all your help. I appreciate it.

Matthew 11:28

"Come unto me, all ye that labour and are heavy laden, and I will give you rest."

Chapter One

Keep moving. Lily glanced behind her as she took a deep breath, willing her pulse to slow down. She almost fell into a tray of surgical tools, cringing as the metal clanged to the tiled floor. Lily peered around the deserted hospital floor. Nothing seemed amiss, but her gut screamed of impending danger. The hairs on the back of her neck stood on edge as she leaned over, catching her breath.

How did the bad guys find her so soon? Days ago, her boring life was enough to put anyone to sleep. But everything changed when she walked into her brother's apartment, finding him half-dead from a gunshot wound. She frantically tried saving his life. She hadn't gone to medical school most of her adult life to lose her only family to a bullet. Her efforts were useless. The bullet pierced through his chest and he lost too much blood. She wasn't a miracle worker, but neither was God. As a little girl, she begged God to spare her mother's life, but cancer snatched her life away. No, God was definitely not a miracle worker.

Lily's fingers trembled as her brother's hushed words popped into her mind. *I'm not who you think I am. I'm sorry, Lilian. I thought I had more time.* She wrapped her arms around his blood-stained t-shirt and brushed a kiss on his pale cheek. *You're not safe. Get as far away from here as you can.* And then violence had claimed another victim, leaving her alone in this big world.

Footsteps echoed down the hall behind her. An ominous stillness engulfed her as she froze in place. What was she supposed to do? There weren't many hiding spots on the ICU floor. The footsteps stopped and the only sound she heard was a rhythmic beeping of a patient's heartbeat.

Get a grip, Lily. There's no one after you. She pulled a strand of her charcoal black hair off of her olive-tinted face. Lily adjusted the white coat around her shoulders and breathed a sigh of relief. Her father always warned her about reading too many mystery books. Yet, she couldn't put the intriguing books away. Her favorite pastime turned her into a paranoid basket case. No wonder she was still single at twenty-seven. Her over-imaginative imagination scared men away.

Lily grabbed a file from the back of the door and mumbled under her breath. The intensive care unit boasted of heartache and pain, but she loved watching modern medicine heal the sickest of patients. It satisfied her soul, knowing she could play a part in reuniting love ones. When their conditions seeped the life out of them, it reminded her of how much God didn't really care. That His limited power reserved for those that were worthy, maybe. All she knew was that God never came through for her. Her empty life proved that theory.

Lily set the file down and slid her cellphone out of her pocket. *Two a.m. No wonder the place felt like a graveyard. Five more hours and my shift will be over. I can go home, watching pathetic Christmas movies and hiding from reality; my brother's dead and I'm so alone. I don't even own a cat.*

As she rounded the corner, she collided with an unexpected obstacle—a solid chest. She could feel the pressure of hands tightening around her arms, sending a shiver down her spine, as the masked figure leaned closer and whispered in her ear.

"I wondered when we would finally meet." His raspy breath made her stomach curl with nausea.

"Let go of me." As Lily tried to yank her arm away, she could feel the guy's fingers digging into her skin. No use. His strength overpowered her by ten. She didn't build muscles by reading mystery novels or watching Christmas movies.

"I think we need to get acquainted." He tugged her arm, the urgency in his touch obvious as he pulled her towards the stairs. As she kicked her legs and flailed her arms, her heart pounded with fear and adrenaline. Lily wasn't strong, but that didn't mean she couldn't attempt to fight.

"Your brother never mentioned how ornery you were." His deep chuckle sent electricity pulsing through her body.

"How'd you know Jason?" She stopped fighting, only for a second. Was this guy a friend or a foe? Like friends really dressed in concealed masks and tried abducting innocent people. Definitely not her friend or Jason's either.

"We go way back." He clutched the side of her arm so tight, numbness radiated down her forearm. "Now, shut up!"

"Where are you taking me?" Lily's words were barely audible. She couldn't let this man abduct her out of the hospital. Once he did, her chances of survival were slim.

"Your brother double-crossed the boss." He pulled a long knife out of his pocket. The sharp blade piercing the skin across her cheek. Blood slid down her face. "Give me what's mine and you live. Don't and you die. It's simple."

Her sporadic heart rate quickened. Sweet popped off her black brow as butterflies floated around in her stomach. *Calm down, Lily. Now is not the time to have a panic attack. You're a doctor, don't give in to anxiety.*

"I have nothing of his." She took a calming breath, trying to still her erratic emotions.

"Want to die among your patients?" His words felt like ice on a chilly day. He lowered the knife for half a second and glanced around the empty halls.

It's now or never. She hit her elbow into the guy's stomach, catching him off guard. He winced in pain and cursed, his grip loosening from the impact. Lily sprinted down the hall, her heart pounding in her ears as she strained to catch any sound of her captor's pursuit. Without a second thought, she slipped into the closest door and leaned against the wall. No sounds or he would find her. She shut her eyes tightly, desperately trying to steady her trembling hands. The touch of hands on the top of her shoulders sent a wave of fear through her body. Lily's piercing scream echoed through the sterile ICU room, muffled by a hand that suddenly covered her mouth.

"Shh." The voice sounded familiar. How had the bad guy found her already?

She yanked on the hand covering her mouth. Lily's heart beat faster than before. She almost escaped. She opened her eyes and stared into the bluest eyes she had ever seen. His eyes were honest looking, full of compassion and gentle. No way was he working with the other guy. She watched as the man tugged on his doctor's coat, revealing his name tag. *Stephen Smith.* Memories of her spying on the doctor from afar made her cheeks redden. Up close, his deep blue eyes held a golden speckle. Unique was an understatement. Stephen Smith was a handsome man.

"Your name's Lily Walsh, right?" He stepped to the door and clicked the lock. Whoever was out there wouldn't get past the handsome doctor. He looked like he could handle himself in a fight. His muscles protruded from the white jacket.

Lily shook her head. She couldn't speak from fear of sounding like a silly schoolgirl.

"Is someone after you?" His voice held a calmness that soothed her tempestuous heart.

She nodded her head again. What was wrong with her, besides almost getting abducted? Jason would have loved to see the day that she actually stopped talking. He always accused her of never knowing when to be quiet. Thoughts of her brother danced in her mind, causing tears to slide down her face.

Stephen touched the top of her face in a reassuring gesture. "You're going to be fine. You have a slight cut on your cheek, but it's not deep, so no stitches."

Lily didn't speak. No words would come out. Standing there, she found herself lost in the doctor's mesmerizing eyes, unable to look away.

"When I get back, I want to hear your voice." A soft smile slide across his face. He was downright gorgeous, and his smile took her breath away.

Lily shook her head and frowned. Now was not the time to gawk at her rescuer.

Stephen casually rolled up his pants leg, revealing a concealed ankle holster from which he smoothly retrieved a small gun. With a giant stride, he approached the door, his face adopting a hardened look. "The joys of working in the ER. Never know what will happen."

She inched closer to him and grabbed the edges of his jacket. Her fingers clung to the cotton texture. "Y-you can't go out there."

"I'm touched by your concern, but no thug is going to make me cower in an empty ICU room." He pried her hand off his jacket, the sound of fabric stretching and snapping filling the air. "Lock the door and don't open it unless you know it's me."

Before she could respond, he bolted out of the door, leaving her heart pounding and hands shaking.

****

Stephen held the gun close to his chest. The metallic feeling sent warmth pulsing through his body. He never left home without it. His father, ex-Marine, hammered gun safety into him from a young age. He learned to shoot before he could ride a bike without training wheels. Stephen glanced at a nurse sitting behind an oblong desk.

"Call security." The silver-haired woman's eyes bulged like golf balls as she glared at his gun, fear obvious in her expression. He didn't have time to explain. The thug was more than likely gone, but he wouldn't take any chances.

Stephen rounded the corner, heart pumping with adrenaline. He was ready for a fight. He'd teach the perp a lesson about traumatizing beautiful women. Fear clawed at her so much she couldn't even talk. He had seen it all before as memories of his sister's abduction swirled into his mind. Three years. It had really been that long ago. Now, she was married to his best bud, the town's only detective, and raising two daughters and twin boys. Life had a way of moving on, only it seemed to move on without him. Besides spending time with his family, he had no social life. Being the town's most eligible bachelor had its benefits, but he had no time for meaningless dates. He wanted to settle down one day, but God would have to drop the woman into his life, because work took top place in his life besides God.

The hollow echo of footsteps reverberating through the empty hall made him instinctively reach for the gun's trigger. In a split second, life could be over. He wasn't ready to die, and he wouldn't take the chance. Stephen knew too well how fleeting life was. As an ER doctor, he witnessed last breaths too often. It never got easier, but God had reasons for not sparing the lives of his patients. Stephen had to trust God. Without God, he'd go insane.

"Dr. Smith?" The white walls amplified the deep voice, making it resonate throughout the hall.

Stephen turned around and faced a security guard, medium height, fit, small scar on his cheek. He didn't look familiar, but security changed as often as he changed his clothes. He prided himself on knowing the staff at the small-town hospital he worked at since his residency. But people slipped in and out, and he was only one guy.

"You are?" Stephen stared at a random name tag, *Jay Walker. I know Jay, and this guy was definitely not the fifty-year-old he waved to every morning when he clocked off duty.*

"New hire. My first day is today." He shifted his arms uncomfortably. "I heard there's a commotion going on here."

Stephen's gut screamed at him as he lowered his head and glared into the icy black eyes of the security guard. He could easily take this guy out, but his brother-in-law would not take too kindly to him picking a fight with a guy just from getting a bad vibe. Actually, Stephen didn't believe in vibes, but he trusted God and the common sense He had given him. Stephen would play along for now, but he wouldn't let his guard down. He leaned over and slid his gun into the holster. Stephen didn't really need his gun for protection. His dad had taught him how to use his hands as a weapon and take out his opponent. Science taught him where pressure points were to eliminate a foe.

"What happened to Jay? I know that's not your name?" Stephen stepped down the hall at a steady pace, never taking his eyes off the guy.

The guard's face reddened as the long scar on his cheek deepened in noticeability. "He let me borrow his name tag. Mine won't be ready till tomorrow. Jay had an emergency come up, so I'm going solo."

No way would Jay give up his post that easily. Jay, former Navy, put as much dedication in his job as he did when he served our country. Something didn't add up. Stephen grabbed his phone out of his pocket and sent a quick message to the police detective. He could go rogue if he wanted, but his relationship with his family meant more.

"Follow me into this room and I'll explain the situation." Stephen hoped Dr. Walsh hadn't fled the minute he left the room. Fear clouded common sense every time. He didn't know if this guy was a lone attacker, so she wasn't safe. Not that bringing a suspected attacker into the victim's presence was a smart move, either. Paul, his detective brother-in-law, would kick him for that later.

"Did the perp harm the female?" The guard followed Stephen into the room. In the chair, Dr. Walsh slouched, her black hair creating a curtain that shielded her face from view. Was she sleeping?

"How'd you know the victim was a female?" Stephen stepped to her side and gently nudged her arm. Her glassy eyes popped open as she almost tumbled sideways out of her chair.

"Women are easier targets, Dr. Smith." He yanked a notepad out of his pocket and stood in front of Lily. "Ma'am, I'm the security guard, Jay Walker. What happened?"

Lily's eyes twitched as she stared at the guard. Did she recognize him? Stephen crouched beside her chair and reached for her hand, trying to calm her nerves. He wouldn't let this guy touch her. One slipup and he'd take the guard down.

****

Lily opened her mouth to speak, but nothing came out. Those eyes. The piercing blackness sent shivers through her body. The security guard looked too familiar. Only the guy who attacked her didn't have a scar on his cheek. But he was wearing a mask that concealed his face. His eyes, an endless abyss of hate, flashed into her mind. It had to be the same guy. Her protector, Dr. Smith, led the thug right to her. Lily took a deep breath, trying to still her nerves. The guard didn't know she was on to his charades. She needed to act ignorant in order to save her life. Easier said than done. Was this the guy who had killed her brother? As her hands trembled, she could feel sweat dripping down her face in small beads. Anxiety. Her therapist claimed it was normal for victims of heinous crimes to experience panic attacks. The exercises never stopped the condition. Her anxiety lurked in her inner being, waiting to destroy her calm.

"Ma'am?" The guard took a step closer to her chair. The smell of tobacco wafted through her nostrils, making her gag. "I think you should come with me. The doctor is clearly making you nervous."

Dr. Smith stood to his full height, towering over the guard. He looked hard and would intimidate her if she had nefarious intentions. "She stays with me." He crossed his arms over his chest as his muscles bulged from his coat.

"I have jurisdiction here, and the right to apprehend a witness." He made a grab for Lily's arm, but Stephen's swift action resulted in the guard's fingers being slapped away.

Maybe she was mistaken about the doctor and he was on to the charades the whole time.

"Stand down, doctor or I will arrest you." The guard's forehead furrowed with hard lines as he tightly gripped his pocket.

"You're not even a security guard." Stephen positioned his body in front of Lily. His eyes were as cold as steel, tempting the thug to touch Lily. "The police are on their way."

With a chilling intent, the thug withdrew a knife from his pocket, the very one he had wielded against Lily. The sounds of her gasps filled the small room, which seemed to grow louder with each passing moment. Her knee felt the gentle brush of Stephen's leg as he stepped closer to her. The heat, like a warm embrace, stilled her fear. She took comfort in knowing the sight of the metal knife didn't faze the doctor.

"Let me take the girl and no one gets hurt." He tried reaching around Stephen, but his solid frame blocked the way. No way was the thug getting past the doctor without getting put in the ER first.

"Drop the knife." Stephen barked out the order as his deep voice bounced off the white walls.

"My boss is more intimidating than you." The guy swung the knife carelessly through the air, not caring who he cut.

Lily's faint cry echoed through the silence, her body freezing in response. If the thug took the doctor out, she'd be alone. She looked around the room for something to use as a weapon. The tiny ICU room, no bigger than a standard bathroom, offered nothing besides a bed and chair. There wasn't even a tv plastered on the white walls. Lily would just have to trust that the doctor was more than capable of taking down a bad guy.

"Last warning." Stephen balled his fist at his side. His white coat looking like it would rip from the movement of his biceps.

The thug took a menacing step towards Stephen, the sharp edge of the blade grazing inches from his face. The doctor grabbed the thug's hand, wincing as the blade grazed the side of his arm, leaving a shallow cut. Blood dripped onto the floor as Stephen kicked the knife under the bed, restraining the thug with his hands behind his back.

"You're bleeding." Lily shook the fear from eyes and stepped into doctor mode. Dr. Smith had saved her life. The least she could do was administer first aid to his gash.

"I'm fine." As the sound of bones popping cut into the air, he tightened his grip on the thug, determined to subdue him.

"My arm. You're breaking it." The guy grunted in pain. "What kind of doctor are you?"

A smile spread across Stephen's ruggedly handsome face. "The kind that stops thugs from harming innocent women."

"I'll press charges." The icy words fell into the air as Stephen loosened his grip, just a little.

Stephen's eyes twinkled with amusement. Even in the face of danger, Lily hadn't seen a man comparable to the doctor. His ocean blue eyes, a window to his heart, deepened as he glanced her way. Her pulse quickened as his gaze rested upon her face. His strength and confident demeanor added to his good looks. Why would a man like him be single? She'd heard the idle gossip from his admirers in the staff room. Each single nurse was determined to win the attractive doctor's heart. She steered clear of office romance or anything that stood in the way of professionalism. Then why was she gawking at his good looks? It was admiration and gratitude for saving her life. Nothing more.

"Doctor Walsh? Did you hear me?" Stephen's voice brought her back to reality.

She shook her head and stretched to her feet. His body was inches from her face.

"Reach in my coat pocket and pull out a zip tie." His voice rang with tenderness, yet authority.

"I'm not even curious why you have zip ties in your coat. You're an interesting character, Dr. Smith." She gently explored the inside of his pocket, her hand swiftly retracting from his leg. Heat climbed up her face as she jerked her hand out of his pocket. That brief contact was enough to undo her vow of dating coworkers. What was it about this guy that made her drop her guard and wish for things she couldn't have?

Stephen slid the ties around the thug's wrists and pushed him onto the floor. He straightened his body and gazed into Lily's eyes. "You doing ok, doctor?" A smile teased the corner of his lips.

Lily took a hesitant step back, her heart racing from his overpowering presence, and collapsed into the chair. Stephen, noticing her awkward swooning, kneeled down and gazed deeply into her eyes. Attraction or awareness zapped between them. What was wrong with her? She couldn't be near a handsome man without acting like a clumsy schoolgirl with a crush?

"Careful, doc, or I'll admit you for observation." He winked his eye as the door creaked open. Lily sighed as a much-needed distraction walked into the room. Whatever was happening between her and the charming doctor stopped now.

****

Paul slid his pen and notepad into his jacket as he ran his fingers through his jet-black hair. "I'll let you know if I get any information out of this thug. You know how it goes."

"Unfortunately, I do." Stephen's attention shifted from the detective to Lily, who was having her face checked by a nurse, and he couldn't help but stare. Her black hair kissed the tops of her shoulders as the silky strands rested beyond her collar. Her bright green eyes met his as he breathed back the heart-pounding reaction. Lily Walsh was not only beautiful, but captivating. Why hadn't he noticed her before? She's not really one to blend into the background.

"You listening, man?" A smirk spread across Paul's face as he patted him on the back, displaying his amusement. "Wait until I tell your sister about this."

Stephen shook his head and faced his brother-in-law. "Because she knows about being a victim?"

"That too, but she's been praying a female would catch your attention. And here we are." Paul's dark eyes flashed with amusement. "If you have the same outcome as we did, you'll be married with kids in a year, two tops."

"What? No. I am a bachelor by choice. No green-eyed beauty will change that?"

"Whatever you say, doctor." The sound of Paul's laughter broke through the tense atmosphere of the room.

"How are your houseful of children doing?" Stephen smiled as pictures of his nieces and nephews popped into his mind, little smiling eyes and drooly faces.

Paul stifled a tired yawn, his eyes briefly meeting Stephen's. Amusement filled his glassy eyes. "The twins barely sleep at night. But the newborn phase ends in a blink of an eye."

"I'll stop by soon and visit Belle, my incredibly talented sister." She managed a household with four children under four, and she remained sane.

"I love talking about my family, but this isn't a social call." As his detective persona settled over him, Paul's face took on a steely expression, ready to solve the mystery at hand. "What can you tell me about Lily Walsh?"

Stephen glanced in her direction. The cut on her face resembled an inch scar he proudly wore on his shoulder from dirt-biking. He had accepted a silly dare as a teen to bike up a small mountain on his dirt-bike. Stephen knew the risks, but couldn't turn down a dare. He earned the respect of the student body, but ended up in the ER with a gash that needed stitches. His mind drifted back to the beautiful woman sitting on the other side of the room. Her eyes fluttered open as their gazes met. Warmth pulsed through his body, but he didn't look away. He had plenty of women that tried getting his attention. Why had this green-eyed wonder broken through his defenses?

"You have it bad, bro." As Paul glanced at Stephen, he couldn't resist rolling his eyes at the unmistakable look of infatuation on his face.

Stephen knew his futile attempts wouldn't even matter, so he dropped it. He found the fellow doctor interesting, but he would not get involved any more than he already was. "You asked what I knew about her. She's been working here for six months, maybe. She's quiet and keeps to herself."

"Have you noticed any admirers or enemies from afar?"

"You're looking at that angle?" Stephen let out a yawn. It had been a long shift. The ER hopped with more activity than usual. He didn't know where all the patients were coming from. It had to be half of the population in their small town in Tennessee.

"I'll check into her brother's death. But I need to look at every angle." Paul looked at his watch and frowned. "My new partner should be at the station by now. Call me if anything changes in the case." The fluorescent lights cast a soft glow on Paul's face, accentuating the twinkle in his dark eyes as he stepped to the door. "You're not so entangled in her life or the case that you can't simply walk away. I have an uneasy feeling about things. I'd hate for you to get in the crosshairs of a killer."

"She needs me. I can't walk away until she's safe." Stephen's mind screamed, *run before it's too late*. But his heart thumped louder with every glance he stole her way. As long as Lily needed him, he'd be available.

"I figured, but I had to at least warn you," he said with a hint of concern in his voice. Stephen watched his brother-in-law slip through the partially opened door, his footsteps barely making a sound.

God, I don't know why are paths crossed, but keep her safe from anyone with ill intent.

With each stride, Stephen's long legs effortlessly covered the small room. He reached out and nudged the top of her shoulder, his touch light and comforting. He needed to get her home, where she could rest without the fear of falling out of a chair.

Her eyes darted open. Fear covered her bright eyes as dark circles twirled under her eyelids. Even with a cut and sleep deprived, Stephen had never seen a prettier woman.

"It's me, Stephen. I'm going to take you home." He reached for her arm and slid her tired body off the chair.

"I'd argue, but I don't think I have enough energy to drive home." She rested her head on his shoulder and allowed him to guide for out of the hospital.

Fleeing from Danger, Jessica West

Chapter Two

As the sun rose, it painted the sky with a mesmerizing blend of pink and orange hues, peeking over the mountains in the distance. Lily rested her head on the back of the seat, feeling the soft fabric against her skin, as she took in the familiar scenes. She had moved to East Tennessee from the ocean town of Manteo, North Carolina, six months ago. The beach life had stolen her heart. She loved it. The smell of the fresh ocean air felt like therapy to her broken heart. No one knew her in the town that boasted of tourist and a simpler life. She worked at the local hospital, then soaked up the rays at her favorite spot on the beach.

But running from her past hadn't been her intention. Or was it? The accident. Her father's death. Heartbreak. It felt like a chain pulling her under the ocean, restraining her breathing. Almost sucking the life out of her. The beach was perfect, but even the squishy sand beneath her toes and the feel of the rushing water on her face couldn't erase haunted memories. She almost perfected the specialty of running or hiding from her past. Her estranged brother's desperate plea for reconnection echoed in her mind. Having a four-year advantage in age, he had stepped into the role of a fatherly figure, needing to shield her. Regrettably, she shut him out completely. Memories flooded her mind, each one carrying the sting of past hurts. Jason and their father had such identical features that they could have passed as twins. Seeing Jason reminded her of what she could never have—her parents back.

Jason's guilt trip weighed heavily on her, forcing her to leave behind her peaceful oasis for a small town in Tennessee. Though she had cherished her peace and sanctuary, she couldn't ignore the obligation she had towards Jason, and so she left with a sense of reluctance. Her foolishness had snatched away her parents from them. Allowing her brother back into her life was the smallest act of kindness she could offer, but it held the potential for immense healing.

"Is your place the two-story farmhouse?" Stephen slowed his Chevy down as he glanced at the house numbers.

Lily opened her eyes. She must have dozed off during the fifteen-minute drive from the hospital. She felt a wave of fatigue wash over her body, causing her to shake her head. "Yes."

Stephen pulled his truck into the driveway, his tires crunching on the gravel, and his gaze instinctively shifted towards her. She decorated the walk-around porch with a line of white Christmas lights, creating a festive atmosphere. The lights dangled precariously from the railing, creating an unsettling sight that suggested meddling. Before her shift, the lights were intact and secured to the porch railing.

Mischievous teenagers.

"This is the White's old place." As he grinned, his face, with its creamy white complexion, seemed to glow. "I spent a lot of time out here hunting in the woods and causing havoc with Paul and Joe. Joe moved last year to the mountains and became a park ranger. It's a shame this house sat on the market for eight months. Guess no one wants to move to a rural town like this."

"I'm a transplant. So, I guess some people are moving here." She sat straight in her seat, fishing in her purse for her keychain. Lily gave the doctor a heart-felt look. Maybe this small town had something she couldn't find before—a charming, protective man.

No. She did not need a man to complicate her simple life. Lily had worked hard making a new life from the ashes of the past. A man had no place in the mix.

"I'm not sure what drew you to this town, but I'm definitely not complaining." The touch of his finger on her knuckles sent a mischievous spark through his twinkling eyes. "Maybe God has a sense of humor."

"God?" As she scowled, her brow furrowed, deepening the lines on her forehead. "Did God…" She let out a puff of air and jerked the door open. "Never mind. It's not worth it."

"Don't leave me hanging. Finish your sentence." He leaped out of the truck and jogged to her side, where she leaned against the truck's door, disoriented and dazed.

"If your God is so loving, why did he destroy my life and snatch everyone I loved from me?" Her green eyes burned with fire as she looked away from Stephen. Now was not the time to think about God. Maybe never was a good time. He had failed too many times for her to believe in a fairy tale God who could grant wishes or answer prayers.

"Wow! That's a big accusation, doc." He ran his fingers through his short, brown hair, as a tight smile donned his lips.

"Let's just drop it. You won't be winning me to Jesus, ever." She brushed past him and glanced at the broken light bulbs scattered on her porch.

"Fair enough. But for the record, I wouldn't push Jesus on anyone. I would, however, help you sort through a few misconceptions on God's part." Stephen gripped Lily's arm and swiftly guided her away from the porch. Leaning over, he smoothly drew his gun from the holster and meticulously scanned the porch with unwavering concentration.

"Just so you know, I find this scene odd." She leaned over the bottom step, grazing his shirt with the tip of her finger. Anything to change the subject. She did not want to think about God or His past failures.

"What?" He whispered, taking a step, his shoe crunching over the broken Christmas lights.

"A gun-wielding doctor." She pulled the back of his shirt as silence echoed back. "I should be quiet, but I blab when I'm nervous."

"The element of surprise is a handy weapon." He pulled her close, the heat between them suffocating the lingering chill of the morning. "I think the perp is gone, anyway." He stuck his gun in his waistband.

Lily wiggled out of his arms, letting out a deep breath, stilling her rapid pulse. "So, doc, can you fix the misconceptions swirling through my mind?"

As he turned around, his eyes, the color of a cloudless sky, gleamed with an unidentifiable twinkle. Stephen Smith defined the word good-looking. His broad shoulders, straight posture, kissable lips. Wait! The very idea of growing feelings for him made her stomach churn with unease. A blush rose to her cheeks as a playful smirk danced upon his lips. Could he read her mind? No way, right?

"How about we go inside and discuss this?" He touched the side of her arm, leading her to the door.

"No." In a reflexive motion, she flinched and pulled her arm away from his fingers. He definitely seemed like the good guy, but why did her pulse quicken and butterflies danced in her stomach at his nearness? "I need to know that I can trust you."

Stephen's eyes lit up light the row of Christmas lights before someone crushed them. "Do you think I'm untrustworthy, doc?"

"N-no." She could probably trust him with her life, but her heart was a whole different matter. She could not trust him or any other man, no matter what his mesmerizing blue eyes said.

"I need context." Her treacherous heart beat faster because of his nearness. What was wrong with her? She had spent an undisclosed amount of time with male patients. Some were good-looking, even if they were unconscious. No man, not even Ronald, caused her heart to long for what she vowed to never have—a man, love, happiness.

"Ok." His breath formed a visible cloud of cool, white mist that mingled with the surrounding air.

To say the morning was cold was an understatement. Early December in East Tennessee was way colder than her paradise on the beach. She rubbed her hands over her arms, generating little heat.

Her body instantly relaxed as Stephen's touch on her forearm erased all traces of the chills. "My dad was in the Marines and my two best buds were entering the police academy. I seriously thought about becoming a soldier or a police officer."

"Why didn't you?"

"My sister Belle reminded me that being comfortable with a gun didn't mean I had to make a profession out of it." A smile filled his face at the mention of his sister. Lily's eyes watered. She longed for that connection with another human, but she was utterly alone, without even a pet. "I entered college with enough credits to start my third year. Medicine and the human body thrilled me."

"So, you became a doctor?" Lily interrupted. She loved a good story, but sometimes she'd flip to the end of the book to read the outcome.

"A streak of impatience, Doctor Walsh?" His laughter floated through the icy air.

Lily knew there was more to that story, but wouldn't push him. Not every doctor's story was as easy as hers—Mom died from cancer, she determined to save the world or at least a life, as a doctor. Lily wiggled her fingers, trying to get some feeling in them again. "I'm freezing."

Stephen's arm slid around her shoulder, and she immediately felt the comforting heat radiating from his body. The steady throb of his heart reverberated through her, sending shivers down her arms. She could get used to hearing his heartbeat and feeling his warm touch on her arms.

"Let's get you inside." He tugged on the edge of her jacket, smiling. "If you want to survive the winter, you need a coat that is insulated, to help regulate your body heat." He stepped to the door. As she approached the front door, the sight of the shattered doorknob and knife marks sent a shiver down her spine. "Stay behind me." He barked out the order as his fingers reached for his gun.

****

Stephen stepped into the ransacked-room. The six-foot Christmas tree lay shattered on the hardwood floors, creating a mess of broken glass and pine needles. He tightly gripped Lily's arm, providing a steady anchor as her gasps echoed through the vast room. Her green eyes resembled luscious grass after a spring shower. Sorrow mixed with an unknown emotion burned in her eyes. He shoved the desire to pull her into his arms away. That time would come, but right now, he needed to check the rest of the house.

He stepped around a marron-colored couch, stuffing pulled out of the cushions. Who would destroy someone's property like this? Someone determined to find something, but who? Stephen pulled his cellphone out of his pocket and sent a text to Paul. He would not like him messing up the crime scene.

"How about we go back to my truck until the police show up?" He imagined the perp destroyed the rest of the house, and he wanted to shield her from the devastation.

"Oh, no." Lily's voice trembled as she darted up the stairs. Stephen following behind her.

He could feel irritation coursing through his body as he vigorously pumped his arms, desperately trying to catch up to her. She was faster than she looked. On his days off, he'd spend hours hiking the trails, rock climbing, anything to keep his heart healthy and his body fit. But he underestimated Lily's stamina. For a woman no taller than five-five, her short legs were fast.

She bounced off the last stair and disappeared around a corner. Stephen puffed out his aggravation. What if the thug that destroyed the house hadn't left yet? She didn't give him time to search the property.

"Lily!" He entered the room with a swift, graceful slide, his fingers wrapping around her arm with an intense, almost painful, force. He stared into her teary eyes as his fingers slipped away from her arm. "You can't run off like that. What if…"

"For the record, I can take care of myself." Her eyes darted to him like fire. She stepped away from him, her knees hitting the floor with a thud as she cradled a pile of shattered jewelry in her hands.

"I'm sorry. I shouldn't have reacted like that." His demeanor was calm under pressure. It was a top qualification for an ER doctor. But watching Lily run off into an unknown situation stirred something dormant inside him.

"It's destroyed. Like everything else in my house." Tears patted the carpeted-floor as she stared at the broken pieces in her palm. "It's all I had left of my mother."

His heart dropped as he stared at the battered woman in front of him. Even with blotchy skin and red-rimmed eyes, she was beautiful. He tugged on her arm and pulled her to her feet, wrapping his long arms around her small body. She fit like a puzzle piece next to his body. His missing half? Stephen caressed the back of her long black hair as he shook his head. Now was not the time to swoon over this beautiful doctor. He didn't have the time for love. If he did, half the women in their town would want a date.

Her quicken pulse and choppy breaths sent warning signs through his brain. Stephen pulled her out of his arms and gently nudged her into the over-sized chair by a bookshelf.

"Breathe." He knew the signs, dealt with trauma patients daily. Panic attacks were no joke. Stephen ran his finger over the side of her arm. "You're not alone. I'm right here."

"For how long?" Tears muffled the words as her body shook. "I'm all alone, and someone wants me dead."

"Slow breaths, doc." He titled her chin to face him. His heart melted into tiny pieces as her sobs tugged on his heart. She deserved to fully enjoy the holiday season without the burden of questioning her own survival. "Look at me. I will not leave you. As long as you need me, I'll be by your side."

Her body stilled, and her pulse regulated. She wiped her eyes on the end of her jacket. "We're practically strangers. Why get involved in my life when I have bad guys after me?"

"Lily, no one should be alone." That was the truth, but he didn't add that being near her stirred up his icy heart, making him want to feel again. And maybe God had a purpose for their paths crossing, but she wouldn't accept that, since her relationship with God was nonexistent.

Her gaze locked with his deep, soulful blue eyes, as if she were delving into his thoughts. With a sigh, she broke their connection and turned away.

Something from downstairs filled the air with a pounding, banging sound as Lily tightly clasped her hands around his wrist. Her chair toppled backward as she sprung up, her fingernails digging into his flesh.

"It's just my brother-in-law, Detective Paul Walkman. You're safe." Sliding his arm across her shoulders, the scent of cinnamon and vanilla drew him closer to her. "Let's go meet him. He's outside."

****

Lily's body shivered, and the icy temperature had nothing to do with it. She adverted Detective Walkman's glare, like she had something to hide. *Who's after you? Do you have any enemies? Anything from your past that might set off a killer? Any disgruntled patients or relatives?* She wanted the rapid fire of questions to stop. Frustrated and overwhelmed, Lily balled up her fists, desperately trying to steady her turbulent emotions. The detective's dedication to his work was apparent in his meticulous approach, leaving no room for doubt in his abilities. With each passing minute, she became more convinced that she had unwittingly become the prime suspect in what should have been a simple routine questioning. And that was ridiculous. Why would she hire someone to take out herself?

She stared into Stephen's soft blue eyes. His flash of compassion melted her fearful heart. This was hard enough, but having him here made the process doable. Maybe God had put him in her life right when she needed a friend. What was she thinking? God had no part in any of this. Coincidence, not God, brought them together. She would not rely on an imaginary God to get her through her darkest nights. If it worked for others, fine, but she needed to rely on someone she could see and who was trustworthy. Like Stephen. Only she dragged him into her web of problems and would subtly offer him an escape before he got buried by everything. He was too good of a man to waste away the holidays by dodging thugs with ill intent. His family needed him. She would survive. At least she hoped that was the case. Alone.

"Ms. Walsh, tell me about your brother?" Paul Walkman's piercing stare zeroed in on her, his narrowed eyes conveying skepticism. His hardened gaze made her squirm uncomfortably on the tattered couch.

I can do this. She repeated over in her mind. *I can resuscitate near-death patients, so this is a piece of cake.* She took a deep breath and immediately regretted it as the stagnant air made her cough uncontrollably.

"Paul, I think this interview has gone on too long." Stephen scooted close to Lily. His spicy scent reminded her of Christmas and the outdoors. He slid his arm around her shoulders as she fought the urge to lean into his solid body. She could easily lose herself in his confident demeanor.

"Stephen, you know the more information I have, the quicker I can solve this case." The steady tap-tap-tap of his pen on the edge of a notepad echoed in the quiet room. His face contorted with irritation, and his eyes turned a deeper shade of brown, flashing with anger.

"That's the problem." Stephen tightened his grip on her shoulders. "She's not a case, but a person. Lily has been through too much this morning. As her doctor, I can't let you continue this interview."

Paul opened his mouth to protest, but stopped as Stephen opened the front door, bringing a wave of coolness that gently caressed the room.

"You have enough information to start your investigation." As Lily looked on, she noticed the stern glances traded between the men, their eyes locked in a silent battle, while Paul silently slipped out of the chair and walked towards the front door. He glanced in her direction, whispering something to Stephen. With a pat on the back, Paul disappeared into the outside. Stephen's mischievous grin filled his face as he closed the door.

"Thanks. I couldn't take any more questions." A sheepish smile spread across her face. What should she do with the good-looking doctor, her self-made protector? She was already getting emotionally attached. Kind of hard not to when he knew the right actions to take and words to speak. But she would not rely on him emotionally. That crossed into dangerous ground, and she did not need a man in her life. Men were excellent protectors, at least some of them, but didn't know how to cope in a relationship when life was normal. She wouldn't skew her perceptions of the doctor by giving him the opportunity to disappoint her and prove her theory of men. He needed an escape route. She would give it to him.

"Paul's hardcore, and forgets human limitations sometimes." Stephen plopped onto the couch next to her. His eyes lit-up with an unreadable emotion. "But he always has my back, and that of a beautiful woman."

I could easily fall for this man. She shook her head and frowned. *But I won't go through that again. Modern medicine and scientific theories are relatable. Heart matters, and emotions are fallible and unreliable.*

"You say that to all the single women?" She didn't really want to hear his answer. Lily knew from staff-room gossip that Doctor Smith was no flirt.

The corners of his mouth curled into a crooked smile, giving him a quirky and endearing appearance. He ran his finger over the edge of her arm. "Only to the exotic beauty with silky black hair and mesmerizing green eyes."

Her wall of defense shattered into millions of pieces. With each intense gaze from the doctor, she could feel her guarded heart betraying her. Startled, Lily leaped up, accidentally bumping her knee against the couch. "Ouch."

Stephen scooted on the couch in front of her, his deep blue eyes never leaving her gaze. "Careful, Doc." He touched the top of her knee as she winced in pain. "If I didn't know any better, I'd think you were running from me."

Electricity shot through her at his sudden touch. What was she like thirteen again — awkward and giddy? No way! She was a grown woman who did not need a man in her life to cause more trouble. A professional. A doctor. Lily scrunched up the fabric on her shirt and sighed. Stephen Smith was trouble and she could not trust her treacherous heart one more minute.

"You should leave." With a sense of urgency, she almost sprinted to the front door, her path obstructed by a mess of ornaments.

A mischievous smile etched across his creamy white face. He stepped inches from her. She felt his warm breath tickling the top of her hair. "Uncomfortable?"

Lily stepped into the door, trying to put some space between them. Stephen's eyes danced in amusement. He knew how his charming personality affected her, and he played off that. She nodded her head, unable to get her mouth to work.

"Calm down." He rested his hands on the top of her shoulders. Heat pulsed through her body at his touch. "I'm one of the good guys."

Lily rolled her eyes at the simple comment. Her fluttering heart could object to those words. "We're practically strangers."

"We're way beyond that point now, doc." He moved a strand of her black hair behind her ear. "I don't want to go."

Lily thought about leaning into his muscular arms, staying until the enemy was gone, but rejected that thought.

"We only met a few hours ago." Although she secretly admired him from afar for months. He did not need to know that.

"When God brings two people together, it's like they've always known each other." He stared into her eyes, looking for a reaction. "God turns the bad into good."

"God?" Lily let out a nervous laugh. He had nothing to do with this. "I think it's time to leave." As she opened the door, she could feel the cool breeze hitting her face, instantly awakening her senses.

"I'll go, but this conversation is far from over." Leaning over, he gently kissed her forehead, leaving a tender touch on her skin. He silently slipped away, leaving only the faint trace of his presence in the morning air.

What conversation? God or their relationship? Because she was not talking about either with him.

Lily closed the door, the sound of the latch clicking echoing through the empty room. As she took a deep breath, she could feel her body relax and her mind become more focused. She looked around the room, her eyes captured the chaos and devastation. If she worked hard, she would clean up the place in time to watch her favorite movie before she dozed off.

Fleeing from Danger, Jessica West

Chapter Three

Stephen hurriedly grabbed his bag from the locker, his keys jingling as he fumbled to close the door. Freedom. His much-needed Christmas vacation started now. Normally, he didn't take a week off during the holidays because the ER never rested. He was always on call during Christmas. Last year, during his turkey dinner, he savored one bite before rushing to the hospital for an accident that left five people severely wounded. Unfortunately, one didn't make it off the operating table.

He shook his head and frowned. Now wasn't the time for morbid thoughts. He loved his job, but he needed to clear his head. Step away. Focus on God. Reevaluate his life.

Twenty-eight, single, no future prospects. Kind of bleak assessment of life. Black, silky hair and with bright green eyes danced into his mind as a smile lit his face. Lily Walsh. The one woman he wanted to pursue, but the one woman who wasn't interested. Any single woman would jump at the opportunity to date him. At least, that's what his sister told him. Why did his heart do flips for someone who put up a wall around her heart? He tried finding her in the cafeteria, or the break room, but their paths never crossed. He wouldn't give up that easily. Not when a female finally broke through his pure-bred bachelor heart.

Stephen jogged up the stairs to the ICU floor. Lily's attempted adductor had either left town or was taking a holiday break. Four days had passed in silence, but that meant nothing. The calm before the storm. He stepped to the oblong desk and gave the nurse his charming smile. He needed info without sending one member of his fan club the wrong message.

The nurse, with her pale face and fiery red hair, absentmindedly ran her fingers through her locks as she placed a chart on the desk. "Doctor? What a surprise. Need a date for any awkward family holiday parties?"

Stephen nearly choked on his salvia. She knew nothing about tact. It never ceased to amaze him. Women hunted him like he was the only deer in a vast open field.

He cleared his throat, shifting uncomfortably. His vacation couldn't start soon enough. "Is Dr. Walsh on call?"

The nurse's eyes blinked in rapid succession, her mouth gaping in astonishment. Nothing. She sat there like a deer in headlights.

"Lily Walsh?" As he spoke, his deep, confident voice commanded attention, diffusing the tension in the air. Clearly, she did not think he walked up three flights of stairs just to ask her out. He didn't even know her name. Only knew her as one of his gawkers. Did the single women have no decency? He was not a game to be won or a prize. Normal men would gravitate to their admirers, but not him. There were no safe zones. Even in church, the older busybodies spent their free time trying to play matchmaker. Did they even pay attention to the sermons? Stephen was pretty sure the pastor preached a message on meddling women last Sunday. He shouted, the only amen. The other men were too hen-pecked to agree verbally.

"Her shift ended two hours ago." The nurse leaned forward, her eyelashes fluttering flirtatiously. "I'm not supposed to disclose this information, but she's on vacation for the next week."

He glanced at her nametag and shot her a half-smile. What was the point of protocol if no one followed it? "Thanks, Amanda."

"Anything else, Dr. Stephen?" He almost busted out laughing at her over-the-top approach to get his attention.

"No." He jogged off, leaving her gawking in silence. Stephen jogged past the ICU rooms and a crowded waiting area.

Before he left for his parents' cabin where the whole family was staying, he needed to check on Lily. Maybe invite her to join them. She didn't have any family, and he could use the excuse to get to know her better. They had a connection going on. That's why she avoided him like the plague. Her behavior intrigued him.

Stephen opened the side door that led to staff parking. He breathed in the fresh morning air. Maybe it'd snow this Christmas. The perfect holiday surrounded by family, food, and snow. And maybe a gorgeous green-eyes doctor. He flung open his truck door, the sound of metal creaking, and carelessly tossed his bag onto the back seat. So much for being a lifelong bachelor. Lily's innocent gaze had the power to make him reconsider his bachelorhood.

He slid the key in the ignition and pulled the seatbelt over his chest. His ringtone of White Christmas floated in the small compounds of his truck. His eyes lit up as Paul's name popped on the screen.

"What's up, bro?" Stephen backed out of the parking lot. "You headed to the cabin already?"

"Belle and kids left a few minutes ago. After I finish a stack of paperwork, I'll join them." Paul's voice held a hint of irritation.

"What's going on?" Stephen cranked up the heater and adjusted the vent.

"Can't a guy call his best bud and brother-in-law without an ulterior motive?" Paul's chuckle floated through the phone.

"No."

"Fine." He cleared his throat and sighed. "The thug who tried to abduct Lily is a seasoned criminal. His rap sheet is as long as my kid's Christmas lists. His name's Justin Cleaver."

"He's not talking?"

"Even worse, he's out on bail." Stephen knew the news agitated his friend. Sometimes the system worked in favor of the perp, not the victim.

"I need to check on Lily." Stephen turned at a stoplight, driving away from their small town. Lily's house rested on a seven-acre lot on the outskirts of town. Remote. Country living at its finest, unless someone had ill intentions. Then the vast fields and woods were eerie. "I'll talk to you later." He set his phone in the cup holder and prayed for God to protect her and keep her safe.

His phone rang again, snapping him out of his prayer. "Hello?"

"Stephen? Someone's in my house." As she spoke through the phone, Lily's voice carried a delicate, whispering tone.

"Where are you?" He pressed on the gas and gunned it down a country road.

"I'm hiding in an upstairs closet." Her voice trembled, and he knew she was on the verge of a panic attack.

"My eta is four minutes. Call the police." The line went dead as a stillness settled around him. "Lily?" His heart raced as he navigated the curve too quickly, adrenaline coursing through his veins.

God, keep her safe.

****

Lily pulled her green, fuzzy socks over her icy feet. She threw a sweater over her damp shirt and pulled her wet black hair into a ponytail. Her refreshing shower did nothing beyond surface level cleaning. She had hoped the steamy warmth would snap her body out of the funk. For days, she tried coming up with an excuse to call the ruggedly handsome doctor that evaded her mind every time she closed her eyes. Better him than the thug who tried to abduct her and trashed her house. No matter the reason, she could not make a habit of daydreaming, causing her fickle heart to hope for something that could never happen. At the hospital, the anticipation of running into him nearly consumed her. Lily wanted to feel his warmth seeping into the depths of her heart. His deep blue eyes searching her soul. But instead of giving in to her treacherous heart, she avoided him like the flu. Eating in her car. Taking the long, uninhabited way to the ICU floor. Bringing lunch everyday so she didn't need to bump into him at the cafeteria. Her sudden lifestyle changes were childish, but she was a coward. Instead of facing her emotions, she ran from them.

She tossed her dirty clothes in the hamper and plopped on her bed, grabbing her phone. With each swipe of her finger, she hoped to drown out the feeling of loneliness, but it only grew stronger. Her phone never chimed from a text. No one ever stopped by. She was utterly alone. And Christmas was the worst time to be so syndical. That's why she clung to Christmas movies, pretending the feel-good vibe was a part of her life. No amount of make-believe could fill the void in her life. Her finger stopped on a picture of Jason. Why did God have to steal her only family from her? He seemed bent on making her suffer. God hated her so much, but why? She had tried the Christian thing as a child until she watched her mother's cancer-eaten body dwindle down to nothing. Her mother loved God, and He repaid her with stage four breast cancer. No amount of begging to God healed her mother. When they lowered her casket into the dirt, she vowed never to fall victim to God's twisted ways. After the accident that snatched her father away, she cemented that resolve in her heart—God was a waste of time.

  The familiar creak of the floorboard at the bottom of the stairs shocked her ears as Lily leaped off her bed. Her heart pounded as she searched the room for a weapon. Whoever was downstairs had not made a friendly visit. She wiped her clammy hands on the side of her pants, feeling the cold sweat against her skin, as she tip-toed to the closet. She needed to hide, to become invisible. Easier said than done, especially in a narrow closet that half her clothes couldn't fit into.

  Lily scrunched her body and slid behind the row of scrubs, blending seamlessly into the tapestry of vibrant hues. A bone-chilling crash echoed from downstairs, resembling the shattering of glass, instantly sending her nerves into overdrive. Was the perp destroying her house, looking for something? Jason's things were in a storage unit. She didn't have enough emotional stability to look through his belongings. Maybe if she had a strong shoulder to lean on, she would have found whatever the perp was after by now. Stephen's face popped into her mind. She needed to call him. He would know what to do.

Lily scrolled through her phone and found his contact info. *No, I can't drag him into this mess again.*

As the footsteps grew louder, the sound echoed throughout the entire staircase, made of aged wood. Time was running out. Her indecisiveness would lead to her death.

Her fingers trembled as she pressed his number. Stephen would call his brother-in-law and wouldn't even have to come to her rescue. Yeah, right, like he would trust someone else to keep her safe.

She pushed his number and smiled as his handsome face etched across her mind. His husky voice vibrated in her ears, causing her pulse to increase.

"Lily?"

"Stephen, someone's in my house." She held her breath, her body tense, as the footsteps abruptly stopped right outside her bedroom door, sending a wave of fear through her. "I'm scared." Her heart thumped so loud; she was sure the perp could hear it through closed doors.

Stephen's words jumbled together as the phone slid from her fingers. She gasped for air as she took shallow, choppy breaths. *You're a doctor. Pull it together."*

A creak resonated from the floor near her door, and then she distinctly heard footsteps hastily retreating from her room and descending the stairs. What was going on? Something had spooked the perp.

Lily clasped her hand over her mouth, trying not to make a peep. There could be more than one bad guy. Another loud crash resonated from downstairs, causing her olive-tinted face to lose its color.

The smell of smoke wafted into the closet, causing her to cough. Smoke? The thug set her house on fire, with her in it! What was she supposed to do? Cower in the closet and possibly die, or escape and possibly run into a trap?

Lily wasn't an impulsive person. She'd rather contemplate her options and go back-and-forth, seeing which option had more facts to back it up. The sound of her deep, throaty cough filled the air, a harsh reminder that time was slipping away. Fear or no fear, she had to act. She slid her phone in her pants pocket and pushed opened the closet door, tumbling to the hard floor.

The faint smell of burning filled the room as tiny puffs of gray smoke seeped in from under the door. If she delayed any longer, her window of escape would be gone. How she wished she could call on God for help. But she knew a fairy tale wouldn't get her out of the fire alive. Reason. Action. Anything but God.

Here it goes. She wrapped her fingers around the hot metal doorknob. With a yelp, she hastily withdrew her fingers from the scalding door and tenderly pressed her lips against the blistered skin.

"It's a fire. Use your brain." In a rush, Lily rummaged through her dresser, scattering various items onto the floor, until she finally retrieved a mask and gloves. As she slid the thick mask over her lips, she could taste a faint hint of cherry flavor, and hurried to the door. She firmly gripped the doorknob with her gloved hands, feeling its familiar shape.

Nothing. Not even a budge.

Her heart raced with fear, causing her to take quick, shallow breaths. Her mind went back to the footsteps she heard earlier. The bad guy must have sealed her door shut, anticipating a slow death or a narrow escape out the window. She rushed to the window and threw the curtain rod on the floor. Her heart beating so fast, she could feel it in her fingertips. Lily peered down into the yard. No shadows or figures lurking around. Safety. Or that's what the person wanted her to think. Put your guard down, fall into the hands of a killer. No time for foolish thoughts. The only way out was through the window.

Maybe someone passing by spotted the fire and called the fire department? She shook her head and frowned. Her closet neighbor lived fifteen minutes out and they rarely stayed home.

Lily grabbed the edge of the window and pulled the window sill with all of her strength. The age-old window didn't budge. She was planning on getting the windows fixed, but that didn't help her now. She paused as the crackling of fire consuming wood roared outside her bedroom door. It was now or never. With a loud thud, she grabbed a bulky book from the bookshelf and forcefully slammed it into the windowpane. The comforting sound of shattered glass filled her room while a gentle breeze carried coolness into her lungs.

With wobbly legs, she climbed out of her window onto a small part of the roof, no bigger than her body. Standing on the edge, looking down, her heart raced as she backed up to the window, feeling the broken glass against her leg.

I can't do this. Fear engulfed her like the flames, slowly eating through her bedroom door.

Her mind raced through all the scenarios: Smoke inhalation-a collapsed lung, jumping to the ground-broken bones, burning in the fire-death. None were promising, but the latter sent icy shivers through her body. The roof could collapse at any minute, sealing her doom. Tears streamed down her face, and she wiped them away, her gaze fixed on the side of the yard. A hundred yards away, the tree sparkled in the sunlight, its branches casting long, stretching shadows. The daylight painted a deceiving facade while distant birds filled the air with their cheerful melodies.

She ran her tongue over her bottom lip and tried calming her nerves. Anxiety creeped through her as every muscle trembled. A crack split through the air as she glanced behind her. Fire raged through her bedroom door as her possessions disappeared into the flames. The alarm shrilled in the distance. A cloud of gloom wrapped around her body. No family. No house. All alone. Life couldn't get any worse unless the perp lurked in the shadows, waiting to end her life. Frozen in fear, she closed her eyes and waited.

****

Stephen barely put his truck in park before he jumped out, adrenaline pulsing through his body. He jerked his gun out of his holster and stared at the flames. His childhood memories came crashing down on him. This place felt like a second home to him. Joe would be sick with grief at the sight. Good thing he lived hours away.

Lily? The weight of his legs made each step a struggle, slowing his progress. She called from the upstairs closet. Did the fire catch her off guard? If she was still in the house, her survival rate was low.

The sound of crackling flames filled the air as he ran towards the door, shielding his face. As the fire raged, the intense heat licked at the edge of his arm, leaving a blistering sensation. He didn't care, he wouldn't let her die. Stephen had to find a way inside the house.

"Lily!" The crackling of the fire drowned out his husky voice, making it difficult to hear. The back door.

Frantically darting around the back of the house, a canister of gasoline abruptly obstructed his path, causing him to trip. He sucked in a deep breath. Not only was the thug an amateur, his determination to catch Lily had gone too far. Once he laid his fingers on the creep…

He stopped in mid-sentence as he spotted a hunched-over figure on the roof. Fire shooting through the window.

"Lily!" Stephen willed his troubled heart to calm down. "God, help me get her before…" His voice trailed off as he sprinted to the shed. He had to find a ladder fast. Lily looked unconscious and the roof could collapse at any minute, sealing her doom. As an ER doctor, he treated many burn victims. Recovery was long and painful. Of course, he never saw the healing, only the burned flesh and disfigured bodies.

No, Lily won't be a statistic. He jerked the shed door open as his eyes adjusted to the dimly lit space. On the far wall hung a fifty-foot ladder. He dashed inside, throwing the metal over his shoulder like it weighed nothing. With a few long strides, he stood in front of the burning house. He shook his head as he propped the ladder against the unstable exterior wall of the house. He was on borrowed time. No way would the dilapidated house hold his one hundred and seventy-five pounds. Stephen could call the fire department and walk away to safety, but he'd be a murderer. As a doctor, he saved lives, at least who God allowed him to save, not watch people die. Lily's charming green eyes and heart-stopping smile danced into his mind. He'd be a fool to think his motives were innocently that of a doctor, trying to save a life. Stephen needed to wrap his arms around her fragile body, hear the steady rhythm of her heartbeat pulsing through her body, and carry her to safety.

He swiftly ascended the steps, effortlessly leaping three at a time, and then gently lowered himself onto the roof, inching closer to Lily. Sweat poured from his face as the heat from the fire licked the edges of the roof. Any hesitation, and they wouldn't make it to see another Christmas. Amidst the roaring flames and the smell of burning wood, he placed her gently on his shoulder and swiftly descended the ladder. He sprinted as far away from the fire as he dared to go. Stephen wiggled out of his fleece jacket, draping it on the icy grass. He laid Lily's unconscious body on top of it as the farmhouse collapsed into a heap of wood.

Stephen's skillful hands glided over Lily's soot-covered face, the sound of sirens growing louder in the distance. His eyes ran along her body, accessing the damage the fire caused. Singed clothes, a few burn marks on her hand, but nothing serious. Minor first-degree burns. As the adrenaline waned from his body, pain pierced through his arm. He glanced at his arm; flesh exposed from his burned sleeve. A second-degree burn, but he'd live.

He ran his fingers down her silky olive skin. Even covered in soot, he'd never seen a more beautiful woman. *Thank You God for sparing her life.*

"Lily?" He swallowed the lump rising in his dry throat. "Sweetie, talk to me."

She moaned as her eyes fluttered open, trying to get her bearing.

Tears threatened to escape his burning eyes as smoke filled the air. The thick smoke made it hard to breathe, but the real reason for his tears was the profound sense of gratitude he felt towards God for sparing her life.

"Stephen, what are you doing here?" With his calloused fingers, he gently cupped her face. Leaning over,

Stephen pressed a soft kiss to her forehead, then drifted down to claim her lips, savoring their sweetness. Which tasted of Christmas and home. With her eyes wide, she leaped back. *Idiot! Why ruin your simple bachelor life for a woman with more problems than a math book?* Stephen groaned. He did not regret the kiss. In the brief time they spent together, she chipped away at the barriers surrounding his heart. No regrets. No turning back.

"What was that for?" She brushed her fingers across her lips, a frown appearing on her face. "Stephen, I…"

"I won't apologize." As he stared into her eyes, a flicker of emotion flashed across her irises. Fear? Longing?

The blaring sirens of a fire truck filled the air as four men sprinted toward the blazing fire. Help had arrived, just not in time to save her belongings.

Stephen had a proposition for her, provided she would accept it. And no, it had nothing to do with wedding vows.

Fleeing from Danger, Jessica West

Chapter Four

"Doctors are the worst patients." Stephen glanced at the chart on the counter, a look of disappointment crossing his face.

He had been in this ER room hundreds of times, but no cases had ever made him feel the way she did. To be an efficient doctor, he rarely let his emotions spring to life. Patients needed professionalism, not pity. That's what family was for. In the not so rare cases when patients were alone, he made sure compassion and sympathy ran freely from the nurses. A few times when children were involved, he'd dash to his office before the tears tumbled to the checkered hospital floor. He had seen the worst of life as the unimaginable limped through the ER doors. Humanity without God fell short every time. Broken bodies, hearts, and shattered hopes. He couldn't do his job without his faith. Administration would have admitted him to the psych ward on floor five by now. His job wasn't for the weak-hearted. God had called him as a doctor, shedding His light to the hopeless, and he filled the halls with his prayers. Prayers for the aching child, lawless criminal, for the patient whose life would never be normal again, and for every person in between. God's presence beamed through this place. If only he could convince the weary-eyed beauty, her olive-tinted skin contrasting against the sterile white sheets of the hospital bed.

"Speak for yourself." Lily tossed the covers off her legs, the sound of rustling fabric echoing in the quiet room, and shifted uncomfortably on the hard bed. "I've been an exceptional patient, but you're not my doctor. You can go on with your vacation. Just leave me be." Her words had a delicate mix of bitterness and frustration.

Stepping towards the bed, he crouched next to her and gently cupped her chin, his touch both comforting and intimate. He could get used to staring into her sea-green eyes every day for the rest of his life. *Woah! Where did that come from?* Stephen rolled his eyes at his emotional tug of war. "You can't get rid of me that easily."

"You're not indebted to me, doctor." Her eyes met his for a fleeting moment before she instinctively withdrew from his contact. "Dr. Williams is a stellar physician."

Yeah, and he's also single, trying to flirt with way too many patients. His bedside manner is lacking. I will not put you through that pain. The words sat on the edge of his tongue. But he had no reason to doubt his colleague's skills. "I never leave a damsel in distress."

Her lips formed a gentle curve, accompanied by a twinkle in her eyes, which blossomed into a radiant smile. A soft laugh floated through the room, causing his heart to beat faster. Why did her nearness affect him so much? He'd been around plenty of beautiful woman, but none of them slipped through his guarded heart. It was much more than her looks. He needed to get to know her better to find out what it was.

"I am anything but a damsel in distress." She lifted her chin in defiance. Yet a smile tugged on her pale-pink lips.

His fingers grazed her smooth lips, each touch a reminder of the passionate kiss they shared, a moment he wouldn't trade for anything. From Lily's sheepish look, she remembered the kiss, too.

"I'm well aware of that." His heart pounded in his chest. One quick movement and his lips could claim her again. The taste of peppermint twined with something spicy, like paprika.

"Stephen…" she breathed out his name as her fingers ran across his forearm, sending tingles throughout his body.

The door abruptly opened as Paul walked into the room carrying a notepad and a smirk on his face. "You two are awfully cozy. May I remind you of your unwed status?"

Lily's face turned five shades of red as she scooted away from Stephen. He rolled his eyes at the familiar words. Stephen might have repeated those same words to a love-struck detective and Stephen's sister Belle.

Crossing his arms over his chest, Paul's dark eyes seemed to come alive with a radiant gleam. "Just repaying the favor, bro."

Stephen sprang up from Lily's side, and with a playful smile, he gave his friend a light punch on the arm.

A hardness rolled over Paul's eyes. His detective persona clearly in place. His deep voice rumbled through the small room. "Not surprising, but we're dealing with an amateur arsonist. We found a fingerprint on the gas can. Once it's run through our system, I'll let you know."

Lily rolled over on the bed and stared at the detective. She wiped the tears running freely down her face. "M-my house?"

Detective Walkman ran his tongue over his lower lips and frowned. "A complete loss. And right before Christmas."

Lily's body trembled as Stephen's arms enveloped her, his presence creating a sense of safety and solace. "Not a complete loss. I keep a small suitcase with all the important documents, ID, bank cards, a week's worth of clothes in my office."

"Intriguing."

"Or someone prepared to run." Paul's steel-as-ice glare caused her to shift uncomfortably. "What are you not telling us?"

Stephen's hands tightened their hold on her shoulders, his lips grazing her ear as he whispered softly. "Trust him and me with whatever you're running from."

She shifted out of Stephen's arms and sat up in the narrow bed, throwing the sheets on the floor. "My dad died right before my sixteenth birthday."

"How?"

She blinked back tears. "He had left for a meeting, hours away. I sulked in my room that night because of my crush … never mind that part." Her cheeks turned bright red as she glanced at Stephen. Golden specks that lay hidden behind her sea-green eyes sparkled through the tears.

"Go on." He rubbed the back of her hand, dreading to hear the rest of the story.

"I had headphones on and didn't hear the fire alarm. Flames surrounded my room, and I panicked. I passed out and woke up at the hospital."

"Déjà vu."

"Instead of just losing my house, I lost my father." She ran her fingers over her puffy, red eyes, trying to soothe the ache and swelling. "No one knows what he was doing in town. His meeting was hours away."

"He saved your life." Stephen couldn't resist the urge to touch the silky black strands of hair that framed her face.

"And he died." She let out a heavy sigh. "I never knew what caused the fire. My social worker carted me off to different foster homes until I was old enough to leave the system."

"What was your father's name?" Paul scribbled some notes on his pad.

"Isaac Walsh, former CEO of Yorkshire Investments."

"One of the top investment firms in the world." Paul raised his eyebrow. But kept writing. "Any jealous ex-boyfriends?"

"Only casually dated a guy, Ronald Fisher. We broke it off once I learned where his money came from."

"Drugs?"

"He was too knee-deep into it to leave the family business for a foster kid like me." She gritted her teeth as her fingers fisted over the hem of her shirt.

Paul snapped his notepad shut and shoved it in his pocket. "I have a lot of angles to work on. You have any friends or family to stay with?"

Lily's mouth curled into a frown as her lower lip trembled. She shook her head and stared at the floor.

Stephen's serene voice cut through the heavy silence hanging in the room. "She's coming to the cabin with me and spending the holidays with us."

She shook her head, attempting to appear braver than her pale skin revealed. Stephen drew her nearer to his sturdy frame and draped his arm around her shoulder. "My family loves company."

"And Belle wants to meet the woman who finally captured this bachelor's heart." Paul casually retrieved his phone from his pocket, quickly glancing at the vibrating screen.

"It's settled." Stephen's eyes twinkled with pleasure as he stared into her eyes.

Bringing her home was the best idea ever, or the nail that finally doomed his singlehood. Only time would tell.

"I got to go, but Lily, bring the key to your brother's storage unit when you come." Paul slid out the door like he wasn't even there.

"I'll go home with you, but I need to make a quick stop first." In one swift motion, she leaped off the bed and let her feet glide over the tiled floor, finding her shoes in an instant. The stench of smoke was overwhelming, and Stephen couldn't help but notice the layer of soot that covered her clothes.

"Lily, I don't think that's a good idea." With a gentle yet firm grip, he reached for her arm and pulled her body into his embrace. She could have died in the fire, and now she wanted to play investigator and search through her brother's belongings. Someone wanted her dead. Not a good idea.

"And I don't think setting our hearts up for failure is wise either." With a sudden movement, she yanked her arm out of his grip and headed towards the door.

"Lily…" What was he going to do with this Asian-American beauty?

"You coming?" Her green eyes sparkled with mischief.

No way would he let her go anywhere alone. Of course he was going. But they both might regret this decision later. As he leaned over, his hand grazed the reassuring touch of the cold, metallic gun in his ankle holster. At least he had backup.

****

Lily clung to her duffel bag, the only possessions she had left. She ran her fingers through her smoke-scented hair, trying not to gag. Before they left the hospital, she retrieved her suitcase and quickly changed. Too bad she didn't have time to shower. First impressions were important. She wanted Stephen's family to like her. Wait ... what? Her treacherous heart was at it again. She wasn't going to his family's cabin under false pretense, like the next step in her relationship with Stephen. She had to remind herself that the only reason she wasn't spending Christmas alone was because of a maniac after her. It would be easy to fall for the false narrative of family and love. Her life didn't involve any of those luxuries, and it'd be best to guard her wayward heart. Her heart rate increased and her mind wandered whenever the attractive doctor stood by her. But nothing about that was real. Stephen Smith had a long line of admirers, and she would not be one of them. Plus, he believed in God. In all honesty, she believed in God, too. But life had skewed her image of God. He wasn't loving or wonderful. He liked to see certain people suffer, and she was one of them. Lily never felt his love, only His judgement as He snatched everything good from her — no family, home, friends. She was utterly alone, and she blamed God.

"What are you thinking about?" Stephen's voice drifted through the cramped compartment of the truck. Startled, she yanked her head off the seat and met his kind eyes, which seemed to radiate compassion. He made it hard staying neutral towards him. She felt an overwhelming urge to lean into his sturdy arms, finding comfort and protection from the troubles of life. But she vowed off men since Ronald. And she was doing Stephen a favor since God had taken every man away from her — her dad, Ronald, Jason. She was saving his life by keeping him at a distance.

"Too many things." Lily's burns ached as she shifted her body in the seat. Besides a few scraps and burns, she'd come out of the fire unharmed.

"Lay it on me, doc."

"Do you think God has a hit list?" The sun peeking out from behind the distant mountains captivated her eyes to the window like a painting of the sky with a beautiful blend of pink and purple hues.

Stephen's mouth curled into a smile. His fingers traced along the edge of her palm. "Why do you ask?"

She puffed out a sigh and slid her hand under her leg. Lily needed to keep her distance because weakness surrounded her heart. She could not afford to fall for the handsome doctor. "If He does, I'm at the top of the list."

"God isn't like the maniacs after you. He doesn't inflict pain to get a pleasure out of it." Stephen gripped the steering wheel and glanced at the mirror. "I don't always know God's plan, but I trust Him because He knows best."

"I can't trust someone who steals everything from me. It's like I'm always on the naughty list and I'm a decent person." Why was she having this conversation about a God that clearly hated her, with a guy that could never understand the feeling of loss and being utterly alone? "Never mind … this conversation is pointless." She stared out the window, avoiding his quizzical looks.

"Nothing about God is pointless." He clutched the top of the steering wheel, hands turning pale.

"What's wrong?" She gazed into the rearview mirror, her heart pounding fiercely in her chest. "Is that black car following us?"

"Maybe." With a quick motion, he pulled his gun from its holster and placed it securely on his thigh, ready for action. "Just in case."

Lily's body tensed at the sight of the gun. The nightmare seemed never-ending, making her contemplate leaping out of the moving truck to confront the thug in the black car. Of course, she would cower far away from any bad guys.

"Get down!" Stephen jerked the truck, making a sharp right turn.

The sound of a loud pop filled the air as a bullet narrowly missed the front seat and struck the windshield.

Lily's piercing shrills floated around the cab. She didn't want to die, not in a house fire or a shootout. She just wanted to live.

The sound of tires screeching on the asphalt mingled with the gunshot as Stephen fired his gun out of the window. "Target hit."

Lily peeked out of the mirror, watching the black car slam into a dumpster. Stephen must have shot out a tire. The truck slowed to the side of the road as he slid his seatbelt off his shoulder. Panic engulfed her body. "What are you doing?" She dug her fingernails into the side of his wrist.

His gaze, cold and unyielding, sent shivers down her spine. "I'm going to put an end to this senseless violence."

"No!" Lily gripped the side of his shirt, feeling the rise and fall of his chest as she took deep, calming breaths. "Call the detective."

"The perp could be gone by the time Paul arrives." Something flashed into Stephen's deep blue eyes.

"I want this to end too, but not at the expense of your life." She blinked back tears. Lily would never forgive herself if anything happened to the kind doctor.

Despite the forced smile on his face, his cold blue eyes betrayed his genuine emotions. "Fine. I'll take that as a sign that you care about me, even if it's just a little."

She sighed. The problem was she cared about him and that was dangerous ground for both of them.

"I'll text Paul and let him know we'll be at the storage unit so he can take our statements." He ran his fingers over hers. "Everything will be fine."

She wanted so desperately to believe in happy endings, just like she wanted to believe in a fairy tale God who granted wishes. But neither were true.

****

Stephen's low whistle echoed through the storage unit, mingling with the sound of the metal door slamming shut. He glanced at the towering stacks of boxes that reached from the floor to the ceiling and shook his head in disbelief. They'd be here until next Christmas, lost in the sea of cardboard and the remains of a life cut too short. He glanced at Lily, shoulders stooped and a blank stare protruding off her face. She seemed deflated. He needed to use caution. Keep his bachelor status intact. Walk, no run far away from this green-eyed trouble magnet. But he wouldn't. Not needing any excuse to get into her personal space, he trudged next to her, wrapping his enormous arms over her petite frame. Fearing she'd push away; he rubbed circles on her back, trying to offer support. Her body fit perfectly under the umbrella of his arms. Rather than stepping away, she embraced him tightly, burying her face in the fabric of his shirt. The sound of her soft whimpers echoed through the room as tears soaked his white shirt. Her quickened heart rate pulsed against his chest, transmitted through the layers of fabric as she gripped the back of his shirt.

He pushed away slightly to get a look at her face. Big mistake. Her puffy eyes and tear-stained face chiseled the remaining bachelor post around his heart away. Who needed a ridiculous title, anyway? He could commit. He would commit. If she would stop sending him mixed signals and give him hope. Stephen wanted a love like his parents and sister. But love didn't always feel right at first. A big firework display or embraces by a warmly lit fire were not the standard for love. Sometimes, love had to be earned. Love? No way. At least not yet. He could picture waking up to Lily each day, raising a family together, growing old together. The future was easy to imagine. It was the present that seemed kind of shaky. Trying to jar the thoughts in his mind, he leaned over and brushed his lips over her silky-smooth ones. Surprise laced her eyes as she pushed away from him.

"Stephen—" That one word said it all. He was a complete fool. He allowed a damsel in distress to break down his guarded heart, yet she wanted nothing to do with him. *Keep it professional. You have a fan club for crying out loud. Ease into dating with one of those girls.* Stephen sighed as he ran his fingers through his inch-thick hair. He needed space. Room to breathe and think. Her holly-infused perfume kept choking his resistance away. There was no escaping her. He didn't even really want to.

"Let's look through the boxes." He skulked to the other side of the room, his wounded pride lingering on his tongue. Space, distance, a sea of boxes between them. He needed it all before he fell to her feet, begging to let him in.

As she slid to the gritty cement floor, she forcefully ripped open a box. "Maybe I shouldn't go home with you for the holidays."

You think? He set a pile of papers on top of a closed box. "Lily, there're no strings attached. No hidden agenda. You will be safe with my parents." Would he be safe from her beautiful face and the longing her presence created in him?

"Stephen … I…"

"Don't." He imagined her words were empty platitudes and feeble excuses. He wouldn't listen. Not from her. In the short time, she meant everything to him. And that was why he needed to forcefully place his heart back into the guarded walls, locking away the vulnerability.

With a dramatic sigh that filled every corner of the small storage room, Lily pried open a box, careful not to rip the contents inside. "I don't even know what I'm looking for." Frustration laced her soft words.

No joke. And it kind of felt weird going through a dead man's belongings. His treasures. These boxes were the remains of his life.

"Tell me about your brother." Stephen needed additional information, or they'd find nothing useful. And his mom's award-winning apple pie kept calling his name. He could see his dad stealing the last piece of his pie, destroying all the evidence.

"Well … Jason played the age card a lot. Four years older and he knew everything." As she tossed a stack of papers inside a box, a tear rolled down her cheek, which she quickly wiped away.

Apparently, not how to stay out of trouble. Trying to stop the ache in his back, Stephen leaned against the rigid metal wall. "What was his profession?"

"A commercial real estate agent." Her flat tone held no emotions. "Jason worked in Knoxville but commuted home on the weekends. But sometimes…"

"What?" Stephen held a file of papers and walked into the shark zone. So close her spicy perfume clouded his judgement. He almost stepped into her personal space. Almost. But he didn't want to make the same mistake twice, so he plopped on the icy floor an arm's width away.

"He'd be gone for weeks and never answered his cellphone."

"Standard behavior?" He'd never turn his phone off for weeks, no matter the temptation. His sister was feisty.

"We reconnected six months ago." She ran her fingers through her black, silky strands. "And he disappeared so much. I wondered why I left the beach for an absent brother."

"Drugs?" Stephen flipped open the folder and scanned the sheets of paper.

"No clue." As Lily straightened her back, a look of displeasure crossed her face, forming a frown.

"What is it?" He chopped down every excuse his brain could muster on why he needed to hold her. She did not want his comfort, and he needed to respect her.

"Before he died, he made it sound like he was living a secret life."

"Like a wife and kids or…"

Lily ran her fingers over her face. "He told me to get far away from here. I think he was involved in illegal activity."

Stephen's fist collided with his palm, sending a shiver down his spine as he felt the frigid sensation spread throughout his body. Whatever Jason was involved in was coming for her. He had to figure out what to protect her. "Look at this." He handed her a dark-colored folder.

Lily shuffled through the papers as her tongue slid against her bottom lip. "This makes no sense. Jason wasn't a criminal."

Stephen grabbed a folded paper with names and numbers and took a picture with his phone. "Might come in handy later."

Lily dropped the file like fire laced the edges of the paper, burning her with each touch. "It can't be."

"What?" He scooted closer to her, into the danger zone, and grabbed the folder off the cold cement floor. Stephen pulled an ID card off the top of the stack. "CIA?"

"I-I…"

"This changes everything." He slid the card into his pocket. He'd give it and the file to Paul.

"What was my brother involved in?" She took a deep breath. By her rapid breathing, he knew she couldn't take any more investigation for today. "Did his undercover work land him as an enemy to a drug lord? Or maybe he witnessed a murder. Double-crossed someone in an organized crime ring."

Stephen slid his finger over her moist lips. "Shh."

The sound of echoing footsteps filled the hall, sending a chill down his spine as his arm hairs stood on end. Were they followed? They needed to leave fast.

He slid his gun out of his ankle holster and breathed a quick prayer for safety.

"What…" Her voice quivered with fear as her gaze locked onto the gun, her body tensing in anticipation. Her hands trembled as she reached over and tightly grasped the edge of his shirt, afraid to let go.

"I'll get us out of here." With a grunt, he climbed off the unforgiving ground, extending his hand to help her up from the cold cement-floor. He then wrapped his arm around her shoulder, providing both comfort and stability. This mission, he wouldn't fail.

Tears filled her bright eyes. "We're going to die."

Not on his watch. As he pressed his ear against the door, all he could hear was an eerie silence echoing back at him. A ploy? A trap? It didn't matter; it was go time.

He slid the door open and squeezed her hand. "No matter what, run to the car. We may only have seconds to get out."

They walked further into the darkness with every step, their surroundings growing increasingly obscure. Stephen knew his limited ability was nothing compared to God's power and deliverance. He clung to that hope to get them to safety.

****

"I can't believe your parents live here." Lily unbuckled her seatbelt as the full landscape of the cabin came into view. A three-story modern cabin with sleek industrial lines and colors. Snowy mountains as the backdrop. "It's out of a movie." She gawked at a ten-foot pine tree decorated for Christmas with white lights and red bows. White icicle lights dangled from the roof. Picturesque snow covered the brown winter grass.

"My dad designed and built it three years ago. A thug burned down their home, destroying all of their possessions." Stephen slid the keys out of the ignition. "It only made sense moving to the mountains and living their retirement before they retired."

"I love it." Her heart pricked with unease, and beads of sweat formed on her forehead. She knew nothing about family gatherings. Being around a family made her uncomfortable. Of course, she hadn't been around her family since age ten, when her mother passed away from cancer. Before then, there were no family meals, game nights, or chatter around a warm fire. She walked on eggshells, trying to remain invisible, not to disturb her mother. Any unnecessary laughter and her father's chide would leave her wishing she really was invisible. She loved her mother, but her father never let her touch her mother's smooth face or listen to her low-pitch voice whispering words of affirmation in her ears.

Stop being selfish, Lily. Your childish germs could kill your mother. Would you want that? Her father's stern voice echoed in her memory.

Noone planted kisses on her frizzy hair or wrapped her below-average body in a safe embrace. She was the child no one wanted. At least until it benefited them. After her mother's passing, her father lived in his office. She had everything money could buy, except love and human connection. In her twenty-seven years, she could count on one hand all the I love-you's donned at her. And most of those were from Ralph. No wonder she threw herself at his arms. She craved love and didn't care who gave it to her.

Her five foster homes before age eighteen provided shelter from the elements, but nothing lasting. No family or even love. Those years reminded her of how incapable she was in relationships.

Not anymore. Lily didn't need love like she needed oxygen, water, and food. Her life proved that and caused cynicism to grow around her forgotten heart. She needed to remember whatever happened this week was phony and for show, just like the affirmations were as a teen. Stephen wasn't her boyfriend, and she wasn't meeting his family as a relationship goal. Life and death had everything to do with this, not love. She'd do good leaving her heart at the door and not playing pretend. No matter what.

Stephen gently traced his fingers over the soft texture of her Christmas sweater. Her gaze locked with his dark blue eyes, and for a moment, she forgot everything else around her. Why couldn't she have love and family? Lily chewed on her bottom lip, frowning. Because God etched her name on his hit list, and nothing would change that.

"You ok?"

"I'm fine." Lily would put on a front and everything would be fine. Life would go on as normal.

He grabbed her hand and traced his fingers along her palm. "Let me in, Lily." The intensity in his pleading eyes was so overwhelming that she had to glance away, feeling a pang of guilt.

"I said I was fine." Jerking her hand away from him, she could see the frustration and anger contorting his features. "None of this is real. Why don't we simply accept that fact and move forward with this week?"

As his fingers brushed against the bottom of her chin, he gently tilted her face upwards to meet his gaze. "All of this is real, and I'd give you everything if you just let me in."

As Lily exhaled, her sigh seemed to fill every corner of the truck's compartment. "Please don't ask me to give more than I can. I'm not who you think I am. I don't belong here."

With a gentle motion, Stephen leaned over and planted a delicate kiss on her lips, his touch leaving a lingering warmth. Her resolve was melting away, one kiss at a time. Not good. Startled, she instinctively pulled back from him, staring into his face, a mischievous smile playing on his lips. She could fall into his arms and never let go. But that wasn't the practical thing to do. Heartache and brokenness, not love and happily ever after.

"Whatever's going on in your mind, just push it away. I'm not asking you for anything. I won't hurt you." With a tender gesture, he brushed away a stray strand of her dark hair, his smile lighting up his face. "Let's go meet my family."

He was kidding, right? Because she could already see an empty house, a broken heart, and too many bowls of chocolate ice cream.

Chapter Five

Stephen squeezed Lily's sweaty palm, smiling. He had never brought a female home to meet his family. Especially at Christmas time. How he wished this entire ordeal was real and not just part of her protection plan. He hadn't misspoken when he told her he'd give her everything if she'd just let him in. A converted bachelor. He didn't know how these things went, but he knew how his pulse tripled at her nearness and the longing he felt every time he gazed into her green eyes. He had it bad and the outcome would be treacherous, considering she wanted nothing to do with him. Her mind was in a tug of war, and his side might just win.

He took a deep breath and stepped around the inflatable snowman. No doubt added to thrill his nieces. They were old enough now to enjoy the extravagant side of the Christmas decorations. He braced himself for babies crying and toddlers running around hyped on too much sugar. He envied his best bud. Stephen would love to have a house full of children one day. May even have ten children to love and raise in the ways of the Lord. But first, he needed to find a woman worthy of his love. He stared at Lily as she stepped onto the porch. Her skin was pink from the freezing temperatures. Stephen shook his head and touched the doorknob. He had already found the woman of his dreams. Now, he just needed to convince her they belonged together. *What did she mean when she blurted out, she's not who I think she is? Was she hiding secrets?*

The door swung open as a thin, strawberry blond-haired woman stepped onto the porch. She dusted her floury hands on the end of her Christmas tree decorated apron and pulled Stephen into her arms. "Son, it's been too long."

Stephen wrapped his mom in a bear hug, pressing a kiss to the top of her messy bun. Cinnamon and nutmeg floated through his nostrils. The smell of Christmas and his mom's baking. Childhood memories burst into his mind as he stepped away from his mom. God could have given him any other family. Yet, He gave him the best parents who loved and instructed him in the ways of God. For that, he'd always be thankful.

"Mom, I saw you two weeks ago." He wrapped his arm over his mom's shoulder, towering over her by at least five inches.

"What can I say? I love my boy." She tugged on his arm, then stepped toward Lily. His mom's bright eyes shone with pleasure. "You must be Dr. Lily Walsh. It's a pleasure meeting you, dear."

Lily shifted uncomfortably next to his mother's warm touch. "Call me Lily."

Mrs. Smith pulled Lily into a motherly hug and smiled. "Stephens never brought a woman home before. You must be…"

"Mom…" Stephen's voice held a sternness to it, but his face lit up with amusement.

Mrs. Smith pulled out her smartphone and pushed Lily to Stephen's side. "How about a picture before we go inside?"

"Mom." Stephen's eyes twinkled with love and adoration.

"No, a picture would be lovely." Lily's touch on Stephen's arms sent a jolt through his body, leaving him breathless.

He leaned over as his breath fanned the edges of her ear. "Watch out or Mom will have our wedding planned before we leave."

Dropping her hands, Lily created a physical barrier by moving away from Stephen. With a quizzical look on his face, he gazed at her intently. His eyebrows pinched in the middle. Would marrying him really be that bad?

"Where's my manners? Let's get you both inside. The fire is warm and cookies just got out of the oven." Mrs. Smith pulled Lily inside the cabin. The sound of the door closing echoed in the silence. "I hope you like chocolate chip. It's Stephen's favorite."

"Anything you make is my favorite." His chuckle floated through the high-ceilinged room.

His mom dashed into the kitchen and walked out carrying a plate of cookies. The aroma filling the room. "Tired of takeout? The bachelor's life isn't for everyone. God designed marriage."

"Lea, give the boy a break. They just got here." Stephen's dad, Kevin Smith, looked like a spitting image of his son, only with a few wrinkles and gray hair.

"Dad!" Stephen wrapped his arms around his dad's shoulders after taking a bite of his cookie. "Did you get my text?"

"Everything's good to go." Mr. Smith's eyes twinkled like Stephen's, full of life and mischief. "And who is our beautiful guest?"

"He's the charmer of the family." Stephen stepped away from his dad and fell onto the sectional couch.

"Lily, Mr. Smith." She extended her hand in his direction.

"None sense, young lady. Call me Kevin." He wrapped her in a bear hug, laughter dancing out of his mouth.

"Kevin, thank you for allowing me to break up your party." Lily's hand shook as she pushed out of Mr. Smith's embrace.

"We're so glad you could come." Mr. Smith stepped toward the kitchen and smiled. "I think your mother needs my help to sample the desserts."

"Not my apple pie, Dad." A playful scowl etched across Stephen's face.

He breathed in a sigh. This felt like home. His tiny condo wasn't full of life or laughter. It was simply a place to sleep. He needed people to transform it into a home. Stephen glanced at Lily's pale face and trembling hands. Maybe she could help make it a home. He shook his head and frowned. *Don't get caught up in the façade, man. This isn't real, no matter how it feels.*

Lily tightly intertwined her fingers, desperately attempting to regain composure. "Your parents are…"

"Overwhelming?" Joining Lily, he slid closer and enveloped her hand in his own, his large, comforting grip quelling her trembling.

"No, amazing. In a hard-to-believe kind of way."

The sadness in Lily's eyes pricked his heart and caused him to wrap his arms around her waist, pulling her to his side. "My parents are exactly who they seem to be. Relax."

"You have what I've always longed for … a family." She buried her face into her shoulder as a stray tear dropped onto his shirt.

"Lily…"

"We thought we heard voices." Belle stepped into the room, carrying a slobber-faced infant. She handed the baby to her brother and exited the room. Within moments, she reappeared, carrying another baby that looked exactly the same. "Want to hold him?" Belle's make-up-free face and messy hair added to her beauty. She gently eased the baby into Lily's arms.

"Sis!" With a burst of energy, Stephen propelled himself off the couch, embracing his sister in a warm hug while simultaneously cuddling the baby against his chest. "You look amazing and tired at the same time."

"No one else can give compliments like you." Belle stepped closer to Lily, her touch light and comforting as she patted her on the shoulder. "I can see why my brother likes you."

Lily's face turned red as she quickly stared at the sleeping baby in her arms.

"Belle, you're not supposed to reveal my secrets." Stephen's mischievous eyes sparkled with delight as he leaned in and gently pressed his lips against the baby's velvety cheeks. The sweet scent of baby powder lingered in the air. The softness of the baby's skin brought a warm sensation of tenderness to Stephen's fingertips.

"I … um." Lily's body tensed up as the baby wiggled and squirmed in her arms, making it difficult for her to find a comfortable position. "I've never held an infant before."

Amusement danced in Stephen's eyes as he scooted closer to Lily and stared into his nephew's face. "These little humans are totally cool. Nothing to fear. Except maybe piercing cries or milky spit up."

Lily stared at the pink-faced baby as her mouth curved into a smile and her eyes flashed contentment. "He really is so sweet."

Belle's soft laugh floated through the spacious living room. "He's already a charmer, like his daddy. They both are."

Stephen stood to his feet, handing the baby back to his sister. "Where is Paul at, anyway?"

Belle's eyebrows furrowed into a scowl. "In the office. You can't stay away from trouble, can you?"

"Funny. As much as I'd love holding my nephew and giving you a break, I have matters to discuss with your husband." Stephen's voice lowered to a hushed tone as he leaned towards Lily, his words meant only for her ears. "Will you be ok with Belle? If she does anything to make you uncomfortable, scream for help."

"Ok, Romeo, I think she'll be ok a few minutes without your handsome face." Belle swatted him with one hand.

"Handsome? I was going for electrifying, irresistible, charming…" His deep voice trailed off as his eyes lit up with mischief.

"See what I have to put up with?" Belle rolled her eyes as she playfully smacked her brother on the arm. "I'm going to give you some adjectives if you don't leave us alone."

"I know when I'm not wanted." He walked down the hall, turning around and smiling. "Try not to talk about me too much. I have a complex."

"Is he always so…" Lily shifted her body on the couch, trying not to disturb the baby.

"Obnoxious?" Belle blurted out.

"No, spunky, ravishing…"

"I will not answer that." Belle took her baby from Lily's arms. Holding both twins, she nodded towards the kitchen. "Let's go see if Mom needs any help."

****

Lily moved her fingers around in the bowl, searching for any pecans left to open. She had spent an hour listening to Mrs. Smith and Belle ramble on about children, cooking, and everything in between. Instead of being bored, the two women's warm personalities drew her in. She felt like a part of the family, not a victim hiding out. How she wished this make-believe world was reality. She could get used to waiting with the ladies as their men discussed manly things in the office. Her man? Stephen was everything she didn't want in a man. With him, she could dream of forever and always come back to his charming face and loving heart. But that future, although wonderful, wasn't for her. Without warm arms to hold her and a handsome face to accompany her, she would navigate through life alone. The absence of a family meant there would be no shared meals or moments of laughter. A sense of isolation and despair loomed over her future. And it was all God's fault. If He were even real.

She threw down the last shell in the trashcan and stared into a chef's dream kitchen, an eight-burner gas stove, double-door stainless steel oversized fridge, and the wall-to-wall white cabinets. The kitchen was marvelous, but Mrs. Smith made it cozy and an inviting place. Would she ever have chats around her kitchen island while cracking pecans and whipping up desserts? She didn't even have any friends, let alone anything in her kitchen besides frozen food and bottles of water. The down-turned corners of her mouth revealed her displeasure, forming a distinct frown on her face. Maybe she wasn't content to have that lonely lifestyle anymore. But nothing would change. Longing only made a person miserable. She'd get a dog. Then she wouldn't be alone anymore. First, though, she'd have to rebuild her home. She had plenty of money since she sold her father's investment company when he passed away. And she rarely spent her hefty physician's salary. What was the fun of spending money when you were alone?

"You're deep in thought. Thinking about my brother?" Belle's hazel eyes twinkled like the Christmas lights on the massive tree in the living room.

"I have been waiting for him to bring a woman home to meet me for such a long time." Mrs. Smith pulled a pie out of the oven as the apple cinnamon scent filled the kitchen. "If that doesn't lure the men out, I'm not sure what else will."

Heart pounding and eyes watering, Lily shifted uncomfortably on the barstool. Did his mother not know why she was really here? She couldn't break her kind heart. But not telling her would devastate her in the end.

Belle seemed to understand Lily's thoughts perfectly as she carefully settled her twins in the bassinets, gracing Lily with a comforting smile. "We know you're here under difficult circumstances, but God works in mysterious ways."

"God?" At the mention of God, anger slowly spread across her face. God seemed to take pleasure in her misfortunes and her loss. Besides inflicting her life with pain, He was nowhere near her. It helped her to believe God wasn't real than to believe He liked her to suffer.

Mrs. Smith stopped mixing a cake batter and turned facing Lily. Flour coated the side of her rosy cheek. "Sour subject?"

Taking a deep breath, Lily exhaled, feeling the warmth of her breath dissipate into the Christmas-scented air. "I don't believe in God. Or rather, He takes pleasure in tormenting me. So, I stay far away from Him." Lily watched the women's facial expressions. Most people revolted at the thought of her not fitting into their perfect Christian mold. But Mrs. Smith and Belle's faces wore a light smile without scolding. An unusual response.

"I get it. Three years ago, anger towards God poured out of my heart. He took away my husband and watched as my world crumbled a part." Belle adjusted the receiving blanket over her sons. "I doubted He even cared."

"You were married to someone else before Detective Paul?" As the woman spoke, Lily leaned closer, captivated by her story, her curiosity growing with each passing sentence.

"It's a lengthy and twisted story." Belle plopped down on the barstool next to Lily as she grabbed a pecan, tossing it into her mouth. A smiling tugging on the corners of her lips. "Let's just say God turned a mess into my biggest blessing."

I was not expecting that. Lily ran her teeth over the bottom of her lip, catching skin. "Did you ever feel you were on God's hit list?"

"Sure. And not only God's but other people's too. I learned I couldn't blame God for all the bad things that happen in life." Belle tossed another pecan into her mouth. "I'd go through it all over again, because it brought me to my husband and my biggest blessings."

Lily knew a little of Belle's kidnapping and the attempts on her life. How could anyone walk out of that and still believe in God? Was she a superhuman, or something?

Mrs. Smith's laughter floated through the oven-warmed kitchen mixed with spices and apple pie. "Belle struggled a lot, but in the end, God won. No matter what you're going through, don't be so quick to blame God. He brought you here, didn't He? That's a wonderful thing."

"Ladies, how about we sample the apple pie before the men eat it all?" Belle grabbed three forks out of the drawer, passing them out.

"You know what I always say. A chef must sample her own food. It's an essential part of cooking. Let's dig in." She set three pieces of thinly sliced pie on paper plates.

Laughter filled the kitchen, creating an atmosphere of pure happiness. Pleasurable groans escaped their mouths, adding to the delightful symphony.

****

"What are you trying to say? You think she killed her brother?" Stephen leaned against the wall as he crossed his arms over his broad chest. There was absolutely no way he would fall for someone who was a killer. The image of her soft, green eyes flashed in his mind. Lily's eyes were anything but the eyes of a murderer. He refused to believe it, even if his friend had already jumped to that conclusion.

"Man, you're not listening. Take off the love-tinted glasses and hear what I'm saying." Paul propped his feet on the side of the desk, frowning.

"Fine, I'm listening." But he really wasn't. He would not let his friend destroy the doctor's reputation.

"There's no evidence that she was involved in her brother's murder or anything that's happened to her since then."

"But?" Stephen's words pierced his brother-in-law like sharp daggers. Despite their close bond as best buds since high school and brother-in-law's, they didn't always share the same viewpoints. Their relationship was something truly extraordinary, teetering on the edge of uniqueness. They could exchange blows and hurl insults, but their bond as brothers remained unshaken.

"Dude, you're really into her." Paul's dark eyes sparkled under the fluorescent light. "It's refreshing to see you passionate about something other than work."

"That is irrelevant to this conversation." Stephen shifted his leg uncomfortably, his gaze fixed on his dad. "Come on Dad, take a side."

Kevin Smith's steely eyes brightened. As a former Marine for twenty years, he still held the demeanor of a soldier. "Son, I know better than to get mixed up in your squabble. But I will say, the lover boy look works for you."

"Yeah, it does." Paul's laughter erupted from his lips.

"Fine, jab all you want. But I won't invite you two to the wedding." At the corner of his mouth, a crooked smile slowly formed, giving a mischievous look to his face.

"There won't be a wedding if you don't notch up the charm. She seems ready to bolt at any minute." Paul tossed his feet on the carpet as the thud echoed through the small room, bouncing off of the wall-lined bookshelves.

"I won't take love advice from a guy that waited six years before he reconciled with my sister."

"Everything complicated it."

"Love always is worth it." Kevin stepped toward the desk, arms resting behind his back. "Do I need to get you boys some tea and cookies to go along with your love fest? Or do we have a case to solve?"

"Fine." Paul touched the top of a closed envelope. His fingers tracing along the edges of the folder. "To be perfectly clear, Lily did not kill her brother. But maybe she knows who did."

"Why?"

"Looking at her father's death, there's no way that fire was an accident. Someone attempted to murder her, but they ended up successfully killing him. Surprisingly, he was incredibly wealthy, worth a fortune."

"And the money went to her?" Money was always a powerful motive for crime.

"You guessed it."

"Let's not forget that Jason was a CIA agent. He could have crossed the wrong guy and that had begun Lily's torment." Stephen furrowed his brow, his fingers automatically reaching up to scratch his head as he struggled to come up with an idea. "Lily said the thug that tried abducting her mentioned Jason's name."

"Could be a coverup, or she landed herself in the middle of a criminal organization by association."

"Did you check out her ex, Ronald Fisher?" Stephen slid into the chair across from the wooden bookshelf, crossing his leg over his knee.

"Nothing more than a few speeding tickets. The guy likes to drive fast, border-line suspended license fast." With a straight back, Paul remained fixated on Stephen, his eyes never wavering. "Not much to go on. But I'm going to keep digging until we find any leads or the perp messes up. Desperation causes carelessness."

"What about the list of names I found in Jason's belongings?" Stephen's gaze shifted to the clock on the wall, its faint ticking filling the room. Two hours. He'd been away from Lily for two hours. She could take care of herself and Belle could shoot almost better than he could, but he needed to be near her himself. Not because his heart swooned every time his eyes locked onto hers, but because he was investing in this case. *Yeah, right? Keep thinking it's all about protecting her.*

"I'm still looking into that. It is Christmas week, and you gave me the list hours ago." Paul moved the file into the drawer, a smile spreading across his face. "You're ready to bolt. Missing Lily that much?"

Stephen's face turned a bright shade of red as he dramatically rolled his eyes. "Pure-bred bachelor in the flesh."

Paul's eyes crinkled with delight, and his rich laughter resonated throughout the room. "Whatever you say, bro."

"I'm splitting boys. Two hours and all the pies might have mysteriously disappeared." Kevin Smith trudged to the door, the weight of exhaustion visible in each heavy step he took, and gave a tired salute to his boys before disappearing down the hall.

"Shoot straight with me. Do you think the thugs after Lily will tire and leave her alone?"

"As your friend, I'd advise you to stick close to her. Even the top-notch security system could be breeched with the right skills." In one swift motion, Paul jumped out of his chair and rushed to the door, his excitement palpable. "My new partner is joining us for supper and your cousin

Kayla is dropping off Mary and Katie. I need to swipe a few cookies before they eat them all."

"I don't know how you stay in shape with that sweet tooth of yours." As Stephen flipped the lights off, he gave him a reassuring pat on the back.

"Touche." As Paul closed the door behind him, his eyes sparkled with laughter, adding a touch of mischief to his expression.

"Let's go. I've got two princesses eagerly awaiting their uncle to shower them with love and affection." Stephen walked down the dimly lit hall, enticed by the aroma of freshly baked cookies and apple pie.

****

Lily passed the mashed potatoes and tried ignoring the feeling rising in the pit of her stomach. What was it? Joy? A feeling of belonging? She smiled at the chatter and foreign energy of the people gathered around the table. This feeling of family was something she got from watching a cheesy movie, not something she actually partook in. She shoved a bite of chicken into her mouth, trying not to frown. The food and company were great, but none of it was real. Under normal circumstances, she'd be home alone, dreading another holiday. Not feasting at a table spread with delicious food, laughing at jokes and making memories of a family she didn't even belong with.

She had to keep her heart guarded or her treacherous heart would long for more than her lonely existence could give her. Lily felt warm fingers wrapping around her sweating palms. Stephen. She had never met such a charming and caring man. But she wouldn't explore a relationship no matter what happened. None of the things he wanted were in her future. No marriage, children, or happiness. The sensation of brokenness enveloped her body, making her fingers tremble uncontrollably. Images of lowering her parents' caskets into the ground sent chills through her body. God took everyone from her. She would not allow Him to take Stephen's life because of her. He deserved better than her and God's judgement.

As Stephen leaned over, his arm lightly grazed against hers, sending a shiver down her spine. "Are you ok?"

Lily fought back the tears, desperately willing them to stay hidden. "I'm fine." Lily couldn't bring herself to meet his gaze, afraid that his compassionate stare would cause her to break down.

"Remember the time my mom left you in charge of the house for two hours during an emergency?" Kayla's laughter floated through the dining room, pinging off the wall-papered walls. Lily studied the twenty-year-olds animated face. Her blue eyes sparkled with mischief.

"Not that story!" Stephen tossed a dinner roll at his cousin from across the table.

"Food fight!" Mary grabbed a spoonful of mashed potatoes with her small fingers, holding it in the air.

"Drop it young lady." Her father's stern voice didn't match the playfulness in his eyes.

"See what I put up with." Mrs. Smith, while hiding the corners of her smiling lips with a napkin, shook her head.

"Who votes that I continue my story?"

In an instant, all hands shot up into the air while Stephen's face flushed a bright shade of red. He slouched down into his chair and nudged Lily with his arm.

"You too?"

"Hey, I'm all for good stories." Lily took a sip of her tea and leaned back in the chair.

"Stephen had just turned thirteen and Aunt Lea was at the doctor with Belle. Stephen didn't want to go to the doctor with them, so he stayed with us. But my mom had an emergency at her store. She left Stephen in charge with me and my sisters, three kids under five."

"I never tire of hearing this story." With a sly grin, Belle winked at her brother, silently conveying her amusement.

"My sisters and I mixed up the soaps as a simple prank. Well, Stephen wanted to be super man and have the house clean and supper on by the time my mom came home."

"I had good intentions." Stephen threw up his arms in exasperation and rolled his eyes in annoyance.

"What happened?" Lily scooted her chair closer to the table, eagerly devouring every word that came out of Kayla's mouth.

"Let's just say my aunt wasn't happy that a fireman greeted her at the door and thick bubbles covered the floor, from the kitchen to the laundry room."

"My sister never asked him to babysit again." Mr. Smith shot his son a comical look that seemed out of character for the tough ex-Marine.

"Ok, I know how to run a dishwasher and washing machine now." A warm, subtle smile graced Stephen's lip. "And I hardly ever burn anything in the oven."

"That's because you live on takeout and microwave meals." Paul gave his wife a high-five and tossed a piece of food into his mouth.

"That's low man." With a slight push, Stephen moved his chair back, creating a small gap between him and the table, allowing him to peer directly at Lily. "Care to join me outside? Away from my jokester family."

As Lily held his gaze, she couldn't help but imagine the warmth and affection that would radiate from his smile if he directed it at her, mirroring the love he showed his family. "Sure." She pushed her chair away from the table and set her napkin on her empty plate.

"Come on, man. I was only joking." Kayla's face turned red as she stared at Stephen. "Memories and laughter are good for the soul."

"It's a good story. But I need some fresh mountain air." As Stephen clasped Lily's hand, a sense of warmth and connection surged through her. She jerked her hand from his as they made their way towards the back door. "Save us some pie."

****

The snow fell heavily, creating a white blanket on the ground, as Stephen felt the frigid mountain air cling to his body, causing his arms to tremble. Feeling the biting cold, he rubbed his hands over his arms, seeking some relief. The seclusion of the cabin was a refreshing escape, yet it also carried an eerie sense of isolation. As he peered into the darkness, he saw nothing. Not even a streetlight. He never liked city life, but seclusion was definitely not for him. He'd miss the nosy neighbors who knew his entire schedule and brought him casseroles on late evenings after working in the ER. Not sure he'd miss his fan club, but the women meant well. He never encouraged their school girl crushes or obsessive behavior. Their attention should have flattered him, but he wasn't a prize to be won. That's why Lily's presence was so refreshing. Rejection ordered her affection, or lack thereof. She didn't swoon over his every word or make giddy remarks at his nearness. Did she even like him? Stephen sensed an attraction between them, but the beautiful-faced doctor would never admit it. Something was definitely going on with her. That's why he needed fresh air. Not just for his sake, because he could take his family's jabs, but because she looked ready to bolt. He cast a sideways glance in her direction. Her eyes were closed as she sat, arms wrapped around her body. She seemed peaceful, but the frown lines on her face said otherwise.

  Stephen plopped down next to her, pulling her into a warm and comforting embrace. Core body temperature was very important. In the snowy mountains, hyperthermia could set in fast. She wouldn't refuse this gesture of survival as anything but professional. Would she? Who was he kidding? They were feet away from a warm house not lost in icy terrain.

  "What's going through your mind?" He nudged her arm, basking in their closeness as her cinnamon-scented locks engulfed his body.

  "I'm fine."

  He didn't dare look at her face. They were so close, her nearness might tempt him to brush his lips over hers, offering warmth and security. And honestly, he didn't know why he kept doing that. It's not like he went around kissing beautiful women. Quite the opposite.

"I have a sister." There was a hint of amusement in his words, making them dance with lightheartedness. "I learned fast that fine meant anything but, and I had to watch my back."

Lily exhaled, and her breath formed a misty cloud that lingered in the air. "Stephen, why are you wasting your time with me? I have nothing to offer you. Even if I did, I wouldn't give it to you. I'm a dead-end road."

Feeling his heart shatter into countless fragments, he realized he couldn't endure any more rejection without it bruising his ego. However, he refused to give up easily; he was determined to be resilient and not let her push him away.

Lily Walsh needed a friend. Him. And after the police arrested the thugs after her, he'd leave her alone if that's what she wanted. Until then, she was stuck with him.

"I truly think that God brought us together for a reason," he said, gently running his fingers along the sleeve of her jacket, savoring the comforting heat of the fleece fabric. "As long as you're in harm's way, I won't leave your side."

Her body stiffened at the mention of God. "That's the problem. God does nothing good, at least not for me. We won't ever agree on that. Your faith makes you a wonderful man, whereas my cynicism and contempt make me a realist who in not compatible with you. We won't ever happen." She scooted away from him, staring into the darkness. "My life isn't the only thing at stake here. Both of our hearts might not make it out of this intact."

Stephen's brain whispered, *Run before it's too late.* But his heart wouldn't abandon her in her time of need. Who was he to argue with God? God had a purpose in their crossed lives and he wouldn't miss out on a blessing because of fear.

He tightly clasped her hand and observed her eyes filled with tears, and her skin tinged with a delicate pink hue. "No matter how hard you push me away, I'm not leaving until you are safe."

A soft whimper escaped her lips. "Why?"

"I don't run away from problems. Let me carry some of your burdens. It'll make your load so much lighter." He ran his fingers down the frown line on her lips. "No strings attached."

Her eyes blinked back tears as she scooted closer and leaned against his firm body. "I'll buy it for now."

The sound of his laughter wrapped around them, creating a sense of coziness and joy. "Why Ms. Walsh, you're making me blush."

Lily playfully swatted at his fingers, smiling. "What have I gotten myself into?"

"Only time will tell." Stephen's smile slid from his face as a gush of icy air pounded on his exposed skin. "What were you thinking at the dinner table?"

"How fortunate I was to partake in a family meal. Even if it's not real."

"Explain."

"My family had a lot of money growing up, but hardly any love." Her eyes took on a faraway look, like she was eighteen years away. "We never had family mealtime. Not even during the holidays. Every germ could have made my mom sicker, so my father pushed me away. He robbed me of a relationship with my mother." Lily's hand formed a tight fist at her side, a visible sign of the anger she was holding back.

"That's rough." He squeezed her hand, offering comfort and support.

"After my mom passed away, things were awkward between my dad and me. We never had a relationship, by his choosing. Bitterness severed any connections I had with him. His selfishness robbed me of my childhood — mom, dad, brother." She squeezed Stephen's hand and continued talking. "He disappeared after my mom died. His secret life stole him away from me."

"What do you mean?"

"He prided himself as the CEO of a successful investment firm. With success came many admirers." Lily's breath quivered in the disappearing fog, vanishing into the chilly night air. "I have no proof, but I think he had a secret family."

"That's a big accusation. Why do you think that?" He pushed away slightly, taking in the haunting emptiness in her eyes. Enlarged pupils, pale face, shaking body. Fear had wrapped its ugly arms around her body, trying to choke the life out of her.

"He stayed away from home for days at a time, making his presence known only when it was a convenience to him." Lily's fingers instinctively sought comfort as she rubbed the arms of her jacket, her nervousness palpable in the chilly air. "I started investigating and found pictures online of him with an extravagant red head. They looked too cozy to be work associates."

"It's not a crime dating after a spouse passes away." As the words poured out, his tone remained flat, devoid of any emotion.

"No, I guess not, but the secrecy behind all of it seemed wrong." As she ran her fingers through her dark hair, a slight frown creased her forehead. "One night, when he had come home from a week-long absence, I snuck into his office and hacked into his phone. The pictures I saw stabbed my ten-year-old heart. I wanted a family and smiling back at me was my dad, one arm wrapped around the red-haired woman and another holding a small baby. He looked so happy."

"Any idea of the woman's identity?" Stephen's heartbeat raced, the sound pounding in his ears as he stared into the ominous darkness.

"Julia Price." The words tumbled out of Lily's mouth, sharp and bitter, as if she were desperate to purge herself of a poisonous substance. "Throughout the years, my father never mentioned her, but deep down, I knew he had a hidden family. The mystery of why he kept this from me, denying me the chance to know them, always puzzled me. Growing up, Jason lived at a boarding school. So, it seemed like I was an only child."

"Did you ever see her in person?" Another lead to the threats against Lily's life.

"I glimpsed at her at the funeral. She sat hidden under a black cloak. I'll never forget her tear-stained face and red-rimmed eyes. In that split second, when our eyes locked, a shiver ran down my spine, for it felt as if I had come face to face with the embodiment of evil itself. If looks could kill, it would have been a double funeral."

"Any contact with her since then?" None of it made sense. Sixteen-year-old Lily could have imagined the whole thing, but he doubted it.

"None." Lily stood to her feet, stretching her legs and arms. "My dad's secret family, Jason's murder, and the attempts on my life can't go together."

"Anything is possible." He stood up to his full height and slowly approached Lily, feeling a slight unease being out in the open, even in the middle of nowhere.

"Why wait eleven years to come after me?" She shivered as the chilly wind swooshed on the porch.

"The child, assuming it was your father's, would be almost eighteen by now. Money plays an enormous factor in a lot of crimes. It's worth looking into."

"I'd hate thinking a half-sibling I never met is trying to kill me over money." The words tumbled out barely above a whisper.

"Millions of dollars." Scratching his head, he gazed into the distance with a puzzled expression on his face. Did he just see a small light in the field a few hundred yards from the cabin?

"So, you did a background check on me?" Lily's reddened face shone with displeasure.

"Its standard procedure." He wrapped his arms around her shoulders. "Do you see that faint light in the distance?"

Lily stared into the field as trembles overtook her body. "They've found us. I need to leave right now. I'm putting your family's lives at risk."

"Calm down. It could be anyone." The temptation to kiss her and soothe her overwhelmed him, but he suppressed it.

"On private property?" Her question was valid and made sense. Whoever was out there wasn't having a joyride on the outskirts of the mountains.

An ominous prickly sensation crawled up his arms as the light came closer. "Let's get inside fast." With their fingers entwined, he led her into his parents' house, where he immediately felt a sense of security. Whoever was out there would not get to her. Not on his watch.

Chapter Six

The heat drew Lily into the warmth of the kitchen as she stepped into the cabin, rubbing her numb hands. She glanced at Stephen's family, who were clearing the table and sweeping the floor. Unity. They worked well together because of love and familiarity. Home looked like this. A common love and determination to serve and help each other. Her eyes traveled to Belle as envy tried pouring through her veins. She had been through deadly circumstances, yet here she was with a renewed faith in God, and a dedicated husband and four precious children. She had it all, and she had to trudge through the fire just to receive it. That would never be Lily, though. God wasn't who He claimed to be, and no amount of fire would change that. With a heavy sigh, she took another step into the kitchen. The hum of the dishwasher breaking her out of her daze.

What happened to Stephen? Her pitiful mind made her lose track of Stephen and the other men. The intruder. Stephen must have quietly left without her noticing. Obviously, he wouldn't stay hidden within the safety of the walls when danger was lurking outside. She felt a rush of air leaving her lungs, causing her to bend over and gasp for breath. If anything happened to Stephen, she could never forgive herself.

As on cue, Stephen dashed into the room, gun in hand, followed by his dad and Paul.

"There's an intruder on the premises or a lost hiker. Either way, we're doing a perimeter sweep. No one goes outside." Lily felt a sense of security as he pulled her close, his arm enveloping her waist with a gentle yet firm touch.

His breath fanned the edges of her ears. "Breathe. You're okay."

The look on his face, combined with his mesmerizing ocean blue eyes, caught her completely off guard. Love? Compassion? Longing? At that moment, Lily longed for things she had no business thinking about. Lily was only setting her heart up for tragedy. She would not, no, she could not, fall for this extremely handsome man. She needed to keep her distance to protect *him*.

I'm such a fool. Why did I ever agree to stay with his family for Christmas? I'm too weak. My heart has deceived me. This stops now.

Not sensing her inner turmoil, He leaned over and pressed his lips to the top of her forehead. Chills pulsated through her body as she watched him step to the door.

"When I come back, I'll treat you to a movie and ice cream." His smile disappeared as he followed Paul and his dad into the dark night.

A movie and ice cream would not work for her. Not if she wanted to shield her heart anymore. A movie and dessert while watching a cheesy Christmas movie, with a potential spouse, sat high on her longing list, but also on her not-going-to-happen list. Potential spouse? Stephen was the biggest bachelor in town, and she was not interested. There, she thought it. It did nothing to stop the butterflies slicing through her stomach, though.

"You look how I feel." Mrs. Smith tugged on Lily's arm, pulling her to the kitchen table. "I saved you a piece of pie. It helps calm the nerves."

Lily slid into the chair, picking up her fork and smashing the pie into pieces.

"Oh, my. What did the pie do to deserve such treatment?" The sound of Mrs. Smith's laughter danced through the warm and inviting room.

"Don't worry about my brother. He is a skilled marksman, and he has two tough guys watching his back." Belle handed her daughters a cookie, watching them run out of the room, as crumbs tumbled onto the tiled-floor.

Kayla stepped into the kitchen, grabbed the twins, and walked to the doorway, smiling at the babies in her arms. "I promised Mary and Katie one more story before you get them ready for bed. I thought the boys wanted to hear it, too."

"You're amazing, Kayla." Belle's eyes sparkled with delight as she watched her cousin disappear into the next room, her children in tow.

"No, I'm just the fun cousin. You do this every day and make it look easy." Kayla's voice sounded from the other room. "I want to be like you when I grow up."

"Flattery won't get you anymore cookies." Belle swatted her hand in the air toward the living room. "Kayla's studying to be a teacher. I would want to be in her class."

Mrs. Smith set a cup of hot apple cider next to Lily's plate. "God sure blessed us when He put that firecracker into our family."

Lily shoved a big bite of cinnamon and apples into her mouth. They did not need to hear what she thought about God.

"It's an icy night to be tramping through the mountains. I hope the men return soon." Mrs. Smith absentmindedly rubbed her fingers over the rim of a glass, staring in the distance.

"Mom, nothing bad will happen to them. They probably saw a bear or something."

"With a flashlight?" The words escaped Lily's mouth before she could even consider the potential consequences.

"Oh, dear." Mrs. Smith covered her mouth with her trembling hand. "Someone has breeched our security."

Lily pushed the chair back with her legs and stood to her feet. "It's my fault. I brought danger into your sanctuary. I'll pack my bags."

Fool. She was more concerned with her own safety than the wonderful family that stayed here. She needed to draw away the bad guys, even if it meant death.

"Don't be silly." Belle pushed a chair toward the high-to-reach cabinets, the legs scraping against the floor. She pulled out a metal container. "You're not going anywhere. Besides, we protect our own."

"I don't belong here. Nor is it fair that I'm endangering your children." Lily took a step away from the ladies. She had to get out of here before anything bad happened. She'd spend the week in a hotel, indulging in room service and binge watching her favorite movies. "What's in the box?"

Belle entered a code and pulled out a small handgun. Her fingers ran across the smooth surface. "It's best to be prepared than wish I had it later. And don't worry, my dad taught me how to handle a firearm."

Lily took a short, choppy breath. She needed to calm down, not break down, and have a panic attack. Around her stood women of strength and courage. Lily would not give in to fear.

In a single minute, a sharp popping noise, followed by the shattering of glass, disrupted the air. As terror consumed the house, a chaotic blend of screams and frightened childish voices filled the room.

"Kayla!" Belle took off running toward the living room, Lily and Mrs. Smith following behind.

"We're fine. Just shaken up." Kayla stepped over pieces of glass, staring at the broken window.

The living room window bore the evidence of a bullet hole, a stark reminder of the violence that had occurred. The bullet could have injured one of Belle's children. This had to stop, now. Offer myself for them. They deserved none of this.

"Now's not the time to play hero." Mrs. Smith tugged on Lily's arm, frowning. "Let's get to the safe room and wait for the men."

Lily trembled with fear, her body consumed by anxiety. Despite feeling on the verge of collapsing, she resolved to be brave. The women led her into a compact room, and a shiver ran down her spine as the weighty metal door slammed shut behind them. The men would soon arrive, unless the perpetrator got to them first. In that scenario, it would be them against a ruthless killer.

****

Stephen skillfully and silently trudged through the field, guided by the soft glow of a distant light. He had only hiked through the property once, so the unfamiliar terrain was to his disadvantage. But his dad knew the land that creeped up to the mountains as any decent park ranger would. Three against one. They would find the thug who dared invade private property. Assuming he was a lone stranger and not working with someone else.

Stephen watched as Paul slithered further into the darkness. He couldn't see his dad, but they weren't exactly carrying flashlights. Paul wanted them to go rogue so as not to alarm whoever was out here. They needed to draw the perp away from the women and children. Unless it was a lost straggler who got turned around in the vast mountain range. His parents' property included twelve acres of wooded areas and rolling hills. Their property extended into mountains and forests. At the start of the mountain range was a state park. Anyone could easily get lost in the dense forest and treacherous mountains. He had no intention of finding out. Stephen thrived in an outdoor setting, but unfamiliarity caused confusion. It amazed him how he chose a career where he rarely traveled outside and never hunted bad guys. He enjoyed the thrill of following clues and apprehending bad guys. Although he had never captured a criminal or rescued a heroine. All just mock games he'd play with his buddies, honing his skills. Stephen loved being a doctor, but the work was demanding and life-consuming. Some days, he barely had time to sleep. With a doctor short, the ER never rested. Being the single doctor, he took extra shifts so his coworkers could be home with their families.

He'd once thought no woman would ever tie him down. But lately he longed for the simpler life—a wife, kids, people to share his life with. Two years from thirty might have helped put life into perspective. Time passed in a blur, and before he knew it, he was waking up to another day, feeling old and lonely. Not his future anymore. When Lily was safe, he'd ask her out on a date. If she refused, he had plenty of options. But none gripped his heart like she did.

"Stephen." His walkie talkie came to life, bringing him back to the mission at hand—find the perp, keep the women and children safe.

"I'm feet away from the spot I saw the perp at." As Stephen kneeled down onto the wet snowy ground, he could hear the soft crunching of snow beneath his knees and see his breath forming mist in the chilly air. He stared at the lantern, its flickering light casting dancing shadows on the white landscape. "I have a bad feeling about this."

"I'm coming up behind you." Lowering his gun, Paul stealthily snuck up behind him, his eyes fixated on the mesmerizing glow. "A set-up."

Kevin Smith's voice cut through the darkness as he slid next to his son. "And we fell for it."

Stephen rose to his feet, his gaze fixed on the cabin. Fear surged through his body, causing him to mutter senseless words under his breath. What an idiot. What a fool.

The perpetrator led the women's protectors away from the cabin, providing him with ample unguarded time to commit any atrocious crime. The lights shining through the windows were barely visible to him. They had walked too far. He made a mental note to stay with the women next time.

"Do you hear that?" The sound of gunshots pierced through the stillness of the night, causing Paul to freeze in his tracks.

"That was way too close." With a vigorous shake of his head, Stephen dashed off towards the cabin, his footsteps echoing in the distance.

Fleeing from Danger, Jessica West

The deafening screech sharply broke the unsettling tranquility of the surroundings. There was definitely something happening, and he had a bad feeling about it. He fervently prayed to God, asking for the safety of the women and children.

"Guns drawn, be on alert." Paul inched next to Stephen. "No rushing into the cabin until we access the scene."

"It could be an ambush." Mr. Smith's hard-as-steel voice broke through the night sounds. "It's go time, boys."

"Stephen, you sneak inside. We'll cover you."

Crouching low, Stephen moved stealthily toward the back of the cabin. His heart raced so loudly it convinced him that any bad guy in the vicinity could hear him coming. *God, still my racy heart.*

He pushed open the unlocked back door and slid inside. Everything appeared normal. A cup and plate of pie sat on the countertop. The dishwasher hummed in the background. Light glared from the ceiling. But one thing was amiss—silence. The cheery atmosphere missed one important feature—people. It was unlike his mom to leave a room without cleaning it. Something or someone surprised them.

Gun drawn, he stepped into the living room. His eyes scanned the room and stopped at glass splattered over the hardwood floors. He crouched next to the broken window, glaring at a scant amount of blood. Not a sign of a serious injury, but the bullet had injured someone.

I can't risk calling out to the ladies in case the thug is still here who shot out the window. He slipped into the hall, aware of every hiding place. Stephen opened closets, bathrooms, and checked in every nook he could find.

Nothing. Relief flooded his soul. But where were the women and children?

A thought smacked him in the face as he jogged toward the last door at the end of the hall. His dad's paranoia encouraged him to build a safe room in the cabin. Not even a bullet could get through the steel-enforced walls. Stephen leaned over, panting for a breath of air. He was in shape, but horrifying thoughts penetrated his mind, stealing his energy.

"Mom? Belle? Lily?" He tapped on the door, leaning against it, listening for any movement. They have to be in here. If the thug took them…

The heavily constructed door squeaked open as his mother, wide-eyed and pale, fell into his arms. "You're ok. Is your father and Paul…"

Stephen rubbed his mother's back, taking in her freshly baked cookie scent. "They're fine. Just paroling the front of the house."

"What took you so long?" Kayla moved out of the shadows, carrying a baby. "Oxygen was depleting fast."

"I'm glad you're safe too." Stephen rolled his eyes at his cousin's bluntness. "The bullet grazed you?" He pointed to her bandaged arm.

"The shrapnel grazed my arm." Kayla's faint smile disappeared. "Your lady friend, Doctor Lily, fixed me up."

"Lily?" He poked his head inside the room, searching for Lily. She leaned against the wall, eyes closed, holding Mary's tiny hand.

Longing creeped inside his heart as he snapped a mental picture of the woman with his oldest niece. The soft light from the fluorescent light bathed them in a warm glow, casting gentle shadows on their faces. She looked like a natural, her calming presence sending comfort to a frightened child. The faint scent of freshly baked cookies, with the smell of stale air, created a weirdly welcoming atmosphere. Before he could convince himself otherwise, he took two long strides, the sound of his footsteps echoing in his ears, and wrapped Lily in his protective arms.

She snuggled her face into his chest, her rapid breaths creating a small breeze against his skin. The warmth from her touch sent a jolt of awareness spiking through Stephen's body, every nerve ending coming alive. He realized at that moment there would never be another woman for him, that this connection was irreplaceable.

"When I heard the gunshots, I thought I had failed you, and…"

Lily placed her trembling finger over his lips, silencing him. Her touch felt both delicate and electric, sending shivers down his spine. "Stephen, we need to talk. Now."

His hands fell to his side, stepping away from her, the absence from her touch, leaving him longing for more. Something was clearly bothering her, and all he wanted was to hold her again, feeling the steady beat of her heart and the closeness of her breath.

****

Gratitude welled up inside Lily as she stared into the face of the man that risked his life to protect her again. Without his help, the bad guys would have already won. Her survival skills weren't enough to keep her safe. Sure, she could stitch up gunshot wounds and all that, but it meant nothing if she were already dead.

Reluctant to venture outside, Lily cautiously led the way to a dimly lit back bedroom, which she presumed to be the office. The musty scent of old books lingered in the air as she entered. She felt an urgent need to persuade Stephen to abandon his role as her bodyguard and allow her to escape from him and his family. The looming danger made her heart race, as gunshots and the sound of frightened children shattered the usual tranquility of Christmas week.

She yearned to vanish, to disappear, until the deranged individual harassing her would leave her in peace. And if that never happened, she contemplated disappearing forever. With her bank account brimming with more money than she could ever fathom spending, the means for her disappearance were readily available. Yet, could she bear to leave Stephen behind, never again experiencing the warmth of his embrace or the intensity of his gaze? Her heart would instinctively protest, but the reality remained that they were never truly a couple. In protecting him, she shielded both their hearts from a love that could never blossom. As she reflected on her history of losing loved ones, her mother, father, Ronald, and her brother, she vowed not to add Stephen's name to that tragic list.

Lily slid to a chair away from a window, close to a floor to ceiling bookshelf. She needed space to gather her thoughts away from the intriguing and handsome doctor.

Jumbled words swirled in her mind, a chaotic symphony of confusion. The words tumbled out of her mouth, a desperate plea for escape. "I'm leaving."

A bittersweet smile etched itself onto Stephen's pallid face, his lips curling with a mix of resignation and understanding. The sound of his breath hitched, almost imperceptibly, as if catching on the weight of unspoken thoughts. Did he, too, yearn for the safety that distance could bring? Her presence had become a shadow of danger, threatening his very kin. In this moment, the choice of ice cream to complement his apple pie seemed trivial, a frivolous indulgence compared to the gravity of their predicament. But the biggest decision he should make this week.

Stephen's arms folded, his fingers leaving creases on the fabric of his sky-blue shirt. The color, like the calm expanse of the ocean, accentuated the intensity of his gaze. His eyes, the color of a summer sky, held a flicker of agreement. "Maybe you're right."

Even Stephen had now turned his back on her, aligning his desires with her own. It was what she had hoped for, after all.

"Really?"

"Look Lily, I didn't understand the magnitude of your danger when I invited you here." His eyes bore no emotion as he stared at her. "I misjudged my abilities to protect you. My dad's combat skills should have helped, along with Paul's top-notch detective skills. I was wrong."

He was really pushing her away. She shifted uncomfortably in the high-backed chair. Where would she go? Would she survive the morning?

"I'm a level-headed guy, but I felt compelled to take you in like I would a stray dog." Stephen rubbed the sides of his chin. "I can save lives in the ER, but you shouldn't trust me outside of the hospital."

Something was going on. His words sounded too familiar.

"You brought this upon yourself. If you would have mended the broken relationship with your brother, he would still be alive. Whatever hidden secrets he bore, he would have revealed to you. Your stubbornness aided in his murder. I don't want to have any part of that."

His harsh words struck Lily's heart like a sudden surge of electricity, leaving her breathless and disoriented. The room seemed to darken as his words hung in the air, suffocating her with their weight. His voice reverberated in her ears, each syllable cutting deeper than the last. The faint scent of despair and regret lingered in the air, mingling with the tension between them. As Stephen took a step forward, a rush of wind swept between them, intensifying the cold emptiness that settled in Lily's chest.

Lily's eyes watered at his blunt words. His words were the truth, but hearing them out loud caused bile to rise in her throat.

Stephen crouched down in front of her, wiping a stray tear from her cheek. His touch sending butterflies into her anxious stomach. "Sound familiar?"

Her mouth fell open at the realization of what had just happened. "You spoke every argument that I would have used against you, but you reversed it and attacked me with my own thoughts."

He brushed his fingers against the edge of her cheek. His eyes shone with love and longing. "How did it feel?"

"Miserable."

He reached out and gently intertwined his rough, calloused fingers with hers, drawing her closer to him. "I am familiar with every argument, but none of them hold any truth."

"Stephen…"

With a gentle touch, he pressed his finger against her lips, bringing his face so close that his lips brushed against hers. In a sweet, electrifying moment, her heart stopped as she realized she could never simply turn her back on Stephen.

****

Stephen shot Lily a sideways glance as he pulled the keys from the ignition. She hadn't spoken five words as they drove into town, carrying a list of supplies from his mom. He didn't want to leave the cabin or the safety of knowing his brother-in-law and Dad had his back, but Lily looked on the verge of a breakdown. She needed to take her mind off of everything and just relax. Not true for him, but his sister claimed retail therapy calmed jittery nerves and refocused energy. Lily needed both things. It took some persuading as an extra Smith and Wesson strapped to his side, but Paul agreed with the trip if it got Belle off his back. Stephen ran his fingers over the hard, sleek metal. His pulse quickened, feeling the reality of the situation. A thug was determined to silence the beautiful woman next to him. He could not pretend their trip into town was a normal outing of two people in love. Love? That word again? Pure-bred bachelors didn't love a woman other than their mother, sister, or any other female relative. He slid his fingers over her balled up fist, awareness and flutters flowed through his body. He couldn't ever go back to bachelorhood, not after Lily's piercing green eyes wedged a place in his heart.

Life wasn't about random takeout food, nights out with the guys, or even watching sports in the loneliness of his condo. He wanted, no, he needed, so much more than that. And everything revolved around the petite woman, trying so hard to keep the barrier cemented to her heart. She didn't want a relationship, at least not with him. Every once in a while, the spark of longing radiated from her eyes, sending him enough hope to dream of a forever-home with her. Besides, God had a plan in bringing them together, whether it was more than him being her protector, he didn't know, but prayed so.

Lily stroked the top of his knuckle before jerking her fingers away from his touch. Tears threatened to pound from her face as Stephen found the only parking spot of a make-shift mall.

"Sweetie, I'm right beside you. The bad guy won't get his filthy hands on you again." Sweetie? Where did that come from? Yes, they lived in the South, but he never went around using names of endearment for any female besides his nieces.

Lily's misty green eyes pierced through his body, reaching to the depths of his soul. Shifting uncomfortably, he slid his cellphone in his pocket, checking his mirrors. Nothing out of the ordinary besides a guy carrying an enormous inflatable turkey. Not something he saw every day. And he saw a lot of crazy stuff in the ER.

"Maybe if we hurry, we can eat lunch at my aunt's diner." Stephen hopped out of his jeep, circling around to the passenger seat. Lily stood staring into space, like her mind was millions of miles away.

"Your aunt lives around here and has a diner?" Lily slid her gloved-hands into her coat pockets. Which helped him fight the urge to clasp his hands between hers, claiming something that didn't belong to him.

"She moved to North Carolina, but she manages the restaurant with Kayla's help, and she visits often." He wrapped his arm around her waist, feeling the silky texture of her coat leading her to a side entrance.

"Must be nice having so much family."

It did, and he would willingly add her on that list if she let him. Stephen shook his head at the foolishness of his thoughts. *Keep yourself in check, man.*

He pulled her closer to his body. And it had nothing to do with protection. The eerie sound of silence punched him in the gut. With a parking lot full of cars, cheerful chatter, screaming children, and Christmas music was what he had hoped to hear, not silence.

They stepped past a man dressed as Santa, ringing a bell, and rushed through the nearest door. Something about Santa seemed off. His eyes followed their every move, causing pricks to dance to his neck. Maybe he had too many eggnogs. Or maybe … no, Santa wasn't an undercover criminal. Stephen shook the fogginess out of his head. Not everyone had a sinister plot in mind. Most people were enjoying the Christmas holiday. He should try it.

Lily's body stiffened as her gaze fell on a crowd of twenty people pushing their way through the busy aisles, carts full of last-minute Christmas items.

Speaking of which, Stephen yanked out his mother's list, staring at her sloppy handwriting. After all these years, he still couldn't read her handwriting. Stephen smiled to himself as he spotted Santa dashing through the aisles like a rabid raccoon. What was going on? He curled his fingers around Lily's arms, pulling her to his side as the sound of glass breaking mixed with groans filled the air.

"Give me the woman and the girl lives to see another Christmas." Santa had his arm around a pale-faced girl's neck, a gun poking into her skull.

"No, my baby!" A woman's violent screams jumped from the aisles, slapping Stephen in the jaw. Good thing he wasn't a cop, because they'd have fired him a long time ago. His one job of protecting Lily failed. How was he going to get out of this mess? With a quick motion, he sent a text to Paul detailing the situation. He couldn't rely on his buddy though, not when a good thirty minutes separated them.

"Freeze or the kid gets it!" Santa's blood-shot eyes narrowed in on Lily. "Woman for the child. Fair trade."

Stephen tightened his grip on her arm, pulling her closer to his body. He leaned over, his breathing fanning the edges of her ear. "I need you to trust me."

She pushed her body away from his. A look of defiance flashed in her eyes. "If I were dying, your skills would be life changing. But you're not a detective, and I won't have a child die for me."

She took a step closer to the thug, letting out a soft sigh as she moved her trembling body in front of him.

"No, Lily!" Stephen reached for his gun seconds too late. A crashing sound exploded around him, sending him toppling over into the darkness.

Chapter Seven

Stephen moaned as he fluttered his eyes open. Where was he? What was that cinnamon-fishy-infused smell? It was enough to make him vomit. Stephen rubbed his eyes as he climbed off the icy tiled floor. His head felt like a sledgehammer pounded the life out of him. A familiar voice sounded from behind him.

"Hey there sleeping beauty." A firm hand clamped onto his shoulder. "It's good you're awake."

Stephen wrapped his fingers around the sides of Paul's jacket, gazing into his humor filled eyes. "Where is she?"

"Calm down, man." Paul brushed Stephen's hands off of his jacket, grabbing his arm to help steady him.

Stephen slapped his buddy's hand away from him, taking deep breaths. *God, she has to be ok.* "Where is Lily?" His voice rising above the chatter in the store. If Paul didn't answer fast, Stephen would probably spend the night in jail for assaulting a police officer. He didn't care.

Paul, sensing the mood change in Stephen, leaned over, whispering, so no one could hear. "We have a hostage situation."

God, no! Stephen winced like someone sucker punched him in his stomach, vomit threatening to spew at any moment. "I'm an idiot. Santa got the drop on me."

"If it makes you feel any better, the guy had a partner; female, around five two, dirty blond chin-length hair."

Stephen ran his fingers through his hair, trying not to let his emotions assault him. Since childhood, he had a deep understanding of the power of emotions. The overwhelming sensitivity that used to drive his parents insane now served as a guiding force in his role as a doctor. In the bustling emergency room, he felt the raw emotions of every person who stepped through the doors. He prayed for every patient on top of the medical intervention he provided.

Stephen, a macho, gun-wielding doctor, was no stranger to the barrage of emotions that threatened to overpower him. But from a young age, he had learned to relinquish control to God, allowing his faith to steady his choppy emotions. However, in this moment, his senses heightened by adrenaline, the intensity of his emotions was undeniable.

Paul, with his hard-as-steel eyes, locked his gaze on Stephen, as if he could read his thoughts. The weight of his words hung heavy in the air.

"The description of the woman matches the mother of the girl that Santa threatened with a gun," Stephen replied, his breath escaping in a furious rush. Realization hit him hard - this whole situation was a meticulously planned setup, and it had succeeded.

"She is in custody," Paul informed him, his voice laced with a hint of satisfaction. "A few hours in jail should loosen her lips."

Stephen's gaze wandered around the empty room, the once vibrant holiday activity now reduced to abandoned shopping carts filled with forgotten merchandise. The atmosphere was thick with fear and tension.

"What about the girl?" Stephen asked, his voice tinged with concern. His eyes darted around, searching for any sign of Lily.

"Kidnapped," Paul confirmed, his tone grim. "But we reunited her with her real mom."

A small smile tugged at the corners of Stephen's lips, relief washing over him. "How long was I out?"

"Not long enough to rescue a hostage," Paul replied, motioning towards the door as an EMS truck pulled up outside. "You need to get checked out."

Stephen crossed his arms, a defiant stance challenging his friend to remove him from the store. He treated head injuries; he knew he didn't have a concussion.

"Doctors are the worst patients," Paul remarked wryly.

"So are cops," Stephen retorted, stepping away from Paul and surveying the aisles. Where had the thug taken Lily? One obstacle hindered his determination to see her - his brother-in-law.

"Leave the situation to the professionals," Paul advised, his eyes flickering towards the back room, a forbidden area reserved for employees only. "State police are assisting me, and a hostage negotiator is on the scene."

"But this is your case?" The words hung in the air as Stephen took off to the back area, not letting Paul reply. He slid down a darkened hall, following the faint hum of electronic devices. Stephen's heart raced as he envisioned finding Lily, his determination overpowering any fear. He entered the first room with an open door. The dim lights casting eerie shadows on the walls. Men in tactical gear huddled over a table, their intense gazes fixated on him. The air felt heavy with tension, charged with anticipation. Stephen ignored their hostile stares, his focus solely on rescuing Lily. He had always prided himself on obeying the law, but with protecting his loved ones, rules became insignificant. Stephen respected his detective brother-in-law, Paul, but he couldn't stand idle while a deranged lunatic threatened Lily's life.

"Sir, this area is off limits," a stern officer with a SWAT team logo on his chest addressed him, rising from his seat.

Undeterred, Stephen folded his arms over his chest, daring the men to arrest him. Lily needed him, or he needed her. She was worth spending the night in jail.

Paul confidently entered the room, his badge clinking against whatever he had in his pocket. "He's with me," Paul announced.

The officer begrudgingly nodded, resuming his seat and focusing his attention back on the screen before him.

Paul gestured towards a chair in the room's corner. "Sit down and stay out of the way," he instructed Stephen. "Don't make me arrest you myself."

Stephen obeyed, puffing as he fell into the chair. He'd do it their way for now. Any sign of escalation and he'd go rogue, and take the fall back later, once he had Lily secured at home.

Paul's gruff voice pierced through the thick fog of silence. "The perp is antsy. We need to make our move soon."

Hostage negotiator, Larry Black, chimed into the system, having direct access to Lily and her abductor. "Let the woman go. Abduction is a lower sentence than murder."

"My rap sheet is longer than a kid's Christmas list." The voice bellowed out; gun pointed at Lily's chest.

Stephen jumped out of his seat, moving to a better view of the cameras. His hands instinctually gripping the gun in his shoulder holster. As a doctor, he knew the signs of a panic attack. Seeing Lily in a fetal position, face pale, rapid breaths, he'd say she needed medical intervention fast.

Paul reached for the stack of paper a team member scooted in front of him, reading the rap sheet. A scowl etched his face as hard lines stretched between his eyebrows.

"Bill King, the jig is up. Let her go."

"She's my insurance out of here. Just buying time until help arrives." He shifted the gun in his hand. "Since that incompetent woman…"

An ambush? No way would he stick around for that to happen. Stephen crouched forward, yanking the microphone from an officer's fingers. "King, this is Doctor Stephen Smith. My patient is on the verge of a panic attack. Unless you are aware of the proper calming mechanisms and resuscitation, I'd advise you to let her go now."

Paul cast a bone-chilling eye toward Stephen, prying the microphone out of his fingers.

King's voice croaked over the speaker, breaking the minute of silence that had felt like an eternity. "Doctor? My wife was a doctor before she died. I'll give you ten minutes to revive Ms. Walsh to her health status. My boss doesn't need a sick female dying on him until after she gives us what we want."

"Unlock the door." Stephen stared at the hard eyes piercing through his body. Within seconds, he had somehow angered six state police officers and his ex-detective best friend, landing himself on their enemy list. Oh well. While they stared at a monitor, he'd rescue Lily.

"You can't go in there. You're a civilian." An officer jumped up, knocking his chair to the tiled floor with a thud. "I could arrest you with obstruction."

"I'm a doctor and she needs medical help. So, while you're twirling your thumbs and daydreaming, I'll be rescuing a hostage." The officer lunged forward, knocking over a stack of papers.

"Cool off, Rodney." Paul pointed to a chair in the back of the room. "This is my case."

"What's taken so long? No funny business." King's voice played over the speakers. "Time is ticking."

Stephen stepped to the door, nodding at Paul. Fumes etched across Paul's face. The plan, or lack of one, infuriated Paul, but he'd get over it. No way would he let Santa get the drop on him twice.

Paul grabbed Stephen's shoulder, leaning in and whispering, "I've got your back, bro."

Stephen knew Paul would be right behind him apprehending the thug, as long as nothing went wrong.

God, use me to rescue Lily, and show her Your love.

After a quick prayer, he edged out of the room, leaving behind the safety that filled a room full of police.

****

Breathe, I won't die today, at least at the hands of this maniac. Who impersonates Santa just to commit a heinous crime? Lily should have stayed in the security fortress of the cabin. Even though the bad guy shot up the place, so security measures mean nothing to him. She took short, choppy breaths, trying to beat down the anxiety swirling in her stomach. Lily bowed her head in disgust. She would not have a panic attack, not now. But no matter how many calming techniques she tried, the pit in her stomach burned with worry. What if this guy killed her? Did that kid make it to safety? Would anyone care if she died? What would happen after death, a sea of nothingness? Was Stephen okay? He crumbled to the floor faster than a sandcastle in high tide. He needed medical help. If she could get out, she'd administer medical care.

Lily peeked at the guy staring into space, the gun jammed into her chest. He had stripped his Santa suit off hours ago, or it felt like hours ago. His round stomach resembled the cookie belly of Santa Claus, but this guy looked forty years younger, with barely any white hair gleaming through his chin-length brown hair.

Oh my goodness! The woman set me up. Lily's mouth dropped to her chest. Why was she always thinking with her heart and forsaking logic and reasoning? Not entirely true. As a doctor, she stuck to the logical side of medicine. Science could explain every miraculous thing in the world, not God or the Bible.

Lily's mind drifted to the good-looking doctor, who stared at her with such intensity, she could almost see the windows of his heart. Treacherous situations never ruffled him, causing him to panic. What made them so different? Both doctors dealing with stressful jobs, only he had someone carry his burdens. She didn't.

God. The taste of the word left a foul linger in her throat. God, the Christian excuse for everything and the name the lost, hated. He was a fable at best and a cruel taskmaster at worst. If God was real, He had cast Lily aside years ago. It would be nice having someone else carry her burdens for a while. The weight was so heavy, it could crush her in an instance. But people like her didn't find peace in God or anyone to carry her anxiety. No wonder her attacks creeped in all the time.

Santa set the phone down, staring at her like a fragile porcelain doll. Who was he talking to? She didn't hear any of his conversation, too lost in her thoughts.

A tap rattled at the door. What was going on? Backup or another thug intent on delivering her to their boss? The door creaked open as a familiar face popped into view, only he looked hard, professional even.

"Doctor Smith, you have ten minutes." The guy faced the door, like an ambush would happen. Only silence echoed back.

Stephen stepped to her side, crouching next to her. He leaned close, his breath tickling her ears. "Play up your anxiety."

This was his plan? A big performance? Not an actress by character, but she'd do anything to breathe fresh air instead of the stale air of the tiny break room. Not to mention breathe without the metal tip of a gun poking into her body.

"Ma'am, I'm Doctor Smith. I'm a consultant with the local police, who called me at the first signs of your illness. Can you open your mouth for me? He asked, shining a light into her throat.

Lily stuck her tongue out like she'd instructed so many patients.

Stephen shook his head, frowning. "You're worse than I thought."

Stephen's talent shined through his performance. "You're not only on the verge of a collapsed lung, but you have streptococcus pharyngitis."

Strep throat. Laughter threatened to escape from her lips, blowing the total act. She hoped Santa didn't know medical terms. If he did, they were in trouble.

Santa turned facing them. "It sounds serious." He waved the gun in the air, thinking. "My boss won't like this."

"Highly contagious." Stephen felt along Lily's skin, stopping at her pulse points. His touch fluttered along her arm, causing heat to creep to her face. So much for paleness.

A tight grin filled his lips before being replaced with another hard look. He leaned toward her; his words barely audible. "No blushing. I need to play off your paleness."

Then get out of my personal space. Lily wanted to flash the words at him, but she peeked at Santa's gun and wondered if he was buying any of this.

Time to play it up. Lily bent over, hacking like her lungs would jump out of her mouth. Santa jumped to his feet, wiping perspiration from his face.

"The air is too thick in here." Santa stood to his feet, waving his arms and gun in the air. Santa was losing oxygen to his brain fast. Or that was Lily's explanation for his eradicate behavior. "Plan B."

"What?" Lily roared out another deathly cough, wondering if she was really sick.

"I'm getting out of here." He pointed to the door. "We're getting out of here. Doctor, you've seen too much. I can't let you live. A shame, really. My Bernice loved her work, and I vowed to never harm a doctor. Well, she's dead and life goes on."

Stephen heightened to his full stature, towering over Santa by inches. No way could the guy who looked like he worked out by inhaling cookies take down the doctor, whose biceps poked through his shirt.

In an instance, Stephen not only had his gun drawn, he had disarmed Santa, holding his hands behind his back.

"Get off me!" Santa growled like a lion ready to devour its prey.

The door crumbled open as Paul burst into the room, gun drawn. He apprehended Santa, tossing him to the officer behind him.

"She won't get away. No one ever gets away from the boss."

"Take him out of here." Paul grumbled as he looked at Stephen and scowled. "Mighty dumb thing you did back there."

"What were you waiting for? Santa to deliver your presents before you apprehended him?" Stephen wrapped his arms around Lily's waist, steadying her to the door.

"Cute." Paul wiped the smirk off his face. "We're all making a trip to the precinct. I have two perps to interrogate, and you can give your statements to my partner."

"Great. Let's get out of here." Stephen pulled Lily's body closer to his. She felt his strength zap through her weakened frame like bolts of electricity. And she never wanted him to loosen his hold on her again. Because for a moment, she pretended there wasn't a gulf separating them, and a future together could happen.

****

"Why are you staring at me?" Lily stretched the last piece of tape on a red-checked wrapping paper.

Stephen set the pile of unwrapped presents aside, grabbing Lily's silky hands. Yesterday, he thought he had lost her to a lunatic. Today, he needed to keep her close. Not just for her safety, but for his peace of mind. He had no right demanding her nearness, but he couldn't shake the images of her hunched over, gun shoved into her chest. What if his plan had backfired? If anything would have happened to the amazing woman beside him, he wouldn't have been able to move on. He spent the night praying and thanking God as he paced the hall in front of her room. Her light snores squeezed his heart, sending comfort and love bubbling over. When she ran into his life, Stephen boasted in his bachelorhood like it was a trophy. None of that mattered anymore. Because when he allowed himself to dream of the future, Lily's smiling green eyes laughed back at him. He had known her for days, maybe a week, tops, but he couldn't convince his heart of that.

"Do I have dried icing on my face?" Lily rubbed the sides of her cheeks, causing pink blotches. "I almost died. A girl can indulge in a few dozen cookies to clear her head."

Stephen's hearty laughter filled the office as the sound ricocheted off of the floor-to-ceiling bookshelf. "My mom hasn't stopped shoving food in your face since we got back from the store."

"Don't I know it?" Lily's face crinkled into a silly grin. "I foresee a shopping spree in my future. Especially if I can't pry my jeans on anymore."

"You're perfect just the way you are." He ran his fingers along the backside of her hand. "God made no mistakes when He made you."

Lily dropped her hands away from Stephen, her eyebrows furrowed into a straight line. At the mention of God, a scale fell over her face, hiding all emotions. "Do we have to talk about Him right now?"

He didn't understand her animosity toward God. Stephen desired a future with Lily, but not at the expense of forsaking God and tossing the Bible out of his life. "No, but I have one loaded question."

As tears welled up in her eyes, Lily fought to blink them back. He couldn't bear witnessing the turmoil etched on her face, but she couldn't evade God's presence indefinitely. "What?"

"Why do you clam up at the mention of God?" He wanted to take her in his arms, promising a love-filled future together, if only she'd turn to God. But the relationship topic caused visible pain, and he didn't want to scare her away.

Lily fidgeted with the empty tape dispenser, clearly uncomfortable with the conversation. She looked anywhere but at him as the words tumbled from her lips. "I'm on God's hit list. Just knowing me the last few days, you can vouch for that."

What could he say without scaring her off? God didn't have a hit list because unjust rage and retaliation didn't fuel Him. If she looked around, the mercies of God were keeping her alive. Leaning over, he gently brushed a strand of silky hair behind her ear as he whispered, "What I see is evidence of God's love and protection for you."

Lily pulled away from Stephen's touch. Hurt filled her eyes as her lips trembled. "There's a gulf between us, and it's best for both of us if we keep our distance."

"Wait! We already have a wall separating us and it's eating at my heart. I can't lose you, not when I finally found someone worth throwing my bachelorhood away for." He wanted to pull her into his arms, but crossed his arms over his chest instead.

"None of this is real."

"It feels real to me." Why couldn't she see that hurt, not hate toward God, pierced at her heart? Her hurt needed healing, and he could help if she'd let him.

"I can't be the Christian woman you desire. Our paths don't lead in the same way." Lily took a deep breath, obviously frazzled by the conversation.

He'd play along, but he couldn't shut off his emotions. His heart belonged to her. No turning back now. Stephen would just have to convince her he was worth taking a chance on. And that her whole being screamed for a relationship with God, but fear controlled her.

Before Stephen could respond, the door jolted open. He stared into the hard-lined face of his buddy, knowing that his look meant bad news.

"Can we talk?" Paul moved his head to the side, motioning to the hall.

Stephen jumped to his feet. He needed a moment to breathe, and distance from Lily.

"Wait. If this is about me, I deserve to hear whatever recent developments you've come up with." She heightened to her five-foot-three height and folded her arms over her chest.

A tight smile tugged at Stephen's lips. He admired her powerful personality, but now wasn't the time to be obstinate.

"Just so you know, I'll follow you wherever I need to in order to get the information about this case."

So much for keeping our distance. Stephen threw his arms in the air, sighing. Could he really say no to her forest-shaded eyes and silky smooth lips? Not when everything about her added to their attraction. "Fine, but if this causes another panic attack…"

"That's cold, man." Paul playfully punched him on the back. "Way to talk to your lady."

Lily cleared her throat as both men's eyes darted toward her. "I'm not his anything, and I can handle it."

Stephen's heart exploded at her icy words. She could deny it all she wanted, but they had a relationship, and he'd fight to preserve it. God had a plan, and he intended to find out what it was.

Fleeing from Danger, Jessica West

****

    Lily pinched the inside of her palm, trying to keep her tongue from slipping. Exhaustion. That's why she couldn't keep her mouth shut. Normally a quiet person by nature, not a fiery, obstinate firecracker. She almost burst out laughing at the sour look on Stephen's face as she stood trying to look intimidating next to his giant stature. She defied him and the detective, but since her near-death experience, it scared the boldness out of her. No turning back now.

    She shook the haze out of her mind, glimpsing at Stephen in a not-so-subtle way. Did Lily really want him to back off? God's hit list flashed before her eyes. Because of God, she couldn't have a relationship with Stephen, even if her treacherous heart beat just to feel his touch and stare into his ocean-blue eyes. Stop! Lily wanted to scream at herself for letting the gentle-handed doctor into her heart. Most of her life, it had just been her. It felt nice having someone care and fuss over her, but at what price? Did Stephen deserve God's wrath because of association? Absolutely not.

    What I see is evidence of God's love and protection for you. Stephen's words bore a hole in the inner layer of her heart, causing tears to well-up inside her eyes. What if everything she thought about God her whole life was a lie? No hit list. No determination to destroy her life; one person at a time. Just an ill-conceived notion and a bitterness that pulled a scale over hear eyes, causing hatred and hurt toward God. Lily rolled her eyes. She did not have time for fanciful thoughts. Stick to the facts and throw out all the what-ifs.

"You're a light year away from us. Care to share what is going on in your mind?" He leaned toward her, his breath tingling the side of her ear. For a second, she thought her words had sliced at his heart; a look of pain etched across his face. But the twinkle in his eyes and his mischievous grin returned.

Heat shot up the sides of her cheeks as she focused on anything but the man next to her. Didn't she just tell him they needed to stay away from each other? He didn't take her seriously because of her flip-flop emotions.

"If you lovebirds would focus on me for a few minutes, I've got four kids waiting for story time with Dad."

That didn't help her rosy cheeks. It didn't seem possible, but her heated cheeks flushed more. She took a noticeable step away from Stephen, giving her brain time to function. From the smirk on his face, he knew exactly what his closeness did to her.

"Bill King, at the advice from his lawyer, wasn't talking." Paul ran an agitated hand through his black, wavy hair. "But the female, Betty Tail, sang like a bird."

"What did she say?"

"She needed money for the holidays, and she's not a seasoned criminal." Paul fidgeted with a pad of paper, pulling it out of his pocket.

"Do you believe her?" A cloud of unease flashed before Stephen's eyes.

"No rap sheet or anything to disprove her story."

"Did she know why someone is hunting me like prey?" Lily blurted out, tired of the staleness of the case.

"No. She's the lowest on the totem pole. No one told her anything."

"Great. This case leads nowhere fast." Stephen puffed out a breath of indignation.

"I wouldn't say that." A faint smile spread across Paul's face. "Mr. King blurted out some useful information before his lawyer arrived."

"And?" Lily and Stephen said simultaneously.

"Mr. Cortes doesn't play games. Whoever is on his hit list never lives to talk about it," Paul said.

"Lovely." Lily wrapped a piece of hair around her finger, gazing at the row of books on the bookshelf. "Guess I won't start planning my twenty-eighth birthday." *At this rate, I won't live to see it. What was Jason involved in?*

"When is your birthday?" Stephen cast her a full-faced smile, twinkling his blue eyes. If he didn't stop being so charming, she might lose her resolve to keep her distance, doing everything her mind warned against.

"Not until May, but…"

"I see moon-lit walks on the beach, feeling the squishy sand between our toes, and listening to the ocean waves crash into the shore." He met her eyes, no hint of humor in his face. "I can picture so much more if you give us a chance."

Normally persistence drove her crazy, but coming from him, it tugged at her heartstrings, stripping the cords away one at a time. *Stop! I can't let anything happen to him. If it were just the perps after me, maybe we'd have a future one day, but I can't put him in the crosshairs of an angry God. That's if He even exists.* Horrible luck, or a wrathful God, was to blame for most of the situations in her life.

"We live in East Tennessee, landlocked and away from any beaches." She ignored his plea for a relationship. She needed to focus on the case.

Paul tapped his fingers on the side of his folded arms. "Time is ticking. You don't want to face a wrathful Belle because four kids are screaming for Daddy and I'm stuck with you both."

"Fine. What were you saying?" Stephen spoke, never taking his eyes off of Lily. She squirmed under his intense glare.

"Mr. Cores was the head drug lord of the Cores family. Hard-lined criminals."

"Was?" Lily didn't like the sound of this. Whoever was chasing her took out a high-profile criminal?

"No one's spotted him for days."

"Why are they after me?" Reading books and watching sappy movies hardly gets a person on a hit list.

"Your brother was CIA. The Cores family could have been one of his cases or…"

"No! My brother wasn't a double-agent." Lily threw her arms in the air. Jason was loyal. He'd never turn on his country. Although she barely knew him. Time pushed them apart and her obstinate ways never mended their relationship.

"I'm following leads and digging into his background. I'll let you know when I find more information." Paul turned around and slid through the door.

Stephen closed the gap between them, offering a shoulder for support. Of course, her short stature could never reach his shoulders. But she rested her face against his chest long enough to feel the soothing rhythm of his heartbeat, gleaning from his strength. Lily pushed away from him, trying to silence her conflicting emotions.

"I don't feel like wrapping presents." She stepped to the door, pausing enough to get a quick glance at the handsome man she was leaving behind.

"Lily, no matter how much you push me away, I won't leave you until you're safe. And even then, it's your choice."

With nothing to say, she slipped into the hall, staggering to her room before the gush of tears fell down her face.

Chapter Eight

Keep your distance. Stephen glanced at Lily as she picked up a handful of snow with her gloved-hand, rubbing the powdered substance between her fingers. Her fascination with the snow added to her youthful charm. Baby-faced and short in stature, she barely looked old enough to drive, let alone be a doctor. He figured that's why her fierce determination etched through her character. Stephen jammed his hand into his coat pocket, before he regretted pulling her into his arms. He had seen no other woman as beautiful as her. His heart thudded steadily, swelling at her gleeful laughter and wonder.

He had spent an uneventful morning playing with his nieces and nephews and doing last-minute holiday prep for his mom. Christmas being four days away, his mom was in full prep mode. She wanted everything perfect for Lily, who had never experienced a genuine family holiday, and for the distant family members who hadn't arrived yet.

Lily seemed overwhelmed and excited at the chaos surrounding the cabin. One minute a wide smile plastered over her olive-tinted face, the next minute tears sparkled in her eyes. She was being true to her word and keeping her distance from him. Her iciness broke his heart; shattering it into so many pieces. She'd barely spoken five words to him all morning. And she acted like looking at him was a deadly poison.

Through much prayer, he begged God to take away his love and affection for her, but God didn't answer some prayer. Especially when all he wanted to do was to pull her into his embrace, never letting go. His mother, sensing his inner torment, suggested they go for a stroll in the freshly fallen snow. He'd never turn away alone time with her, but he felt like a third wheel; Lily and the snow, a wonderful distraction from having to face him.

The threat on Lily's life loomed in the back of his mind. The thugs were crafty and determined. He needed to shake the cobwebs out of his brain and focus on her safety.

They trenched farther away from the cabin, trailing the outskirts of the wooded mountain range. Their leisure stroll wasn't supposed to turn into an expedition through uncharted land. Why had his wandering mind led them so far from the cabin?

"I think we should turn around and go back." Stephen glanced at the snowy footprints.

Three sets? His eyes darted to the rough terrain around them. Were they not alone and being watched? By a hunter or a thug? He couldn't take any chances. He tugged his gun out of his ankle holster, pulling Lily into his arms.

"What are you doing?" Her chilly tone iced his body more than the below-freezing temperature.

Just as he was about to explain, a sudden pop echoed above them, and he swiftly pushed Lily down onto the snowy ground.

"Are we under attack?" she exclaimed, the sound of gunfire echoing in the distance. Her words stumbled out of her mouth, barely audible above a hushed breath.

Stephen scanned the terrain in the location of the shots. He couldn't see anyone, but someone had seen them. Another shot zoomed through the stale December air, causing goosebumps to attack his skin. The police had three suspects in custody. How many hired hands did the Cores family have? Would this ever end?

"Were going to die." Panic-laced words slid out of Lily's mouth as she laid as low as she could on the snowing ground.

If he couldn't find a way out of this mess, they would. He pointed his gun toward the perp and fired. Gun powder attacked his senses as he glanced around for a place to hide. To their advantage, they were in a wooded area, but being unfamiliar with the land didn't help him any. And if the thug camped out on the mountain, they were visible to him no matter where they hid.

"I can't stay face down in the snow. My limbs are tingling and my toes are numb." She flipped over, staring into his eyes with a look of pleading. "If the bullets don't kill us, hypothermia will."

She had a point. Their winter clothes were appropriate for the weather, but not for hugging the icy ground or prolonging their time on the elements. "Can you reach into my back pocket and yank my phone out?"

She motionlessly sat on her feet, running her hands along the edge of his back pocket, searching for his phone. A feeling of relief flooded his soul as she pulled it out, gripping it between her gloved fingers.

"Paul is number four on speed dial." Maybe the shooter had retreated. Seconds ticked by with no more bullets soaring through the air. But he couldn't let his guard down yet.

"No signal." The phone dropped from her trembling fingers. She looked like a snow princess; blue-tinted skin and all.

He slid his arm around her shaky body, pulling her close to his chest, trying to share his body heat. He pressed his lips on the top of her snow-infused hair, basking in their closeness. Her pounding heart beat pulsed through her jacket, reminding him of the danger they were in.

Another bullet zoomed through the air as Stephen bit back a yelp of pain. He glanced at his arm, feeling the burning heat travel through his body. Blood seeped out of a hole in his arm. *Nice move getting shot. At least Lily was unharmed.*

"You're bleeding." She whispered close to his ear.

"Nothing serious, just a graze." He gritted his teeth. Just a graze felt like his arm would explode. Even worse, he couldn't return fire with an injured arm. "Can you shoot?"

"I'm about saving lives, not ending them."

"If you want to save your life, take my gun and fire a round in the direction the bullet came from. We're an easy target, and we can't leave the woods because he could take us out in a second in the clearing."

Her eyes narrowed in determination as she squeezed the trigger, sending a bullet racing through the air. She placed the gun in Stephen's uninjured hand. Lily yanked at the end of her shirt, ripping enough of the fabric to use as a bandage to soak up the blood until it stopped bleeding. She tugged his arm out of his jacket, examining the wound.

He floated in the realm of unconsciousness as the pressure gnawed at his arm. Cold sweats popped off his brow.

"Stay with me." Her urgent plea and light tap felt like a warm, fuzzy blanket.

"I'll stay with you forever if you let me." His weakened-words flowed out of his mouth.

"Always the charmer, even in the face of death." She tugged on his arm harder as he bit back the urge to scream.

"I'm not dying, just feel like it." He leaned toward her, blinking back the urge to sleep. He had to stay awake.

"Have I ever told you how hypnotizing your green eyes are?"

"You're delusional."

"I'm a man in love." He touched his lips to hers. Electricity shooting through his body.

"Stephen—."

His eyes drifted shut as a familiar voice danced into his mind. His eyelids wouldn't open, so he sank onto the moving platform as darkness engulfed his body.

****

Lily snuggled under the layer of covers, finally feeling warmth and movement from her numb limbs. She stared at the curled-up figure on the hospital bed. His legs hanging over the end of the bed by inches. Stephen laid lifeless on the bed, his bandage protruding from under the covers. The bullet wound was a clean in and out; no damage to any muscles or arteries, a flesh wound that would heal with no lasting effect. Paul and Mr. Smith had heard the gunshots, and had probably saved her and Stephen's lives. The thug had disappeared into the wilderness like he wasn't even there, leaving behind trails of blood.

Stephen stirred in the bed, his color returning to a safe shade. Lily wanted to check his chart, making sure he received the proper care, but her body lacked the energy it took to get out of the chair. And even if she did, her mind wasn't in doctor mode. Stephen's dad stood guard outside the door, giving them time to heal without another attack. Thankfulness flowed through her body at the safety surrounding her.

His mom had stepped out, searching the cafeteria for more coffee. She was so hyped on caffeine; she couldn't sit still. Lily glanced at the Bible lying on the end table. *Must be Mrs. Smith's.* Never in her life had she picked up one of those books. She didn't believe in fairy tales or the words scribbled between the pages of the Bible. Her mind drifted back to hours ago when Stephen's blood loss had concerned the doctors. Mrs. Smith hadn't paced the floors, wearing an invisible hole in the tile. She just sat, flipping through her Bible, a look of peace etched on her face.

What if the cure for her panic attacks lay between the pages of the Bible? Lily's body trembled as she picked up the Bible, resting her fingers against the worn-out leather. She wouldn't get her hopes up. Lily wasn't searching for a revelation or a life-changing phrase, just something to take her mind off of the brazen attempts on her life, and the man who lay too still in the uncomfortable hospital bed.

The shock must have overwhelmed him, as he blurted out those three little words: "I love you." She could count on one hand the number of times she had heard those words in her twenty-seven years of life. A frown tugged on the corner of her lips. She could not let his feelings for her develop. A gunshot wound. Next, something more serious. Lily would not allow Stephen's feelings for her to put him in the path of God's wrath.

Lily glanced at the Bible cradled between her arms. This book gave hope and life to so many people. But who was she kidding? It wouldn't work for her. She tossed it back on the end table, never removing her fingers from the worn leather. It wouldn't help her, but it wouldn't hurt her either. She yanked the Bible off the table, plopping it into her lap. She strummed her fingers along the silky-worn pages as her eyes scanned the foreign words.

"The Lord is my light and my salvation; whom shall I fear? The Lord is the strength of my life, of whom shall I be afraid?"

Lily's eyes scanned to the bottom of Psalm 27.

"Wait on the Lord: Be of good courage, and he shall strengthen thine heart: wait, I say, on the Lord."

What did it mean? She had plenty to fear, and no make-believe God would change that.

She flipped through the pages, stopping on a portion of red words. *"Come unto me, all ye that labour and are heavy laden, and I will give you rest."*

Rest? When was the last time she actually rested without fear creeping into her heart? She couldn't answer that question. As if being bitten by a poisonous snake, she threw the Bible on the table. Enough of those confusing words.

Lily pulled the blanket to her chin, trying to wipe the verses out of her mind. Why had she picked up that book, anyway? It did not offer comfort or peace of mind to her, but confusion.

Her pulse quickened and her palms turned sweaty. She felt caged in, like the words of the Bible brought torment, not peace.

I need to get out of here. The walls were closing in on her. Feeling an overwhelming need to lash out and scream, she jumped out of the chair. Lightheartedness and dizziness whirled around in her head. Fearing the worst could happen about everything, thoughts attacked her common sense. *What if the bad guy finds me here? What if Stephen never wakes up? What if my anxiety debilitates me?*

Lily rubbed the sides of her head, bending over and heaving. The thoughts were worse than the enemy's bullets.

In bed, Stephen rolled over, his eyes wide open and brimming with a love that gently erased all traces of Lily's anxiety. "Come here." He motioned with his uninjured arm.

Lily stepped to him like a wounded animal to its master. She edged onto the side of the bed, wiping tears from her eyes.

Tenderly, he brushed a tear from her pale cheek, responding to her anguish with a comforting glance. "Whatever thoughts are tormenting you, shake them away."

How did he know the tug-of-war battling in her mind? Lily sniffled back another sob. This man was amazing and didn't deserve her broken, tormented life. The best she could do for him would be to leave. She could change her identity and leave the country.

He ran his finger across her streaky-red cheek, his blue eyes intense. "I'm not letting you leave. You belong right here." He patted his heart, smiling his charming smile that lit up his face.

All anxiety vanished away at his touch. This man understood her inner turmoil, and it didn't frighten him. If only things could be different. Like her sharing the faith that controlled every fiber of his being. Or not being on God's hit list. They could work through everything else, but the two major things separating them were like deep trenches; no way around them.

"Lily, I don't know the darkest thoughts destroying your peace, but I have a solution." His eyes drifted to the very book she had tossed aside minutes before. Was he serious? None of those words comforted her.

"Stephen, you've grown on me, etching your way past my guarded heart. I wish life was so simple and I could embrace your faith, sealing our story together forever. But I can never accept a God who delights in my pain. A God who takes everyone away from me; leaving me bitter and alone. I don't even know if God exists."

"Lily—"

"No, Stephen." Sobs overtook her body as she pressed her hand over her mouth. "Nothing you say will fix me. I thought life could be different, but that's just lies."

He pulled her trembling body closer to his, wrapping an arm around her. His breath tickling the back of her hair. "Let go of the fear, and let someone else carry it for you."

She buried her face in his chest, letting his antiseptic scent float through her nostrils. If only it were that simple. She cared about him, but her feelings didn't matter. She wasn't good for him. Knowing no one could ever carry her burdens for her.

Their eyes locked as he pushed himself away from her, his lips finding solace on her forehead in a gentle, loving kiss. "I think I love you slipped from my lips in the woods."

"Yeah."

"With the pain manageable, I can tell you I don't regret letting it slip." He clasped her fingers in his. "Lily Walsh, I love you and I'll help you work through everything that's eaten away at your mind. But you have to stop pushing me away."

This incredible man confessed his love to her and all she wanted to do was throw up. This only happened in her dreams, because in reality, no fairy tale endings would ever happen. God's hit list whirled around her mind like a twister leaving no prey.

Air. She needed air.

Lily jumped up from the bed, fumbling with the door handle.

"Lily?" His pleading voice beckoned her to him.

"I can't breathe." Pushing past Mr. Smith, her tear-filled eyes blurred her vision as she sprinted down the hall, desperate to escape the very essence of her heart's desires.

****

What just happened? Normally, a woman didn't run off when a man proclaimed his love to her. He'd never done this before, but that's what he thought, anyway.

Let her go, and move on. Her baggage is too deep for you. His mind screamed warnings as he shifted his body out of the small hospital bed. Stephen brushed the side of his wounded arm against the bed railing, chomping on his lip, trying to fight off the excruciating ache traveling through his body.

He couldn't. No, he wouldn't let her go. She needed space, but she didn't need someone else to leave her. Her pain of loss traveled so deep; it controlled her to the point of insanity. Stephen couldn't give her much space beyond a little breathing room. For whatever reason, Tony Cores had her on his hit list, meaning he could hire the entire state of Tennessee and he wouldn't deplete his monetary resources. Nothing stopped him until now. Lily would not die at the hands of a merciless drug lord. Whatever trouble she inherited from her brother would not destroy her. It looked grim, but Stephen would make sure she had a future. An opportunity to love, marry, and have a houseful of kids, even if it wasn't with him.

Stephen pushed out of bed, taking a minute for the world to stop spinning. He had to find Lily. He jerked open the door, nearly running into his father's broad chest, tackling him to the tiled-floor.

"What's this about, son?" Mr. Smith placed his arm on Stephen's shoulder, steading him.

"Dad, no time for a chat. I need to find Lily." No matter how hard he tried to mask the pain, his dad's deep understanding of him allowed him to see right through it.

"You're in no condition to tromp off to wherever and dual the scumbags after Lily." He nodded toward the hall. "I'm coming with you. She went that way."

"Thanks, Dad." Stephen jogged next to his dad; the silence so thick he could cut it with a pocketknife.

"What's going on?" His dad gave him a stern side glance. He was a no-nonsense kind of guy.

"I think I scared her away." He ran his fingers through his disheveled hair, sighing. "But she's not really running from me, but God."

"Son, shoot straight with me." Mr. Smith paused as a nurse darted past them, pushing a cart of supplies. "What are your intentions with her?"

Feeling like an adolescent all over again, the weight of his dad's disapproving gaze made him buckle under its intensity. Memories of a similar conversation in high school flooded his mind, bringing with it a wave of awkwardness that he could never forget.

His dad had warned him about the consequences of toying with a girl's heart, urging him to be cautious and less flirtatious. The memory of that conversation still lingered, the stern words echoing in his ears.

Stephen knew he wasn't a flirt; he wasn't the one responsible for the relentless attention he received from females. As a Christian young man, he did not encourage their scandalous advances, which only seemed to fuel their pursuit. Even to this day, women continued to chase him, hopeful of becoming the one who could capture the heart of the eligible bachelor doctor.

But none of them stood a chance. His heart belonged to an olive-skinned beauty, who held the keys to his heart, even if she didn't return his love.

"I … uh." Stephen wiped the perspiration pouring from his forehead, feeling the slickness of sweat against his skin. The corridor was suffocatingly hot, the air thick, making it impossible to regulate a normal body temperature.

The sound of silence echoed through the empty hall, amplifying the tension in the air. Mr. Smith scanned the desolate surroundings, the silence piercing through the stillness. He pointed to the nurse's station, his footsteps echoing against the linoleum floor as he strode purposefully in that direction.

"Just wondering why my son would jump in front of a bullet for a woman that means nothing to him. I raised you to be fearless, not brainless."

Stephen moved to the side of the hall, seeking relief from the oppressive heat, his back finding solace against the coolness of the white walls. Doubt plagued his mind as he wondered if his father regarded him as a foolish man, someone who didn't understand the consequences of protecting a woman. Stephen knew the logical outcome of all the attempts on Lily's life. And yet, he'd willingly take a bullet for her again, if it meant she could live and be free from fear. Beads of perspiration continued to trickle down his face, mingling with the furrowed lines of worry etched on his forehead.

"Dad, when the bullet pierced my forearm, I didn't want to die, but as I stared into her deep green eyes, I knew I'd do anything to keep her safe. My life flashed before me, and all I could see was her. The thing is, dad, I can't live without her."

A small smile spread across Mr. Smith's face, the lines of concern momentarily easing. "That's love, son."

Stephen nodded, feeling a mix of relief and trepidation. He pushed off the wall, the coolness of the surface now a distant memory, and made his way towards a gray-haired, plump nurse standing behind a desk. The sound of his footsteps echoed in his ears, his heart pounding in his chest. He could feel the weight of his emotions pressing against his ribcage, threatening to burst free.

"I love her, but my love scared her off."

Mr. Smith offered a comforting pat on his son's back, the warmth of his touch providing a brief respite from the internal turmoil. "Give her time. Women can't resist the Smith men's charm. It helped win your mother over. And wash her over with prayer."

"Can I help you?" The nurse shuffled through a stack of papers, barely making eye contact.

"Did a young woman, an Asian beauty, with deep green eyes and long black hair, come through here?" Stephen's voice held tension as he fidgeted with his shirt.

"She did. I waved to her as a gentleman swung his arm around her shoulder, tugging her toward the stairs."

"We're too late."

"I'll call Paul and meet you downstairs." Mr. Smith set his pistol in Stephen's palm. "I locked yours in my glove box."

"Thanks, Dad." Stephen dashed toward the stairs.

The scent of antiseptic lingered in the air, mingling with the faint aroma of freshly brewed coffee. Stephen's heart pounded as he dashed down the stairs two at a time. He had to find her before the thug dragged her out of the hospital.

He wouldn't lose her. Amidst his pulsing heart and the fear that clawed through his mind, a peace that only God could give, washed over his body, giving him strength to find the woman he loved.

****

"You won't get away with this." Lily grabbed the fierce hand gripping her arm, trying to loosen the hold. Her arm had lost feeling seconds before.

"Mr. Cores always gets what he wants." The deep-pitched voice laughed as chills assaulted her body. "And right now, he wants you."

"Why? I know nothing." Panic bubbled inside of Lily like an active volcano. How would she get free? She ran off when Stephen confessed his love for her. Lily doubted he'd rescue her again. Even if he wanted to, how would he know a thug had abducted her?

"Your incompetent, double-crossing brother." He tightened his grip on her arm, yanking her down another flight of stairs.

Jason.

"Please, I haven't spoken to him in months. I didn't know he was a CIA agent." Her voice was breathy as she fought for each labored breath. Her insides screamed with panic.

"CIA?" His boisterous laugh rumbled from his fat lips. "That's what they're calling it these days?"

What was he hinting at? Jason could not have been involved in drug trafficking. Right? Her brother's steely dark eyes popped into her mind. Lily couldn't recall basic information about Jason. Like what was his favorite food or movie? The realization sent a shock through her body. She had been living in a make-believe world; cut off from the people around her. What kind of person knew nothing about their only blood relative? Was she so closed off that the warning flag for Jason's wellbeing never registered in her mind? Maybe he asked her to move to Tennessee to help him turn his life around, and she failed him. That's assuming Jason was on the Cores' payroll. How could she believe a scumbag holding her at gunpoint? And how many flights of stairs did this country hospital have? It shrank in size compared to the hospital she worked at. But the stairs seemed endless, to her advantage.

She tugged on her arm. Lily needed air, and she needed her pulse to regulate. It wasn't a stall-tactic. She felt on the verge of passing out or throwing up. "Let me go."

"Feisty." He loosened his grip, as an angry laughter floated through the staircase. "At first, we needed you to pay for Jason's backstabbing ways, which you will do. But, after this closeup view, your exotic beauty might save your life. Boss is always looking for a new bride. He killed the last one." He paused, choking back a coughing-laughing fit.

"I'm not for sale." She bent over, heaving. How would she get out of this mess?

"It beats the alternative." He tugged on her arm again, causing her to trip over a step, landing on the hard floor below the staircase. "Why am I telling you all this? Doesn't matter. You won't get free."

Pain shot through her leg as she tried massaging the knee that took the brunt of the fall.

"Get up, princess. Your chariot awaits." He pointed to the exit in front of them. Her freedom lay between a foot of nothing, separating her from a vehicle that would carry her into bondage and possibly death.

Her legs turned into jelly, and the taste of vomit burned in her throat. The urge became overpowering, and she could no longer resist. As chunky thrown-up particles covered the ground, she turned her head and saw the man's shoes barely eluding her bodily fluid.

"What the…" He jumped back, trying to distance himself from the sour-smelling substance.

Lily wiped her shirt sleeve across her mouth, scraping any remaining pieces off her face.

"I did not sign up for this." The man paced in front of the bottom staircase, waving his gun in the air. "I don't need you messing up the leather upholstery on my new SUV."

Maybe losing her breakfast was a blessing in disguise. A blessing? She sounded like Stephen. Not a blessing, but luck was on her side.

"Think, Dwayne." He mumbled loud enough for her to hear. "What's wrong with you?"

Anxiety. A panic attack. Fear. "Must be a twenty-four-hour bug." She hung her head down as her stomach screamed for relief.

"Twenty-four-hours?" He ran his fingers over his bald scalp. "No way are you puking in my SUV for that long. But if I don't deliver you to the boss, I can kiss my SUV and everything else goodbye."

Dilemma. Should she make a run for it while the gun swung wildly in the air, Dwayne not focused on her? Maybe help would arrive soon. Stephen's painful look crossed her mind. Why couldn't she acknowledge her feelings for him, giving him some hope to cling to? Because danger followed her and it wasn't just the Cores family who wanted her to suffer; but God. She needed to keep her distance to protect Stephen from the very God he loved.

"I'll call Peewee in. He drives a rusted can." He slid his phone out of his pocket. "No funny business." He shifted his body away from her, speaking on the phone.

Now's my chance. Hoping her legs would cooperate, she wobbled to her feet. Dwayne threw his arms in the air, having an animated conversation. She'd use that to her advantage. She gazed up the staircase. No way she'd make it to the top without him noticing. Especially with a bruised knee. But she wouldn't go outside; making his job of abduction easier.

Lily tip toed up the stairs, relief flooding her as Dwayne disappeared from view. Too easy. She heard cursing and heavy steps as the pursuit was on. Lily ran as fast as she could, heart pounding in her chest. She would not give in to anxiety when it meant her freedom.

She heard a gunshot zoom past her, barely missing her arm. Mr. Cores needed her alive, but it didn't mean the bullet couldn't injure her.

Keep moving, Lily. One step at a time. She exhaled, stepping over another stair. Hearing Dwayne gaining on her, she covered her mouth, trying not to scream. The cold metal railing slid across her skin, sending awareness floating through her body.

With a pounding heart and short, choppy breaths, she glanced back, colliding with something firm. A scream escaped her lips. How could Dwayne be pursuing her from both sides of the staircase? Must be Peewee. Before looking in the face of her assailant, she felt kind hands rubbing her arms.

"You're safe." Stephen moved her body behind him, pointing down the stairs. "How many?"

"One, maybe two." Before she finished her sentence, he slid his gun out of the holster, motioning her to be quiet.

Her heart dropped as Stephen disappeared down the windy stairs. Seconds later, gunshots echoed through the enclosed space. She crouched down, hoping Stephen was safe. If anything happened to him, besides the gunshot wound he already had, what would she do?

An eternity later, or so it felt, footsteps stomped up the stairs, sending her anxiety into overdrive. She clung to the railing as f it would protect her from her assailant. Stephen's charming face fell into view. He looked unharmed, but ruggedly dangerous, with a look of steel.

Stephen wrapped his arms around her. Pulling her to the door. "He got away, but not without a leg injury. The police will find him."

She wanted to grab his shirt and kiss him for saving her life again. But that would go against keeping her distance and trying to tame her rebellious heart. Instead, she entwined her fingers with his, staring at his ocean-blue eyes as they stepped into a corridor. From his expression, he knew exactly how her heart beat for him, and how she'd give anything to mend the gulf separating between them. But some love stories didn't end in happily ever-after. There's never could.

Chapter Nine

"I won't go back." Lily leaned against the door of Stephen's truck, fire flashing before her eyes. "I have plenty of money to disappear forever."

What was she talking about? Another one of Mr. Cores' thugs had almost abducted her. They needed to get far away from the hospital before anymore showed up. His skills were top-notch, having grown up with a Marine for a father, but he was only a doctor. Stephen didn't know if he could take on a gang of men. He'd die trying if it kept Lily safe, but best not get thrown in that predicament.

"What are you talking about?" He slid his fingers over the steering wheel, feeling the cool leather exterior. He needed to re-channel his frustrations. And get some sleep. Sleep without fear of bad guys interrupting him. Even though she hinted at going rogue; disappearing forever. He couldn't let that happen. The thought of never seeing her again punched him in the gut. Stephen felt like a love-sick puppy, who would never be happy without the person sitting next to him in his life. God would give him joy and contentment, but he'd never be happy knowing he let the only woman he ever loved slip out of his life. He couldn't let her disappear, not without him. Could he really change his identity, leaving behind his close-knit family, and forsake his calling as a physician to follow her? Stephen glanced at Lily; her eyes closed. Fear etched lines under her eyes. Yes. It would break his heart, but he'd do anything for her.

"Listen Stephen, I appreciate your protective stance in all of this, but it's not your fight. It's my fight, and I'm not putting your family in any more danger."

Uh, oh. She had a point, but she couldn't push me away that easily. Stephen let out a low breath of air. They were sitting ducks in a parked car in the hospital's parking lot. He needed to speed up this conversation and get her to safety. "It's not your fight either. It was Jason's."

"Whatever the reason, it's mine now. And your family means too much to me to allow any more harm to come their way." Lily ran her fingers through her blackened strands. "I don't need your permission to leave."

Sleep. I need to sleep to clear my head. I don't need to blow up at this beautifully obstinate woman. "Lily." Just saying her name melted the heat away from his heart.

She stared at him through tear-filled eyes as a stray tear slid down her face. Stephen leaned inches from her face, wiping the tear with his finger. He loved this woman, and nothing else mattered. "Please understand my desire to protect your family."

He traced his thumb across her reddened-cheek. Love spewing out of his heart, etching onto his face. "I get it, but pushing me away will only seal your death. And I can't get this picture out of my mind of you, me, and forever together."

Lily's body stiffened under Stephen's loving touch. "This thing you're feeling for me can't be real." She motioned around the truck. "Because this isn't. One day, the excitement of danger will disappear, and I'm not enough to keep you around."

"Look at me." He tilted her chin, staring into her soul-searching eyes. "All I need is you."

"What about God?" The words slipped from her lips, barely loud enough for him to hear.

An electrifying shock stunned his heart at her words. He knew where this was going. God or her? Until she stopped running from God, he couldn't have both of them. He wouldn't forsake God, but he couldn't let her face the thugs alone.

"If you stay with me, God will banish you and put you on His hit list." A soft sob eluded her lips. "There's no earning favor with God. After all these years, He's still taking pleasure in my ruins. Do you really want to reap God's scorn because of me?"

How could she have such a distorted view of God? "Sweetheart," he clamped his hand around hers, needing her to comprehend what he was about to say. "God is not like that. His love, not his wrathful revenge, drives Him. God is beckoning you to come to Him."

She bit her bottom lip, tears mixed with anger filled her face. She jerked her fingers away from his. "He beckons me to come to Him? By destroying my life and stealing my family from me? That's a sick way of showing love."

"Lily, please." *Did I say the wrong thing? God, help me.* She looked like she would bolt out the door any minute. "I need to protect you. Don't push me away."

"We can only be acquaintances." She pushed her body off the door, staring into his face, eyes hardened and lifeless. "Promise me you won't fall in love with me."

Too late for that. What should he say? "I can't promise something that's already happened." He looked out the window, scanning the parking lot. He'd be a fool to think Cores' men weren't around, waiting to pounce on her again. "Tell me you don't feel the attraction."

Lily fidgeted with the side of the seatbelt, staring at anything but him. "That's not the point. What I do or don't feel for you is irrelevant. Our relationship can't go any further. If you can't keep your emotions in check, I'll disappear."

"Why?" Stephen didn't understand her logic. He couldn't just turn his emotions off and stop loving her. Love didn't disappear with a flip of a switch. Love endured the rough patches of life and grew stronger. But he could not tell her that. She wasn't in a stable mind frame.

"Because I can't risk your life or love for me." She gripped the door handle, her fingers turning white. "You're one of God's children. You'd never understand. But I'm protecting you by pushing you away."

How could she think that? Who fed her all these lies? He'd try to help her with her skewed image of God later, but right now, he needed to protect her. He couldn't do that if she pushed him away.

"We need to go soon. I don't trust Cores or his thugs." Stephen turned the key in the ignition, praying she'd go along with him.

"Fine. But we don't go back to your parents' cabin." She raised her eyebrow, challenging him to go against her.

"Alright," he conceded, "we'll do things your way, at least for now." He pulled his truck out of the parking lot, making sure they weren't being followed. "I know the perfect place."

God, show me how to protect her and give me opportunities to show her how loving you are. And guard my heart if she'll never open her heart up to me. But, prove to her how real my love is. How it's not a fluke.

Fleeing from Danger, Jessica West

****

Lily plopped on the worn bed, staring at the scant furnishings. A black dresser full of clothes leaned against the flowery wallpaper and the twin bed that had seen better days. The room gave off a cozy, rustic vibe; being no bigger than a master bathroom. She wasn't complaining. Getting away from the cabin was her idea. Bonus being the tiny room had a tiny shower.

She hopped off the bed, rummaging through the dresser drawers. Clean clothes and a shower sounded divine. Sleep would make it the perfect evening. She pulled out a plaid long-sleeved shirt and a long black skirt. Not her style, but the correct size. She sauntered into the claustrophobic bathroom, noticing a stock-pile of everything she needed. How had Stephen stocked the place with necessities and decade-old clothes? She'd have to ask later, even though she needed to keep her distance. Her icy demeanor would save his heart and life. Lily didn't want to push him away, but what kind of monster asked a man to choose between her and God? Even worse was the look of contemplation, stamped on his charming face. For a minute, she thought he'd leave everything and disappear with her. Not good, but dangerous. Stephen couldn't forsake his amazing family and life for anyone, especially someone like her. She had nothing besides a pretty face to offer. Underneath her olive-tinted skin and unique green eyes laid an empty mass of nothingness.

No way was he in love with her. Fear trickled down her spine. She was unlovable; which her father drilled into her mind at a young age.

His deep, tired voice popped into her mind. "Lily, stop sneaking into your mother's room. You're killing her with each failed attempt. The cancer can snatch her life away in a second. Do you want to aid in her death? She doesn't love you, no one does. So, just stay away from her."

Tears plopped down her cheeks. Sure, he spoke those words in anger, but the damage never left her heart. Her dad didn't love her. Her mom couldn't love her. And God chose not to love her. If Stephen saw beyond her physical appearance, he'd run, too.

Lily turned on the steamy hot water, letting the heat drown out her anguish. Dwelling on her loveless life did no good. She shoved the painful memories into her stony heart, hoping to silence the ache finally.

She showered and plastered on a cheerful demeanor. Stephen towered over other men in everything, and he didn't deserve to see her bitterness and anguish. Lily wanted to push his heart away, not leave him running from her in disgust. At least, not until she was safe. When safety came, could she really walk away like a stranger to Stephen? Her heart ached every time she saw him. He stirred up feelings she never felt before, and when she closed her eyes, his ocean-blue eyes smiled back at her.

Stop it! I can't fall for him. It wouldn't be fair to him. Truth be told, he had already smitten her heart more than she cared to admit.

Lily ran a brush through her long, wet hair. Twisting it in a ponytail, she flipped the bathroom light off. Her flowing skirt swooshed with each movement. The shirt fit perfectly besides the long sleeves. Lily inherited her height from her Asian mother, but her green eyes from her father.

Hunger clawed at her stomach as she opened the bedroom door, stepping out into the cozy living room. The smell of bacon wafted through the air, causing her stomach to rebel with a loud growl. She blushed as a lopsided smile spread across his face.

Stephen slid the bacon onto a plate, setting it next to a bowl of eggs. "I made the entire pack."

"You know how to cook?" Impressive. She lived on takeout and smoothies.

He set a fork next to her plate, smiling. "It's the only thing I can cook. Mom tried teaching me, but my culinary skills were so bad the fire department's number was on speed dial."

A soft laugh escaped her lips as she imagined Stephen as a boy. He probably ran his mother ragged.

"Hey, it's edible. Unless some of the shell slipped in. In that case, it's added protein." He set two bottles of water on the table.

"Where did the fully stocked house come from?" She paused, knowing he would say a blessing for the food.

Stephen took a swig of water, his eyes twinkling. "Kayla stays here when she visits, but she's staying with my parents until after Christmas."

"She wears these clothes?" She laid her arm on the wooden table, revealing the sleeve hanging over her hand.

"I've heard the 70s were back in style." He reached for her hand, but grabbed his bottle instead. "My aunt and uncle own this house. My aunt leaves her outdated clothes here. She can't throw anything away. Y'all are both the same size."

"I feel like a rag doll." She shoved a piece of greasy bacon into her mouth.

"Trust me, you make anything look good." His mischief flashed into his eyes. Stephen busted out laughing. "Ok, that was lame."

A familiar line that she heard a lot in high school. But none of the guys were as charming as Stephen. Dangerous territory. They needed to keep their focus on the case, not on personal matters. She was, after all, trying to stop his heart from growing more infatuated with her.

"Did you contact Paul?" The case; safe ground.

"He should be here soon." Stephen set his fork on top of his empty plate, staring at her. "Belle packed you a bag of modern clothes and whatever else."

"How kind."

"My family extended an open invitation for Christmas day. The ladies miss you already." He leaned back in his chair, folding his arms over his chest. "My nieces are driving Belle crazy, asking when you are coming back."

This whole thing felt too intimate. Like they were a couple enjoying a meal together. "I don't think that would be smart. I'm exhausted." She pushed her chair back as it scrapped across the wood floor. "The bed is calling my name."

"Lily, you can't run from me forever." His eyes bore into her soul, like he could read her darkest secrets.

That's what you think. "No running, just going to bed." Never mind, it wasn't even dark out yet.

****

Stephen rubbed his jaw, feeling the days-old stubble reminding him that a beard would grow soon. Who had time to think about facial hair when a life was at stake? His clean-shaved, carefree days were over, at least for now. When the bad guys were behind bars and Lily returned to her life, he'd what? Watch her leave? Fight for a chance with her? Sort out her skewed interpretation of God? He didn't know what to do. He couldn't watch her leave, ignoring the way his pulse quickened next to her. Or the way forever seemed like a short time, if he could only grow old with her.

"Bro, am I interrupting something?" Paul's stern voice, mixed with a hint of teasing, brought him back to the real world; his aunt and uncle's cabin in the middle-of-nowhere. "You haven't heard a word I've said."

Stephen rubbed the cobwebs out of his eyes. His heart didn't care about thugs or rap sheets. His only concern was for the woman hiding behind the closed wooden doors. He doubted sleep had evaded her body. She was running from him and fast. A smile tugged at the corners of his lips. Beauty and grace were her companions.

"Man, I get it." Paul ran his fingers through his black wavy hair. "Not too long ago, I was in your shoes wondering about Belle, our uncertain future, and the creeps after her."

"You were so clueless, with your droopy love-struck eyes and irrational brain." Stephen leaned over, chuckling. "Only God could have brought you two together."

"You have a mirror? Cause you just described yourself." Paul was enjoying the jabs too much. But not all near-death experiences brought people together. He needed to prepare his heart in case she walked away. If she did, he vowed bachelorhood forever. No other woman could ever measure up to Lily. And he wouldn't waste his time trying.

"Word of advice?"

"From the lead detective on this case?" Stephen asked.

"No. From your best buddy and brother-in-law." Paul leaned closer, staring at Stephen.

"Fine, shoot." He guessed Paul had earned the right to speak honestly with him. But it didn't mean he had to like it. Especially if his advice encouraged distance from Lily. Not going to happen. Stephen moved his arm around, trying to get comfortable. His gunshot wound had healed rather quickly, but every once in a while, his arm muscle stiffened, reminding him of the present threat to Lily's life.

"Lay everything at God's feet. Otherwise, the emotions from being hunted like prey and your love for her will come crashing down, driving you crazy."

Paul spoke from experience, and his warning made sense. Stephen hadn't been praying like he should. A man of faith, yet he'd been carrying the burdens himself. What if God nudged him to distance himself from Lily? She wasn't a Christian, and that fact should have caused him to guard his heart. Too late for that. In his weakness and stupidity, she chipped away every defense protecting his whole being. He couldn't walk away from Lily or God. He couldn't have both. At least, not until she forsook her animosity toward God. A predicament.

"I know Lily's not a Christian." Paul ran his fingers over his khaki pants. Stephen knowing the next words would punch him in the gut. "So emotionally, you need to distance yourself before she brings you down."

Really? No way would Lily bring him down. Stephen rubbed his chin, hating the arrows his eyes shot at his friend. Paul meant well, but his advice stunk.

"I can't just turn off my heart, expecting it to stay neutral around her."

"I didn't say it'd be easy, but I've seen prominent men fall because of a beautiful woman." Paul grabbed his notepad out of his coat pocket, leaning back into the couch cushions. "You've come too far to fall by the wayside."

Stephen's mouth fell open, shocked by Paul's bluntness. Was his friend right? Was he inching closer to turning his back on God and forsaking the faith that made up his core being? God had brought this amazing woman into his life for a reason, and he couldn't let his heart fall so hard that it stepped away from God forever.

"Thanks, man." He'd have to reevaluate his life and spend the night seeking God's direction and begging for his forgiveness.

"I know you love her, but you'll never be the man she needs if you flop out on God. Your strong faith will win her over once she admits to falling for your charm."

"Enough mushy stuff and analyzing my relationship with God and Lily. Let's focus on the case." Vertigo slipped into his body with each thought, trying to overtake his equilibrium.

A smirk tugged at Paul's lips, reminding Stephen of the mischievous teen that used his million-dollar smile to get out of a lot of situations. "I must be losing my edge. I came to discuss hard-blooded criminals, but I end up having a therapy session. Your sister has ruined me."

Stephen's eyes twinkled at the mention of his younger sister. "She's smoothed out your rough patches, making you a likable human being."

"Thanks, I owe you." Paul rolled his eyes as the bedroom door squeaked open.

Lily stepped into the living room, her black hair pulled into a bun, wearing his aunt's old plaid pajamas. He thought his heart would explode. How was she more beautiful than the last time he saw her? *Breathe, man, breathe.*

Lily sheepishly sat on the couch inches from him, unaware of his inner turmoil. All he wanted to do was pull her into his arms, feeling the touch of her silky skin against his chest. He was so far gone; he didn't know if he could distance himself from her, or if he even wanted to.

Paul hit the top of Stephen's shoe, causing him to come out of the trance. "The case? Remember?"

Stephen couldn't think of any words that made sense, so he shook his head and practically sat on his hands before he let the temptation get the better of him.

Paul cast a warning glare at Stephen, reminding him of how wrong Lily was for him until she accepted the faith and turned to God. Stephen was a grown man. He didn't need to be reminded of his situation. He could handle it.

"We found Dwayne's body on the side of the road. Gunshot wound to the heart. He was a loyal thug for Mr. Cores. As a high-ranking member of the drug trafficking ring, he had access to valuable information and resources. Probably why someone killed him."

"When will this end?" Lily curled her legs on the couch, looking like a vulnerable kid.

Stephen bit the inside of his lip until the metallic taste of blood squirted into his mouth. If he didn't put some distance between Lily and himself, he'd fall fast. He jumped up from the couch, hitting his knee on the end table. Pain. Just what he needed to take his mind off the woman watching his every move.

With a raised eyebrow, Lily shot him a quizzical look. "Did you find anything else?"

Paul shifted his body on the couch, folding his leg over his knee. "We have concrete proof that Jason was receiving payments from the drug lord."

"Impossible!" Lily fisted her hands at her side. "He's being set up."

"I'm exploring every possibility, but prepare yourself for what's coming. People aren't always what they seem."

"What's coming?"

Paul pulled on his shirt collar, staring anywhere but at Lily. "My partner found a note in your brother's belongings, dated days before his death."

"And?"

"It's late. How about I come back tomorrow?" Paul stood to his feet, stretching.

"Detective, if you don't tell me now, you better arrest me now for assaulting a police officer."

Stephen stepped behind the couch, rubbing his fingers over her tense neck. He needed space, but she needed to cool down. And he could help with that."

Paul threw his arms in the air in surrender. "He stated that if he couldn't replace the stolen goods by deadline, exchange your life for the stolen items."

"He pushed you in the line of fire, selling your life for his freedom." Stephen moved his hand away from Lily, fearing he'd take his anger out on her neck muscles. "He had no right."

"I'm going to be sick." She dashed off to the bedroom, slamming the door behind her.

****

I feel like a prisoner. I have to get out of here. She paced the small bedroom, wearing the worn rug out more. *My brother traded my life to save his hide, but he's dead and now Mr. Cores wants me. Was Jason really working for Mr. Cores, or was it just a cover for his work with the CIA?* Lily took a calming breath, trying to push down the bile in her throat.

Fleeing from Danger, Jessica West

Why did God let this happen to her? His disdain for her was clearly obvious. She threw her arms in the air as tears poured down her face. "God, why do you hate me so much? Can you not torment someone else? Give me a break." Lily shook her head as a headache pounded in her temple. She had lost her mind praying to a fairy tale God. She couldn't decide if he was real and holding a grudge against her or fake and just something to make weak people feel better. Lily was weak, and it didn't make her feel better.

Lily's eyes scanned the small room for an escape route. The only exit was a window that she could barely fit her hips through. She reprimanded herself for all the late night ice cream pity parties on her days off. It didn't matter. She'd try anyway, and if her hips couldn't make it, she'd find another way out of this prison cell. Stephen couldn't hold her against her will. He wasn't her captor or her protector anymore. She needed space and answers, and hiding out in a secluded cabin with him wasn't helping.

I should march out of this room, grab his keys and leave, never looking back. The thought sent a crooked smile onto her face. Back to the beach? No, too predictable. She always wanted to explore the land of her ancestors. Her mother's family still lived in Asia. Maybe a distant cousin would take her in.

Her mother's lifeless, pale face popped into her mind. So fragile, like a porcelain doll. Naomi Li, her mother, moved to the states as an exchange student, seeking a better opportunity in life than her parents who owned a fish market. Her beauty and brains took her farther than expected, and her paths crossed with Isaac Walsh, from the prominent family whose empire ranged across the country.

He snagged an Asian beauty, and she married into more wealth than she ever imagined.

A short marriage later and a son, their lives seemed perfect. For four years, they lived the American dream until another positive pregnancy test and a breast cancer diagnostic. Her father never wanted her and blamed her for her mother's cancer. Isaac Walsh was a cruel man, and turned to the bottle once her mother passed away. God had robbed her of the mother she barely knew, thanks to her father. And the father she wanted to forget.

Lily shook her head, trying to get the depressing memories out of her mind. She needed to escape, not dwell on debilitating memories. She had to go back to the storage unit, find evidence to prove her brother's innocence. Or why the thugs were after her. Jason Walsh was just like their father and could have gotten in over his head, making her his scapegoat. Her father had no conscience. Maybe Jason didn't either.

Enough! Lily forcefully tossed her coat, its heavy fabric thudding against the wooden floor next to the frost-covered window. She grasped the faded blinds and pulled them up, revealing a view of the pitch-black night. The cold air seeped into the room, carrying the faint scent of pine trees and damp earth. Outside, a pristine layer of white powdery snow, glistening under the pale moonlight. Lily despised the biting cold, but her desperation to escape this desolate cabin and the charming man inside urged her forward. Stephen's dangerous smile filled her mind. He had chipped away the barriers around her heart, leaving her exposed to everything she could never have with the man, but that she desperately wanted.

Determination fueled her as she gripped the worn window frame, exerting force until it finally yielded with a creak. The icy air rushed in, instantly chilling her to the bone, but she pushed through, her fingers tingling as she pounded the window open with open-palm hits.

With a bone-chilling shiver, she straddled one leg out the window before touching the snowy ground with her shoe. Icier than expected, she slid to the ground, staring into the darkness of the night.

Great. Now I'm wet and cold. Goosebumps attacked her body as trembles overtook her. No way was she climbing back through the window. She barely made it the first time. What was she supposed to do? Her brilliant plan had so many holes in it, she'd freeze to death. She would not knock on the door. Her plan involved stealing Stephen's car, going to the storage building, and finding whatever evidence needed to take down Tony Cores. Not cowering like a little girl and alerting Stephen to her getaway. With no keys, her new plan was hiking to a serviceable road and hitchhiking into town. Hiking through twenty acres of freezing terrain, hoping an innocent bystander just drove by? Foolish. Down right dangerous. But no turning back now.

She climbed off the snowy ground, dusting the stuck-on snow off her pants. A numbing tingle shot through her legs, making it impossible to move.

One foot in front of the other. Simple. But her body protested. She wouldn't die in below-freezing temperatures, so close to freedom. Ok, she wasn't anywhere near freedom. But she wouldn't allow herself to die in a relatively safe environment. She imagined Stephen sipping coffee by the warm fireplace, guarding her tiny room from thugs intent on taking her out before Christmas. Stephen would be furious when he discovered an empty room and an opened window. Lily didn't blame him. She wasn't making his self-appointed job easy. Years had swiped away at her life, but she was still that obstinate, unlovable ten-year-old.

Desperate to survive, she let out a piercing scream, hoping Stephen would hear.

The wooden door swung open. Gun in hand, Stephen glanced around the darkened night, taking in the surrounding scene.

He stood over her, shaking his head as a frown covered his hardened face. "Am I such awful company that you have to sneak out in the middle of the night to escape?" He kneeled on the icy ground, swooping her in his arms, carrying her into the warmth and safety of the cabin.

Tears burned her eyes as he lowered her onto the couch, wrapping a thick blanket around her numb body.

"Don't answer that." Stephen jumped away from her like her nearness sent shots of pain through his body. "I'm not your captor, and the least you can do is make my life easier. I set my life aside, protecting you, so you could have a future bathed in freedom."

Lily's mouth fell open as tears streamed down her face. She pulled the blanket to her chin as rapid breaths and sweating palms tried overtaking her.

"The keys are on the table. Leave. I won't stop you." He stomped out of the room, slamming the bathroom door.

Lily knew her failed escape hurt him and she didn't know if she could ever take it back.

Chapter Ten

Stephen dropped to his knees, brushing his feet against the side of the claw-foot tub. Pain worse than a bullet wound pierced through his heart. Tears threatened his eyes as he blinked rapidly. He couldn't believe Lily's attempted escape. Was he so horrible that she needed to climb through a window in the dead of night, in negative degree temperatures just to get away from him? It made no sense. She made no sense. She'd rather freeze to death than face him.

God, Stephen threw his arms in the air. *What is going on? I'm thinking about love and a lasting relationship with her, and all she wants to do is run from me. Why is this happening? I finally open my heart to love and only now do I realize I'm the biggest fool there is. There will never be Stephen and Lily Smith. Will there?*

He pounded his fist on the chipped-tiled floor. His strength evaded him as he sat hunched over in the tiny bathroom, pouring his heart out to his Father. An hour later, he jumped to his feet with new resolve. Until proving otherwise, he'd protect her without getting his heart thrown in the mix. He knew he loved Lily, so could he easily flip his heart switch and feel nothing? No, but to keep any dignity, he'd try. It'd be really hard beating down his desire to hold her and comfort her. But a one-sided relationship was humiliating. Stephen almost prayed that she had taken his car and disappeared. It would make life so much easier.

But, no, he needed to protect her. In the middle of God's plan for Stephen's life, God threw her into the mix. For whatever reason, he had to keep her safe, not analyze a deeper meaning behind getting thrown together. He needed to fortify his heart and prepare for her to walk away for good in the future. Lily acted like a caged animal. She would leave at the first opportunity, tonight being an example of that.

Stephen always had a heart for the underdogs. After med school, he took a two-month trip to Haiti, exploring where God wanted him to serve at. Living among poverty and disease ate away his heart. He spent long hours offering free medical care to the poorest people and slipping in the Gospel, that could deliver them from filth and sin that ate away at their flesh. It was a heart-wrenching job, and he lost ten pounds, giving every part of him to those who had nothing. He came home a changed man, not just physically, but spiritually. God wanted him to serve in the states, helping those brushed under the poverty level. Every four months, he took a mobile unit into the slums of different big cities, offering free medical care. Not just him, but a five-man team made up of nurses, a dentist, and another doctor.

I wonder if Lily would like to tag along next time? No. She'd be long gone, only haunted memories of what he could never have.

A foul, chemical stench floated through the crack under the door, causing his eyes to burn. What was Lily doing? A loud crash echoed through the bathroom. Lily! He needed to find her.

Stephen dashed out of the bathroom, fingers wrapped around his gun, swiping around the thick smoke filling the small cabin.

Lily's body slumped over on the couch, nestled under the thick covers. Was she asleep or passed out? Stephen didn't have time to figure it out. The bad guys had compromised their location, and an ambush could happen at any moment. Stephen grabbed a backpack next to the couch—his wilderness survival kit.

He anchored it securely on his back, coughing as the smoke filled his lungs. They had to get out of the cabin and go where? Stephen hadn't thought that far ahead yet. His mind screamed escape while they still could. He scooped Lily and her blanket into his arms, running to the back door. Gun in hand, his eyes darted over the snowy terrain, looking for anything amiss. Finding nothing, they stepped into the icy mountain air. Goosebumps popped onto his covered-up skin. They weren't alone. Somewhere evil eyes were watching their every move. Stephen breathed in a cool breath, trying to cleanse his lungs of the smoke he had inhaled.

His fingers slid across Lily's pulse point, feeling a steady pulse. *Good.*

Stephen heard the crunchiness of snow, like someone was trying to go in stealth-mode but failed miserably. Running to his truck wasn't an option. The thug camped out by their only means of escape.

Great. The only option was hiding out in the wilderness, praying the thug left before hypothermia consumed their bodies. No turning back. Stephen didn't know how many hired hands were staking out the place, but it wouldn't be long before they realized the cabin was empty.

"What's going on?" Lily whispered, puffing out a mist of air.

"Smoke bomb." He glanced into her face, her features hidden from the darkness surrounding them. Stephen imagined Lily was chewing on her bottom lip, trying not to cry as icy air swept through her bones.

"Where are we going?"

He looked behind him as a light danced off the side of the cabin. They had little time. "Not sure, just away from the ambush waiting to happen."

Her body shivered under his arms. He moved the blanket tighter around her arms. They wouldn't last long. But he only needed a few minutes to call for backup, hopefully not getting lost.

A ping sound darted through the open field as Stephen trudged through the knee-deep snow. He turned, aimed his gun and fired into the night.

A loud groan followed by a thump filled the silence of the night. Target hit.

"Not sure how many men are out there. We need to hide until help arrives." He slid into the darkened woods, disappearing into a mass of trees. "We'll survive, but I can't risk anyone seeing my flashlight."

He felt her body tense in his arms. A minor discomfort was better than a deadly bullet. But the frigid temperature numbed his feet; signs of hypothermia. He had to get a barrier between them and the deadly temperature. Moving deeper into the woods, he spotted a section big enough for them to sit.

"Sit while I secure a shelter." He lowered her to the snow, tossing his survival gear next to his feet. Rummaging through the backpack, he pulled out a satellite phone and a temperature regulating tent. With the extra insulation, they'd be safe from the elements as long as no thugs sneaked up on them. Chances were slim. What hired thug would stomp through knee-deep snow toward wild animals and freezing temperatures? Hopefully none.

Stephen unzipped the tent, throwing in extra wool blankets. The sound of owls in the distance sent a shiver through his body. They would not die in the wilderness. He had to believe it. Placing Lily inside the warmth, he quickly called Paul, relaying the events of the night. Help would arrive soon. They just had to rough it out until Paul got here.

Slipping his arms around Lily's body, he basked in the warmth that her closeness brought. Light snores floated from her body. She needed sleep, but he couldn't afford such luxury, not until they were safe.

Seconds turned to minutes, and minutes hours as he pleaded to God for protection and deliverance from the attempts on Lily's life.

****

What's happening? Lily jerked her body at the crashing sound. She opened her eyes, trying to focus her blurry vision. *Where am I?*

A toasty, icy filling slid through her bones. She wrapped the blanket over her arms, basking in the warmth. *What was going on?* Her eyes darted to Stephen, crouched next to the tent's opening, gun drawn. A bone-chilling shiver ate at her body. Memories of the night before or hours ago, she didn't know which, haunted her mind.

The climb through the window, numb limbs, smoke, Stephen rushing her into the wilderness, gunshots. Guilt flowed through her veins. Was she so self-centered that she actually climbed through a window, trying to escape the man her heart beat for, but her mind warned against?

Stephen's sharp look flashed in her mind, sending butterflies swirling in her gut. His look of disappointment. No, it went deeper than that. His look of betrayal. He opened up his bachelor heart and all she could do was rip it into pieces. Lily wasn't good at heart matters. She was a doctor, so physical heart matters were easier to fix than love, anger, rejection. Emotions were not her specialty. She had killed the one chance she had at finding love and a forever happiness with someone.

Stephen's eyes were like a shield, their hardness serving as a barrier to protect him from any additional hurt. He barely looked her way. His disdain etched around the corners of his eyes. She had lost Stephen's heart and everything she didn't know she wanted, but secretly it drew her in.

No! His contempt for me is a good thing. The words hung in her mind, leaving a bitter taste. *The weight of his disappointment hangs heavy in the air, suffocating me. I don't deserve him or the intoxicating scent of his sweet love that lingers in my memory. It's best for him to realize this now. The ache in his heart will eventually subside, replaced by the vibrant pulse of a new love. A worthy woman will gracefully enter his life, her presence sealing his love life forever. But amidst the symphony of emotions, it could never be me, as the gentle touch of regret brushes against my soul.*

Tears filled her eyes as she fastened her gaze on the man crouched in the tent, glaring into the pitch-blackness of the night. Cold air slid into the tent, smacking her in the face. If life were different, Stephen would be the man of her dreams, but God was like a gulf separating them, and nothing could bridge the gap.

"You're awake." He whispered, barely looking at her.

"What's going on? Why are we still in the frigid temperatures?" His coldness seeped into her body more than the icy air, sending pain shooting through her heart.

"Two henchmen trudging closer to our location, armed with rifles." Stephen stuffed everything back in his backpack, not the tent.

"Where's Paul?"

"There was an ambush at the cabin." His eyes focused on whatever was outside the tent.

"Oh no. Is your family safe?" She couldn't bear the thought of something happening to them.

"Paul and my dad disarmed the thugs, keeping the threat low until local cops could haul the thugs away." Stephen stiffened as he glanced in her direction, all softness gone from his face. "Until Paul can get here, we're on our own."

Lily absentmindedly reached for his arm, needing to smooth out the tension in the air. With a pained look, he jerked his body away from her.

"Don't." He ran his fingers through his disheveled hair. "You can't have me and try to run from me simultaneously."

I'm gonna be sick. His words clawed at her heart. "Stephen…"

"Stop. I don't need any platitudes. All I need is to protect you so we can get this over with and go our separate ways."

His words knocked the air out of her. This was what she wanted, but it felt so wrong.

"Grab your blanket." He slid the backpack straps through his arms. "It's now or never. Let's go."

Lily puffed out a frustrated sigh. What was the point? When Stephen and Paul captured the bad guys, she barely had a life to return to. After having someone in her life, could she really go back to her robotic routine of work, lonely evenings binge watching sappy movies, and a hollow heart? Maybe she wanted someone to share her life with. A good-looking doctor. She stared at Stephen as he rounded the side of the tent, making sure it was safe to proceed. She destroyed anything they might have had. No way he'd even talk to her when this was over. Ocean waves and squishy sand called her name, with a longing she couldn't ignore. When safety returned, she'd rebuild at the beach and get a dog; a big, human-sized dog. She didn't need Stephen or his God to be happy.

"Are you coming?" He stopped in the knee-deep snow, irritation marring his features.

Why did she ever have to climb through the window?

She took a step in the snow, sinking to her waist. Great, she'd get buried alive in an icy grave.

A hardened look spread across his face, sending goosebumps tingling over her arms. "I'd carry you, but I need my arms in case I need to fire my gun."

Likely story. "I don't want to hold you up. You go on ahead, I'll be close behind you." *Wallowing in self-pity and trying not to freeze to death.*

Stephen stopped. A flicker of emotions flashed in his eyes, but only for a split-second. "Lily." He left out an icy breath so cold the mist could have frozen in mid-air.

She took another treacherous step into a pile of sinking snow. Why did she have to be so short? "I'm fine, just go." She couldn't look at him and not feel utterly rejected. This amazing man, who once beamed with love toward her, now hated her and could barely look at her.

"I'll slow down." He leaned against a snow-covered tree, waiting for her.

"Don't do me any favors."

"Do you really want to get away from me so bad, that you'd risk dying in the wilderness or being taken captive by thugs?" His voice held thousands of daggers, all aimed at her.

Of course not, but I can't stand looking at your hostility towards me. I made a mistake. I'm sorry. She wanted to fall into the snow, begging for forgiveness. What was the point? "Stephen, I just can't go on with you anymore." *It kills me watching the damage I've done to you.* Who'd have thought climbing through a window would harden a man and zap his love away?

He yanked her arm, pulling her through a snowy trench. She couldn't go much longer. Not sure she wanted to, anyway. Besides the snow, the moon, hidden by trees, cast a soft glow, making visibility nearly impossible. Stephen's flashlight illuminated inches of terrain, but icy darkness surrounded them like an unending nightmare.

"I can't do this right now." He stalked off in the snow, running away from her, leaving her all alone.

"Unbelievable." She wrapped her arms over her chest as numbing tingles shot up her legs. The urge to close her eyes was so strong, she couldn't resist. *I'll rest for a minute.* Darkness engulfed her as she fell over in the snow.

****

God, I can't do this anymore. He dropped into a soft, powdery pile of snow, his tears freezing instantly upon contact with the icy ground. *I'm shielding my heart from the only woman I've ever loved, and it's like torture. It's impossible to miss the contempt etched on her face. She hates me and my tough-guy persona is only wedging the gap between us. By protecting my heart, I'm being a full-pledged jerk. Why did you bring us together, God? I'm so emotionally weak.*

What about her? She was barely holding it together. It was like God smacked him in the face, knocking his brain back in order.

I ran off, leaving her in the waist-deep snow. Alone. Thugs, wild animals, hypothermia, death. If anything happened to her, he'd never forgive himself.

He dashed off through the woods, not caring who heard him. He had to find her before it was too late. She may never forgive him for running off, but he had to at least save her life. *God, forgive me. I'll never leave her side again while she's in danger. Give me another chance.*

Where was she? He frantically shined his flashlight over the snow, hoping for any clue to her whereabouts. His breath hitched. A few feet away, Lily laid in a crater of snow, lips blue and face ashen-white.

Two giant steps and he scooped her off the deadly snow, cradling her in his warm embrace. "Sweetheart, wake up." His lips brushed over her cold skin, mixed with his tears. He needed shelter fast. The only option was the tent. The henchmen were probably gone by now. Stomping through the snow, he nestled her body close to his. Her pulse was steady, but her pale blue-tinted skin concerned him. Spotting the tent, he did a quick sweep of the area. Nothing. Stephen tore the flap back, falling into the insulated warmth. He wrapped her in a warm blanket, massaging her arms and legs. She needed proper blood flow.

He stared into her face as the color slowly creeped onto her face. *Thank You, Jesus.*

"Stephen?" She shifted her body in his arms.

"Oh, Lily. I'm so sorry for being a jerk." He pressed his lips to hers, basking in the warmth and closeness of her touch. How could he have ever thought he could have walked away from her when her touch lingered on his skin? Never.

She kissed him back before pushing away, staring into his eyes. "I'm sorry for climbing out the window. I just…"

"Sweetheart, I know." He placed a gentle kiss on her forehead.

The tent's opening ripped open as a man with a rifle poked his head into the tent. "I'm gonna cry." His deep laughter filled the tiny space, as a hardness covered Stephen's features.

Idiot. How did they sneak up on us?

Stephen felt the comforting weight of his gun, nestled securely next to his ankle. If he could only stoop and get it. This entire ordeal would end fast. He cut his eyes toward the man. Although he bore a striking resemblance to Santa, Paul had already imprisoned that man days ago. Stephen wondered why the notorious drug lord employed potbelly Santa lookalikes. Only if they were trigger-happy, and that made up for whatever other skills they lacked.

"Step away from the girl." Santa lookalike pressed the rifle into Stephen's back, frustration marring his face.

Yeah, right, like that's gonna happen. Stephen stared at Lily, her face unnaturally calm for a person held at gunpoint. He couldn't let her down, but he also needed to calculate taking this guy down. Too soon and he'd get shot too late and Lily would be gone.

"No funny business." The man dug the gun further into Stephen's back. He could take this guy, but not with a bullet hole in his back. If the bullet hit the spinal canal just right, it could cause complete paraplegia. A shudder ran through Stephen's body. He did not want that to happen.

God, get us out of this mess.

His eyes met with Lily's, sending a secret message begging her to trust him.

"Out of the tent, both of you." The guy's white hair matched the snowy white powder surrounding them. He scooped down and jerked Lily's arm, sending tears into her trusting eyes.

"Don't touch her." Stephen kicked his leg, knocking the man into the snow. Spotting the gun, he threw the man's gun into a thicket of vines. That should hold him off for a few minutes. "Let's go."

Lily clung to Stephen, her arms enveloping his waist, her fingers tightly clutching the edge of his jacket. Pain traveled through his body. A minor discomfort. It meant they were alive, and the feeling of the icy wind against his skin was a constant reminder of the deadly situation they were in. They needed shelter, but also safety.

"I know you're deadly cold and numb, but if we don't pick up the pace, Santa lookalike will be back."

Lily grunted as the sound split through the eerie silence of the darkened woods. The snow was the only source of light. "What will happen if he abducts me?"

Stephen grabbed her hand, pressing a kiss to her palm. "No matter how bleak the situation gets, don't lose hope. God's gonna get us out of this mess."

She snatched her hand away from his at the mention of God.

Lily needed to resolve her animosity toward God, because only He could rescue them from Cores and his men.

"Sweetheart, let it go. God is on your side, no matter what you think."

She mumbled a few words under her breath. Stephen couldn't see her eyes, but he imagined they burned dark green with a fiery spunk that would help her survive.

"Just drop it. I don't need you trying to fix me or throwing God on me." Lily flung her hair over her shoulder. He'd seen her do it before, mostly when she was upset with him. "I don't need God and I don't need you if you don't leave me alone."

Her calm, easygoing personality attracted Stephen to her, like the rolling waves brushing against the shore. Her beauty was undeniable, but it was her spunk that made her absolutely irresistible. Stephen couldn't help but smile at her icy words. He could hear her indifferent words for the rest of his life, and he'd still never grow tired of her spunk. Of course, he promised God he wouldn't pursue her unless she shared the faith that controlled his life. That resolve was easier said than done.

"I could straighten you out on a few things about your God."

"Please do." If he could get her talking about her misguided notions of God, he could straighten her out.

She wrapped her fingers around his arm, nudging into his side. Danger wasn't gone. He needed to remember they weren't carelessly trekking through the snow.

"God sits in heaven planning his next move to destroy my life." Her voice went from hostile to above a whisper in a second. "I don't want God going after you. Maybe you should stay away from me."

She cared about him. Lily couldn't deny it any longer. Stephen felt it in the way she clung to him and in the tone of her voice.

"Lily..." Before he could finish his sentence, heat traveled through his body, his world crumbing into darkness.

****

Did that really happen? Lily rubbed her rope-bound hands on the side of the van's wall, hoping to sever the restraints.

Pointless. The rope was of superior quality, not your average jump rope. How would she get out? She couldn't count on Stephen. He had crumbled like a sand castle brushing against the waves. She stared at his hunched over body. He didn't appear to have visible wounds. The thug didn't shoot him, just whacked him on the back of the head with the butt of the gun. His prolonged unconsciousness worried Lily, the doctor. He'd been out ten minutes and counting.

His injury was her fault. Their abduction was also her fault. If she hadn't gotten him riled up and defensive, he probably would have noticed the creep sneaking up on them. No way Santa lookalike would have taken Stephen under normal conditions. Why couldn't she keep her mouth shut? Her harsh words had the opposite effect on Stephen. He seemed to like her obstinacy. His mischievous smile popped into her mind. His good-looks were clearly swoon-worthy, but his personality chiseled the shield away from her heart. No matter how much she didn't want to fall for him, she couldn't help it. She ran her tongue over her lips, remembering the sweetness of his kiss. If God hadn't separated them by putting her on His hit list and him on His good list, maybe they'd have a chance at a relationship. God had ruined something else for her—their relationship.

Angry curses thundered from the driver's seat as the van swerved into oncoming traffic. She rolled around in the empty seat-less back of the utility van, nothing to hold on to.

Where was the thug taken them? Would he kill Stephen, her selfless protector? He gave up his weeks' vacation to play bodyguard to her instead of basking in the love of Christmas with his family. Who did that?

Christmas. She sighed a labored breath. What day was it? She mentally scrolled through a calendar in her mind. Considering she didn't know the time; Christmas was probably three days away. No way would this be over by then. No, it probably would be over. In a few minutes, she'd either die or become the wife of a notorious drug lord.

Thanks, Jason. She wanted to scream at the top of her lungs. Her self-centered, conniving brother destroyed her life even though he was dead.

Death. She didn't want to die. She wasn't ready to die. What would happen after she took her last breath? Would she wake up to nothingness or to an inferno that she could never escape from? Did God really hold the answers? Was he real or a make-believe crutch that made others feel better?

The Lord is my light and my salvation; whom shall I fear? The unfamiliar words popped into her mind. What in the world did it mean? *Whom shall I fear?* She had plenty to fear. Death. Separation. Never seeing Stephen again or feeling his electrifying touch. Marrying a criminal. Losing freedom forever.

Sweat ran down her forehead. *I can't do this.* She bowed her head, taking calming breaths, trying to still her shaky emotions. *God, help me.*

Did she really just pray to God? The words slipped out, but she didn't mean them. Okay, maybe she meant them. But God never helped her. He punished her. Her eyes darted to the hard-as-steel man slumped against the wall. It took two struggling men to lift him into the van. God had brought him into her life to protect her.

Stop! God had no part in it. Stephen was at the right place at the right time. Nothing divine about that. Her mind wandered to all the close death encounters she'd had over the past few days. Stephen's presence had breathed life into her days, preventing the thugs from taking her life. She'd only related God to the horrible things in life, but God had brought Stephen into her life, and that outweighed every bad thing until this point.

Moans floated from Stephen's lips as he moved his neck around, getting out the kinks. "I have a pounding headache. What's going on?"

"Santa got the drop on you again." Her heart flutter at his nearness. This was what love felt like. No, not love. Admiration.

"I'm never gonna live this down." A small smile tugged at the corner of his lips. "It's time to break up this party. Santa's been naughty, and we won't stay to see what the North Pole looks like."

Stephen, her man, or rather the guy she could never have, but her treacherous heart ached for, was awake. Oddly, her heart sang a strange tune at the way his eyes glanced over her.

"I'm on too many naughty lists this year. Don't want to find out what Santa does to his naughty children." She wiggled her fingers under the rope. Her hands were going numb from loss of circulation.

Stephen gave her a hard look, not even a smirk etched across his face. It was a joke, but apparently, not funny.

"Inside my pocket, I have a knife. I need you to get it." He turned his body to the side, facing her. "Now's not the time to explore what else is in my pocket."

Why would she have free rein in his pocket? A blush creeped on her cheeks, thinking about her fingers brushing against his pants leg. She couldn't do this. For one, her fingers were bound. Number two, entering his personal space seemed wrong.

Not realizing her inner struggle, he winked at her. "Your Christmas gift is in my pocket."

What kind of gift would fit in a pocket? A ring? No, definitely not. When did he even find time to shop?

"No trying to figure out my gift. One clue, it's a gift I'll give no one else." A soft laugh escaped his lips. "I can see you as a child, staying up all night waiting for Santa to bring your gifts."

Lily's smile faded at the mention of her childhood. "We didn't celebrate Christmas. My father didn't want to celebrate a day connected to Jesus. So, no gifts. Yours will be the first." She sounded so pathetic.

"Even more reason to give you my gift. But not now. I need my knife." His compassionate look stole her breath away.

She positioned herself confidently, edging closer to his leg. Her petite fingers, barely reaching, delicately delved into the depths of his pocket, sensing the smooth texture of an object. With utmost caution, she firmly clasped her fingers around the knife, mindful not to let it slip. Lily's constrained fingers released their grip, transferring the knife into his awaiting hands.

"Good work." She couldn't tell what he was doing, but after a few seconds, her hands were free. "After I take the guy out, be ready to bolt."

She didn't know what he meant, or what he'd do to the thug, but she trusted him.

After a grunt, a sharp swerve, and heavy footsteps, the back of the van opened up. "Let's get out of here."

Lily grabbed his hand, jumping out of the back of the van. She didn't know where they were, but she knew Stephen would do everything in his power to keep her safe.

Chapter Eleven

Stephen glanced at Lily as he wrapped his fingers around hers. She trusted him. Trust didn't come easy for her, and somewhere amidst the chaos, he gained her trust. *God, help me not fail her.* Humanly speaking, he'd probably fail her like everyone else in her life had. But he truly didn't want to be a statistic. She blamed God for every bad thing that happened in life, and he didn't want to add to that list. With every prayer, he pleaded for divine intervention, praying that he could be the instrument to dissolve the animosity she harbored towards God.

He loved her. Yes. And he wanted to spend the rest of his life proving that to her. But his motive wasn't purely selfish. To fight her anxiety and bleak outlook on life, she needed to experience redemptive love and God's grace.

"Where are we going?" Her whisper broke through his thunderous thoughts.

Where were they going? He glanced around the darkened road. He didn't know where they were. The sun peaked over the distant mountain range as the darkened wilderness creeped in all around them. Sure, he climbed mountains, hiked, hunted, but normally on familiar terrain. He hadn't traveled this far past the cabin before. Was the hit man leading them further away from civilization so no one would find their bodies, or a wild animal would chew up all traces of them?

A too-close-for-comfort howl pierced through the early morning hour. The thugs were gone, but predatory eyes were stalking all around them. He didn't fear mountain lions or wolves, but he didn't want to pick a fight with them, either.

Low beams from headlights popped onto the deserted country road. He didn't believe in coincidences, nor did he believe random cars traveled on this stretch of the wilderness.

"On the count of three, take off running toward that stretch of forest." He glared into her bright green eyes. "No matter what happens, stay hidden in the forest."

She tugged on the bottom of his jacket. "You're not leaving me out here to fight off wild animals while you get yourself killed." Fire burned in her eyes.

Thanks for the confidence. "That wasn't my plan. No time for arguing." He jerked her wrist, pulling her into the shadows as the car slowed past them.

"Did that person see us?" Her fingernails clawed into his side as she gripped his jacket.

"Doubtful, but we have to keep moving." He pulled her deeper into the forest, touching the edge of his gun for comfort. It meant the goons were probably searching for their fellow thug, and since he wrecked the van into the woods, they wouldn't find the bad guy. At least not until he gained consciousness and called for backup. They'd be long gone by then.

Stephen ducked behind a row of trees. Yanking his satellite phone from his pocket, he dialed Paul's number. After a few impatient minutes, he stuffed the phone back into his pocket. Paul would call him back. They just needed to survive until then.

"What's the plan?" Lily looked like she was on the verge of a panic attack.

He could easily pretend they were on a date, enjoying God's vast wilderness and each other's company. Would she like exploring God's hidden treasure, the wilderness, with him? Her eyes were wide and her stance was feeble. She clung to him so much he had a hard time walking. No, she'd probably enjoy a relaxing walk on the beach to a trek through the unknown any day. A half smile covered his lips.

"Are you really smiling at a time like this?"

Yes, he was. God, a beautiful woman, and the fresh mountain air. What more could he ask for? Maybe safety to go with it.

"Look, my only plan is to enjoy my time with you."

A sting traveled up his arm as Lily fisted her hand. She had a powerful right hook. And he probably deserved that punch. He liked her feisty side. Stephen bit his lip, trying to hide his smile.

"About our time together in this beautiful wintry tundra…" If he could keep her occupied, the anxiety would slip away.

"What is wrong with you, Stephen?" Her fist curled at her side.

"An age-old question." His eyes scanned the trees in front of them. The tall trees could easily hide an enemy bent on destruction. *Keep her talking, man.* He did not want to diffuse an anxiety attack when danger could be close by. "My mom asks me that weekly. Only in a totally different context."

"Seriously!" Lily ran her fingers through her messy hair.

"Son, why are you so bent on living a bachelor's life? God didn't make you for single-hood. I need more grandchildren." He moved his finger in the air like he'd seen his mother do when she scowled at him. "Life's journey is better with someone by your side. Did you see the new visitor at church? She's about your age. She'll outgrow the excessive makeup when she gets my age, son."

Lily stopped walking, flexing her fisted palm. She was the definition of beauty. And she didn't need any makeup to enhance her exotic look. Perfection. Or close to it.

"Daydreaming about a new female at your church?" Lily poked him in the side with her fist. Twinkles danced in her bright eyes.

He wanted to lean over, claiming her lips for him, but her nearness already distracted him enough. "Not hardly. I have a problem, though."

She gazed at his face, resuming their walk in the woods, ever aware of the dangers surrounding them. "What?"

"I can't get a certain beauty out of my mind. Nothing helps." He tugged on her hand, wrapping his fingers through hers. "But honestly, I kind of like it."

Lily squeezed his fingers before jerking her hand away. "What about the self-appointed bachelor?"

"That was before I met you, darling. I can never go back. Even if you ripped my heart out, I'd never get over you." A smile filled his face. "When this is over, we have a lot to talk about."

"Stephen…"

No one had ever said his name like her. It sounded like Christmas gifts and his mom's apple pie mixed in a soothing package.

Before he could hear her excuse why they could never be together, a shot sounded behind them, sending him into protector mode. He pushed her to the ground, scanning the surrounding trees. The light beamed enough to see where they were going without giving away the thug's location.

He unclipped his holster, holding his gun between his fingers.

God, get us out of here. Expecting to feel a bullet penetrating his skin, he stiffened his body. Aware of Lily crouched in the icy snow, he pulled her up, shielding her body with his.

Another gunshot filled the early morning air. If they didn't get out of the wilderness soon, they might never get out.

"Trust me." He whispered close to her ear. Her anxiety was at a peak, her trembling body a clue to that. But he would deal with her mental state later. Right now, he needed to protect her from a bullet.

Walking back toward the country road in silence, Stephen prayed like he'd never prayed before.

Slowing headlights abruptly stopped in the middle of the curvy road. Stephen pushed Lily behind his body, trying to protect her.

"Get in." The gruff voice sounded from the driver's side window.

Stephen took a deep breath, opening the door and shoving Lily into the darkened backseat. His enormous body claiming the rest of the backseat. With a thud, the vehicle zoomed down the road like it was never there.

****

Lily's heart pounded in her chest. Why had they willingly gotten in the car with someone? The driver and his partner hadn't aimed guns at them or restrained their arms and legs. Yet, something didn't seem right. Love and happily ever-after filled Stephen's mind. Maybe clouding his judgment. With each passing moment they spent together, thoughts of a future with Stephen filled her mind, even though she knew it could never be. She needed to get far away from him before he made the biggest mistake of his life. His heart should swoon over someone of like faith like the visitor at his church or anyone else but her. She was so wrong for him, yet he'd never admit it. Infatuation guided him enough to throw his life and beliefs away for her. Squaring her jaw as her posture straightened, Lily determined to disappear for good once the threat to her life was over. No turning back. No matter what.

    She glanced at Stephen. His head bobbed in the air like he had fallen asleep or was fervently praying. She had never met a man like him. He was infuriating and charming concurrently. Her knight-in-shiny armor. The man that … No. Her treacherous heart couldn't fall for him. Truth be told, she was past the falling stage, but she needed to reapply the shields around her heart and step back.

    The car swerved onto a side road, tossing her body next to Stephen. The sun had fully risen over the mountains, causing sunbeams to filter through the car. Maybe the shield of darkness was better. At least it covered the evil intent of her captors. Lily stared at the gun resting in the middle console. If she could grab it and take over the car, she could … What? Save the day? Get them both killed? Stephen looked calm. Too calm for a man about to face an excruciating death. Christians didn't fear death, or so she heard. Her fear attacked her common sense. If the car didn't stop soon, she'd upholster the inside with vomit.

    Lily chewed on her bottom lip, accessing the situation. The two hooded figures appeared scrawny and unprofessional. First assignment, maybe. No matter, she'd make sure it was their last.

"Why are you so calm?" Lily couldn't stand it any longer. She brushed her leg against his, letting her whispers flow into his ear.

"I'm beat." He leaned his head against the seat, closing his eyes.

Unbelievable. She guessed protectors had their breaking point. How could he sleep at a time like this? Maybe low blood sugar or the thugs laced the door handle with a sleep-inducing narcotic. Either way, she'd protect him.

The car slowed in front of a rusty cabin, the wooden planks barely hanging on. An odd odor filled the air in the car. Apple pie? She must be losing her mind. Lily shook her head, knocking the cobwebs out.

I can do this without having a panic attack. She swallowed the bile rising in her throat and in a split second, the small hand gun trembled in her fingers.

"No one move." Her feeble voice shook as she pointed the gun at the hooded figures.

Stephen's eyes popped open; a smile tugged on his lips. How could he smile at a time like this? Something was seriously wrong with him.

"Hand me the gun, sweetheart." His finger wrapped around hers, trying to extract the gun from her hand.

"What?" Was she missing something? Their abductors were going to kill them. Surely, he still had a fight left in him. She peered into his crystal blue eyes, searching for an answer. What if Stephen had played her the whole time, and he was on Mr. Cores' paycheck? No. She couldn't believe that. He wouldn't betray her. Or would he? He had some amazing acting skills.

Lily jerked her hand away from his, gripping the gun. "No!"

"What are you doing?" There was a small twinkle in his eye, even though his face remained stern and unyielding.

"I'm not going down like this." She aimed the gun at his chest, trying to hide her erratic emotions.

"Sweetheart?"

"Don't sweetheart me. Start talking." Her voice boomed through the compact car, sending shivers through her arms.

"What should we talk about?" He seemed calm and maybe a little humored at the situation.

"Don't patronize me." She steadied the gun in front of his body. With one swipe, he could take her out. "How long have you been working for Cores?"

"Huh?"

"Quit the act. You almost fooled me." Almost. She couldn't imagine him working for the enemy, but he willingly got in the car with two thugs and went to sleep, not caring about taking them out.

"Lily, hand me the gun." His voice reminded her of her father's sternness when he rebuked her.

"Not until you tell me the truth."

"Mom, Belle, take your hoods off." He leaned in the seat, tapping the back of the front seat. The women obeyed, as their hair fell to their shoulders.

"They're involved too?" Lily's mouth fell open. All of them deceived her. Stupid! She had to get out now before Cores showed up, demanding his payment for Jason's sins; her.

A soft chuckle floated through the car. Mrs. Smith turned around, smiling. Not a good time to laugh when she had a gun pointed at the woman's son. These people were crazy. Or maybe she was crazy.

"Sweetheart, lower the gun." His fingers brushed against her cheek, sending butterflies dancing in the pit of her stomach. "First time a beautiful woman has held me at gunpoint."

"Stop! I won't allow you to disarm me with your charm." Lily blinked her eyes. What was she doing? These people couldn't be the enemy. Her head spun as confusion twirled in her mind.

Stephen leaned over, brushing his lips over hers, before prying the gun out of her fingers.

"What was that for?"

"You wouldn't listen to me." His fingers trailed to the strand of hair falling in her eyes. "I'd never hand you over to the enemy. I love you."

Tears filled her eyes at her foolishness and the man's confession. "I'm … sorry."

"No need to apologize. This entire situation could turn anyone mentally unstable."

Mentally unstable? She wanted to bust out laughing at his choice of words. She turned her focus to the silent women in the front seat. "What are y'all doing here?"

Belle turned around in the seat, her cheeks pink. "Paul and my dad were in a minor accident. Both are being evaluated at the ER."

"When we received Stephen's message, we knew we had to help." Mrs. Smith continued the story.

"If Paul or my dad hear about this, they won't be happy." Belle rubbed the sides of her face.

"You knew it was them the whole time?" Lily felt like an idiot.

"Yes. I thought you did too until you went all psycho, pointing a gun at me." A smile played on his face. He enjoyed her lapse of judgment too much.

"Stephen…"

"No time for apologies. We need to get in the cabin and figure out our next move." He opened the door, jumping to her side before she got out of the car.

Goosebumps erupted on her arms, the tiny hairs standing on end as a shiver raced down her spine. It wasn't just the captivating presence of the charming man that quickened her heartbeat; it was the ominous knowledge that resolute thugs lurked nearby, their presence hanging in the air like a foreboding storm, waiting to strike.

****

"I love you. Now, go before Dad and Paul realize you both are missing." Stephen set the folder on the dusty couch, gripping the handle of the picnic basket. The food smelled heavenly. His mom was a genuine hero in his mind, bringing him the rest of the apple pie and enough food to last until the new year.

"I'm saving you both a spot at the dinner table at Christmas." His mom leaned up, kissing him on the cheek. "Three more days to figure this case out and come home, where you belong."

Stephen glanced at the sunbeams glowing on the dingy cabin wall. A new day. What he wouldn't give for a hot shower, food, and at least four hours of sleep. He set the basket on the couch. They had food, thanks to his mom. But no way he could sleep when a bunch of thugs roamed the countryside, trying to find them. At least Lily could sleep. He stared at her as love and amazement filled his eyes. Her body curled up on the old couch, head resting on a tattered pillow, soft snores floating in the air.

Sensing her son's thoughts, his mother leaned in closer to his ear. "Son, give her to God. He works all things out."

Stephen crossed his arms over his chest, fighting the urge to swoop Lily in his arms, never letting her go. "I never knew love felt like this; amazing yet terrifying."

"Our bachelor is growing up." Belle gave him a mock smile, holding the door handle. "We need to go. Paul will be so angry if we get caught in the crosshairs of this mess."

"I love you, too, sis." Stephen opened the door, scanning for anything out of the ordinary. "I'll walk you ladies to your car."

"Always the gentleman." Belle pulled her small handgun out of her pocket. "Stay with Lily. No one's going to mess with us and walk away."

"Love you, son." His mom said, disappearing through the unusually sturdy door of the old cabin.

Stephen turned the lock before plopping onto the couch across from Lily. He set the food basket on the floor. His rumbling stomach would have to wait. Stephen would not wake Lily up, and he wouldn't feast without her.

He grabbed the thick folder his mother had brought him, opening to a random page. His stomach cringed at Jason Walsh's body sprawled on the floor. Working in the ER, he saw death and violence, but not through the eyes of whichever detective typed up the case file. Jason's death was unsolved. No DNA or fingerprints of the suspect. No notes or foul chemicals. Just a body. Stephen scanned the words on the document. Lily was at the crime scene minutes before her brother passed away. Probably missing the killer by mere seconds. A few seconds earlier, and it could have been a double homicide. If that didn't scream God's protection, he didn't know what did.

Thank You, God, for sparing her life. See us both through this alive and draw her to Your saving grace and love. I don't want to lose her because she isn't a Christian, but I won't walk away from You, no matter what.

Tears pricked his sleepy eyes as he glanced her way. He wanted to wake up every morning to her beautiful olive-tinted face and swoon-worthy eyes. Stephen wasn't an impulsive guy, but she brought out the spontaneity in him. He propped his legs on the couch, feeling the little box shift in his pocket.

At his family's cabin, his dad had chucked his grandma's ring at him, telling him he knew what to do with it. He never thought he'd ever give the heirloom to anyone, but then Lily ran into his life, and his whole thought process collapsed. Life was pointless if he couldn't spend it with her. He loved her and the short time they knew each other didn't matter to him. He'd seen her at her worst and admired her strong, compassionate character. The only thing holding him back from popping the question, besides the thugs after them, was her animosity toward God. Love couldn't truly develop apart from God. He wouldn't push her, just pray for God's love to touch her stony heart.

Her relationship with God aside, Lily's back-and-forth with him, didn't convince him she'd accept his proposal. One minute, her eyes yearned for their closeness and a relationship, the next contempt etched across her face, warning him not to touch her. She confused him. Love confused him. Stephen rubbed his eyes as sleep threatened to consume his body. That couldn't happen. He tossed the folder to the empty couch cushion, grabbing the picnic basket. He'd just peek inside at the feast his mother packed for them.

How deep was the basket? It seemed like a never-ending container. He pulled out a gallon of his mom's famous sweet tea. Licking his lips, he set it on the hardwood floor. Stephen shifted through the pie, chicken, cinnamon rolls, sandwich meat, bread, and anything else he imagined they might want. He didn't know how long they were hiding out, but at least they wouldn't starve.

Stephen looked at the sleeping bags by the door. His mom and sister really came through for him. He knew they would. His sister packed a duffel bag of clothes, toiletries, and a coat for Lily and a bag for him.

Lily stirred on the couch. Her disheveled hair covered the sides of her face as he moved closer for a look. He treaded on dangerous ground. He was beyond the point of bouncing back if she rejected him. How had his determination at bachelorhood crumbled so fast? For twenty-eight years, he prided in his unattached lifestyle. No one telling him what to do or his heart making foolish decisions for him. In fact, he used to pity the guy tied down to a woman; hen-pecked. Now, he wanted to be that man more than anything.

Stephen took a slow step forward, his fingers gently sweeping her silky black strands away from her face. The scent of her hair filled his nostrils, a delicate floral fragrance that intoxicated him. As his eyes stared at her sleeping, a breathtaking sight, his breath hitched, his heart skipping a beat. The room seemed to fade away, as if they were the only two souls in existence. In that moment, he realized that he no longer craved freedom or weekends with the guys. All he yearned for was her and the lifelong journey they could embark on together. The highs, the lows, and every beautiful moment in between.

Fleeing from Danger, Jessica West

"Stephen?" Her faint whisper sent electricity shooting through his body. If he didn't back away, he might do something he'd regret later. Maybe he wouldn't regret it, but now wasn't the time to claim her for himself. The ring hit against his keys as he scooted closer to her. His mind fumbled over all the reasons proposing right now would be a terrible idea.

His mom always told him not to pray for patience. But he needed divine intervention, or he'd toss himself to her, worrying about the consequences later. He backed away from her, retreating to the window.

Focus on the mission, man. Her love or rejection will come soon enough.

****

Lily clutched her growling stomach, feeling the hunger gnaw at her insides. How long had it been since she last ate? The days blurred together, leaving her disoriented and unsure of her surroundings. Images flashed through her mind, a truck tossing her body all over the place, the sharp sound of gunshots, the tightness of zip ties around her wrists. She faintly recalled Stephen's strength overpowering their captor, their frantic escape to safety. But where were they now?

Her body yearned to open her eyes and take in their location, but exhaustion weighed heavy, pulling her back into the comfort of something soft, though musty. Where was Stephen? His handsome face danced in her thoughts, his eyes revealing his depth of emotion. Whenever she looked into those calming blue eyes, she felt love. He clearly loved her. But did she truly love him, or was it just a fleeting affection? That was the dilemma. She cared for him, maybe even loved him, and she should be grateful that someone finally loved her after all these years. Yet, the price of her love felt too steep.

God had taken away everyone she cherished, and she feared that walking away from Stephen was the only way to protect him from a future filled with heartache. He deserved better than that. No matter how much she hoped, God's hand of destruction continued to loom over her life. It'd always be the same tear-jerking story; she could never have love. God wouldn't allow it, and she couldn't offer what Stephen deserved.

Against better judgment, she opened her eyes, blinking to fight off the blurred vision. Her heart dropped at the empty room. Where was Stephen? Did he slip out of the cabin, having had enough of her problems? What would she do if she were truly alone? Cry? Have a panic attack? Run away and hide? She did like that option. No one would miss her, anyway. The fire destroyed her earthly possessions, mainly her farmhouse. Lily would keep that option open. She shifted her body, trying to get off the dusty old couch. Fighting with the covers, her legs twisted in the fabric, causing her to tumble onto the hardwood floor.

Ouch! That's going to leave a mark. Lily threw the covers next to her on the floor. Stephen popped his head into the living room, a slight smile on his weary face. Stephen. He hadn't left her. He stepped into the room, grabbing her hand and pulling her off the floor.

"You're here." The foolish words tumbled out of her lips before she had time to think about them.

Stephen pulled her body so close to his, exposing dark circles forming under his eyes. He probably hadn't slept in a long time. She gazed into his face, trying to memorize every feature and scar for when she left. She'd always remember this moment; safe in his embrace. Stephen leaned over, planting a soft kiss on her lips, claiming her for himself. A hundred reasons popped into her mind, why their closeness was a horrible idea. At that moment, she didn't care about reason. She wanted to pretend they were a normal couple without thugs trying to end her life or a vengeful God, bend on destroying any happiness she had.

"Lily, if you'd have me, I'd spent the rest of my life holding you." He tightened his arms around her petite body, sending warmth pulsing through.

What was he saying? Surely, he wouldn't propose. No, he was caught up in the moment. Eventually, she'd break his heart. Best not to entwine their hearts together so much that it destroys her when she leaves. Lily stepped out of his embrace and immediately regretted it.

"What's wrong? Why can't you love me in return?" Stephen dropped his arms to his side, hurt etched on his face.

She wanted to kiss the worry lines off his face. But her mixed signals were breaking his heart. Lily took a deep breath, fighting off the tears that threatened to explode from her eyes. *Why can't you love me? Oh, Stephen, I think I love you, but we would never work.* How she longed to lay her emotions out; ugly and raw. But she couldn't.

"Talk to me." He lifted her chin, pleading with her to let him in. "What's wrong with me? All I want is you."

Lily's heart sank deeper into her chest. Bile rose in her throat, causing her to fight the urge to vomit right on the floor. Or curl up into a ball, wallowing in her self-pity.

"I guess we want different things." A shadow of hardness flashed over his features as he shoved his fingers in his pocket.

"Stephen…" Her heart screamed at her to open up to him. Proclaim her love and affection for him, but she couldn't.

He shook his head, stepping to the door. "I can't keep doing this. When this is over, there won't be enough left of me to survive."

"Stephen…" She couldn't get past his name. What was wrong with her?

He yanked the doorknob, pulling the door open. Cool, crisp evening air drifted into the small cabin, sending shivers through her body.

"I need to patrol the perimeter." He slipped into the hazy evening, ripping her heart out as he left.

Lily threw her body on the couch, soaking the old couch with her tears. Why was God allowing this to happen? Didn't He care enough about Stephen to shield him from heartache? From her?

At daybreak, she'd leave. She'd sacrificed Stephen's life and love too many times. This would be better for both of them. She rummaged through her pocket, yanking a scrap piece of paper and a pen out. She'd write her last goodbye and slip out before he knew it. Lily folded the note, sticking it on the cushion. Through the sobs, she drifted into a fitful sleep.

A calloused hand slid over her face, trying to cut off her air supply. What was going on? Her eyes shot open as a masked man's face came into view. What happened to Stephen? She wanted to scream, fight off her attacker, but she had no strength.

Fleeing from Danger, Jessica West

"Scream and your boyfriend's dead." The gruff voice echoed through her ears.

Whimpers eluded her lips as the man dug his fingers into her neck.

"Do exactly what I say and no one gets hurt." He smelled of cheap cologne and garlic. Lily's eyes scanned the cabin, searching for a weapon. The room was bare. Her only hope; Stephen. But he wouldn't come for her because of the note. He'd think she willingly left. Stephen would be so angry and heartbroken he'd never want to see her again.

"Out the door, now." The guy said, pulling her to the door and into the icy, dark night.

All hope of survival fled as she stepped into the crunchy snow.

Chapter Twelve

Stephen wiped a tear from his icy face, kicking the snow with his booted-foot. Why couldn't she love him? What was wrong with him, that the only woman he loved romantically wouldn't return his love? Was her rejection a sign from God? No matter what she said, or didn't say, he knew she felt something. He'd catch the gleam of longing in her eye before she'd blink it away. Should he walk away, still keeping some dignity? Or follow her like a love-sick puppy dog until she finally gave in to his charm? Would she ever proclaim her love for him? Memories of her soft kisses and gentle touch sent more tears streaming down his face.

God, why is this happening to me? I was content with bachelorhood? Why bring her into my life only to tease me? What am I supposed to do?

He wanted to scream into the darkness. The darkness? How long had he been patrolling the perimeter? Well, he wasn't actually patrolling anything. Hiding out was more like it. He just needed an excuse to flee the cabin and the woman he'd do anything for. Even if she never returned his love, Stephen would not turn his back on her now.

With new resolve, he marched back toward the cabin. He'd reassure Lily that from this day forward, he'd be her bodyguard, nothing more. No stolen kisses or embraces. Stephen would place a lock on his heart, vowing to release it only if she returned his affections. Putting it in her hands meant dying with a broken heart. Living alone, never knowing the joys of marriage. No matter what, he wouldn't throw himself to her feet, begging for her love. He was a fool, maybe, but not desperate.

Stephen stomped the snow off his boots before stepping into the tiny cabin. A shiver ran down his neck as he stared into the empty cabin. The rooms were visible from the door; living room, kitchen, bathroom. All empty.

"Lily?" Eerie silence echoed back as he searched the three rooms. Would she really just sneak into the night, never telling him goodbye or looking back?

Stephen pulled the covers off the couch, revealing a folded paper. He unfolded the scrap paper, staring at Lily's handwriting.

Stephen,

I'm sorry about everything. I never meant for you to fall in love with me. By the time you read this note, I'll be gone. Don't find me. In a different world, maybe we would have ended up together. I'm sorry.

Stephen crumbled up the paper, throwing it against the wall. This was not happening. Anger. Hurt. Confusion. It felt like a ton of bricks were attacking his lungs and he couldn't breathe. She really left him; pushed him completely out of her life. The urge to punch something pulsed in his body. Instead of destroying the brittle cabin walls, he crumbled to the chipped hardwood, tears streaming down his face. Was he really that awful of a guy that she'd risk her life just to flee from him? Before Lily, he believed he was the biggest catch in their small town. Not so much anymore. More like damaged goods. No matter what, he loved her. Love wasn't forceful or demanding. He'd give her the space she wanted. His broken heart screamed for him to fight for her, but his mind repulsed at the thought. She made her choice. Now he needed to get away from town. Maybe resign from the hospital. Start a life somewhere away from her memories. Time would heal all of his wounds. Maybe he'd find a woman worthy of his love.

He rubbed the sides of his face. If he couldn't have Lily, he didn't want anyone. Period. Stephen rested his face on the musty couch cushion. *God, I don't know what to pray for anymore. Show me something. Wherever she is, protect her. She's not out of your care.*

Stephen ran his fingers along the edge of the couch. He felt something long and coarse. Pulling it out, his eyes scanned a used cigar. *Where did this come from?* He stared at the duffel bags by the wall as he jumped up from the floor. *Lily ran away with nothing at all. High unlikely. What if she didn't run away, but someone forced her away?*

Reaching for his gun and satellite phone, he exploded through the door. Using the flashlight on his phone, he scanned the hardened snow for any clues. Two sets of boot prints. *How did I miss some thug sneaking into the cabin, stealing Lily? Distraction.*

Images of the note popped into his mind. Either way, she was going to leave him. He'd deal with that later. Right now, he had to find her.

He wanted to roar like a mountain lion, beat his chest, and pounce on someone. Instead, he dialed Paul's number. *Pick up, bro.*

"The prodigal son has returned." Paul's deep voice echoed through the phone.

"Bro, she's gone." Stephen followed the tracks away from the cabin, toward a hidden path in the woods. "I let my guard down, and she's gone."

All hints of joking erased from his voice. "We'll find her. I'll be there soon."

"Weren't you in an accident?" Stephen shifted the gun in his hands.

"Minor. And the doctor gave me a clean bill of health. Your dad and I will be there soon. Stay out of trouble until then."

"Don't you have a partner?" Stephen stopped as a white van came into view.

"Yeah, but his mom is in the hospital. He's in Virginia for a week. Zach is missing all the action."

"White van off the hidden trail across from the cabin. I'm investigating."

"Be careful," Paul said as Stephen slid the phone into his pocket.

God, help me foil the abductor's plan. Stephen inched closer to the van; gun drawn. Screams pierced through the night air. Lily! He took deep, steadying breaths as he rounded the corner of the van. A man, much younger than his Santa-look-alike colleagues, held a gun to Lily's side. Ashen white covered her face as she fought her abductor. He glanced at her ripped pants, no doubt from the struggle.

"Let her go!" His voice thundered through the darkness.

"Stephen. You came." Her breathless voice yanked on his heart. His insides quacked at the gun, digging more into her side. In a split second, the gunman could end her life.

"Of course I came. Love fights." Stephen stepped closer to Lily; eyes trained on the thug.

"Lover boy, drop the gun or she's dead." Stephen couldn't make out the guy's features, but he was sure the thug was smirking.

"You don't want to do this. Under strict orders to bring her in alive, what will Cores do when he finds out you killed her?" Stephen went out on a whim, hoping his assessment was accurate.

"True." He shifted the gun toward Stephen. "But one of you will die tonight."

"No!" Lily desperately kicked the man's leg, her boots sinking into the hardened snow. The chilling wind whipped against her face, causing whimpers to escape her lips. He watched the man yank her jacket, sending her sprawling into the cold, unforgiving snow. Her body hit the ground. And then, in the blink of an eye, a deafening blast shattered the silence, a bullet whizzing past Stephen's arm, a flash of danger that plunged him into a world of darkness. The last thing he heard were Lily's sobs.

****

He's gone. It's all my fault. Lily beat down the wail rising in her throat. Her bound hands shook uncontrollably. Her breathing quickened as her heart rate spiked. Images of Stephen's lifeless body tumbling to the snowy ground haunted her mind. He took a bullet for her. No way he could have survived that close-range shot.

Lily glanced at the dark-haired driver. His hard-as-steel face cocked into a tight smile. "Lover boy's gone. Now it's time to move on."

"How dare you?" Lily crossed over the middle console, trying to strike the man with her bound hands. Fire burned in the pit of her chest.

"I like 'em feisty." His deep laugh filled the air in the utility van. "I might have to fight Cores for you."

"You're evil." She threw her body against the front seat, trying to come up with a plan. No one would come to her rescue. She was alone in the battle. Her only ally, dead.

"Evil?" His throaty laugh filled the space between them, burning her ears. "Good and evil. What a bunch of lies. I figured you were smarter than that."

"Killing a man is evil," she said through gritted teeth.

"That's your opinion." He turned his focus back on the curvy country road.

Darkness creeped all around them as the van skidded along, further away from familiarity and safety.

If there's no God, who decides what is good or evil? Right and wrong would change from person to person. That doesn't seem right. Lily shook her head in frustration. Why was she consumed by thoughts of a God who cruelly took the most remarkable person she had ever met from her life? Against her better judgment, tears flowed down her face. *Why did You steal him from me? I knew this would happen. I tried pushing him away, and You still punished him by associating with me. Why do You hate me so much?*

"Dodging bullets, kidnapping someone, or even taking a life doesn't faze me, but the sight of a woman in tears unnerves me." He shivered, gripping the steering wheel tighter. "Stop doing that before you render me helpless."

Play on his weakness. Lily let twenty-seven years of bottled anguish roll down her face. Her whole life she wanted someone to love her, not just in words, but in actions, too. She finally found someone that looked beyond her pretty face and actually saw her, and she never gave him a chance. Sure, he slid through the surrounding barriers of her icy heart, but he didn't know that. She fought him every step of the way. Now, she was horribly alone.

What would his family think, knowing she robbed them of their loved one right before Christmas? No more ocean-blue eyes hovering over her, reminding her that love still existed. That second chances were likely. Lily wiggled her face, trying to get the tears away from her nose. With bound hands, she couldn't wipe her face.

"Enough!" Her abductor pulled to the side of the deserted road, setting the gun in the middle console.

She sniffled back a tear before staring into his black eyes. Cold, lifeless eyes. Now was the time to escape. Lily dry heaved like her life depended on it.

"Wh-what are you doing?"

"I'm gonna be sick." Lily bent over, gagging.

"Not in my van, you're not." He jumped out of the driver's seat, mumbling words under his breath. "Get out." He yanked her body out of the passenger's seat.

Lily's body shook from the chilling night air and from the anxiety swirling in her body.

"You best not throw up on my shoes." He growled the words, staring at her like she was vermin.

"Untie me." She muttered the words through a mouthful of vomit.

"No."

"Fine. If you want to smell throw up all the way until we get to your boss, it's fine with me." She tried whipping her tangled black hair out of face, clunky drops of throw up, clinging to the locks.

"You try anything, I promise I'll shoot you." He leaned over, forcefully yanking the rope from her wrist.

Lily massaged her wrist, staring at the rope marks. Freedom. Okay, not really freedom, but she'd take whatever minor victory she could get. Now, how would she lose this creep and escape? Dilemma. Lily leaned over as chunky vomit decorated the snowy road. Her head pounded like a hammer continuously, banging on her skull.

"Gross." He stepped away from her, frowning. "Boss had to assign me to the nutcase."

Fleeing from Danger, Jessica West

Their encounter didn't thrill her, either. The country road felt suffocating, and she sucked in a breath of fresh air. This might be her only chance to escape, and she had to seize the moment. Lily's heart pounded in her chest, a hollow feeling gnawing at her insides. The scent of fear hung in the air, mingling with the foul odor of the wilderness. Desperate for solace, she considered praying to an imaginary God, hoping it would bring her some comfort. But deep down, she knew it was all a fantasy, a futile attempt to find solace. In this moment, she was alone, devoid of any divine intervention or the reassurance of a strong, charming man. She had no one to turn to, her strength waning. She had to push through, fight one more time, and escape. Gathering her resolve, Lily gave herself a pep talk, her voice resolute but trembling. Suddenly, a buzzing noise shattered the stillness, jolting her out of her thoughts. Her abductor pulled out his phone, his voice echoing through the empty road as he shouted into the receiver.

I'm glad I'm not at the receiving end of that wrath. What was she thinking? He'd do worse to her once he found out she'd escape. *So be it. I'm gonna die, anyway. I'd rather die fighting than being a coward.*

A thick canopy of trees sprouted out of the woods a hundred feet from her. One step at a time and she'd disappear into the thick foliage. The man leaned against the white van, lost in a battle of words. Ugly curses flowed from his mouth. Lily closed her eyes, taking soundless steps toward safety. She could do this. Her pulse quickened so rapidly she felt like she'd pass out on the edge of safety. Or relative safety. *Breathe. One step at a time.* Lily took a calming breath, matching a breath with a step. Minutes passed by as she ducked into the thicket of trees. *I made it.*

Her victory was short-lived as a gunshot pierced the night air. Her abductor knew she had escaped and was coming for her. She expected to hear footsteps stomping through the woods or feel a bullet penetrate through her back, but nothing happened. Amazed and terrified, she pushed a limb out of her face, traveling deeper into unknown territory.

The haunting night sounds whispered in Lily's ears, sending shivers down her spine. Goosebumps prickled her skin, intensified by the dim moonlight that barely illuminated her path. The suffocating darkness seemed to engulf her, urging her to keep moving. Would it be death by the hands of a merciless thug or a ravenous, wild beast? She forcefully banished these morbid thoughts from her mind, determined to survive. Lost in the vast wilderness, she felt the weight of being hunted by man-eating creatures, plagued by the ever-present threat of dehydration and hypothermia. The thought of these perils made her cringe, yet her logical mind relentlessly conjured up worst-case scenarios. But no matter what lay ahead, she refused to turn back now.

****

"No!" Stephen gasped for air as he caught himself tumbling in the darkness, falling into nothingness. Where was she? The deafening sounds of a gunshot shrieked into his ear, causing his body to rebel in pain. He tumbled around with something restraining his legs as he fought to his feet.

"Easy." The familiar, deep voice snapped him out of his trance. He opened his eyes, laying on a floor, tangled inside a white blanket. Where was he? But more importantly, where was Lily?

He kicked off the thin-layered blanket, rubbing his hands against the squeaky-clean tiled floor. Pain shot through his body as he tried climbing off the floor.

"Want to explain how you ended up on the floor?" His mother's voice floated around the room, hugging him from afar.

Strong arms lifted him off the cold tiles, placing him back on the too-small bed. Stephen fell back onto the pillow, staring at his bandage. Gunshot wound, different arm, same story; clean in-and-out, no damage.

"Want to explain how I got here?" Stephen twisted the cover between his fingers so hard his hand turned ashen white. *No way I would have come to a hospital when Lily fought for her life with a hired thug.* Lily. Tears burned in his eyes at the thought of his girl, alone, fighting off whatever evil the creep threw upon her. His girl? In his dreams. She made it pretty clear with the note that she wasn't his anything, and he wouldn't stand in her way of escaping to a new life. No matter the reason, he had to find her.

If he kept getting gunshot wounds, the next one could be fatal. Stephen straightened his body in the bed, curling his socked feet under the covers. It didn't matter. He'd take a bullet for her again and even give his life to keep her safe.

God had a purpose in this storm. Stephen just needed to figure out what it was. *God, I can't, but You can. Protect Lily.*

"I followed the GPS from your satellite phone, leading me to your location." Paul stepped next to the bed; arms crossed over his chest. "Good thing 'cause you were unconscious and bleeding."

"Lily?"

"No trace of her. I put a BOLO for the white van you saw at the scene. Nothing yet." Paul slid his phone out of his pocket, staring at the empty screen. With a shake of the head, he set it back in his coat pocket.

Stephen threw the covers on the floor, trying to climb out of bed.

"Where are you going, young man?" The sound of his mother's scolding voice reverberated in his ears, causing him to reconsider his decision to get out of bed.

Stephen set his hard-as-steel eyes on his mother, who didn't even flinch. "I'm not five, and you can't keep me here."

"Then stop acting like a child and get back in bed." His mother pointed her finger in his face. "I don't want to lose a son before Christmas. Which is two days away."

"Mom," Stephen's voice trembled with emotion, "I love you, but there's another woman who has captured my heart. I can't let her disappear into a crime ring, whether by death or marriage." His heart raced in his chest at the mere thought of Lily, his mind filled with her laughter and his arms longed for her gentle touch. Determination surged through him as he stood up, hurriedly slipping on his shoes.

Tears welled up in his mother's eyes, reflecting the mix of joy and sadness in her heart, as she leaned in to kiss her son's cheek. "God has answered my prayers. He didn't create you to be alone. You've finally embraced love."

A soft chuckle escaped Paul's lips, blending with the ambient sounds of the room. "Our boy is growing up," he remarked, his voice tinged with pride and amusement.

Mrs. Smith playfully swatted her hand at Paul, her frown accompanied by the subtle scent of her perfume lingering in the air. "Stop that, or I'll have to put you on the naughty list," she warned, a playful glint in her eyes.

Paul dramatically clutched his chest, adding a touch of theatrics to the moment. "Anything but that," he gasped, his voice infused with mock horror.

A tender smile etched across Mrs. Smith's face, radiating warmth and love. "What am I going to do with you boys?" She mused, her words accompanied by a sense of gentle exasperation and affection.

"Don't want to break up this touchy moment, but I need your car keys." Stephen extended his hand toward Paul, wincing at the pain from his wound.

"Not gonna happen, bro." Paul slid his keys out of his pocket, dangling them in the air. "I'm driving."

"Fine. Let's go back to the crime scene." Stephen kissed his mom on the cheek as he gathered his wallet and phone, sliding them into his pocket.

"Don't forget this." Paul held out a gun, which Stephen quickly secured in his ankle holster.

"Be safe." His mom wiped a tear from her eye. "I'll handle fall back from you discharging yourself."

"Love you," Stephen said, slipping out the door.

Minutes later, he rested his head against the leather seats in Paul's truck. Exhaustion trying to steal his focus away.

"I've looked into Lily's dad's mistress, Julia Price." Paul zoomed his truck down the small downtown section of their rural town, bypassing the major road into town. They didn't need tractors blocking their way out of town. The crime scene was over an hour away, nestled in the mountains on the way to Pigeon Forge.

"And?"

"She's been out of the country, as CEO of her design company." Paul slammed on the brakes as three deer darted across the road, oblivious to any danger. "She's pretty well off. Her business is thriving, so she opened a new storefront in Europe."

"So, probably not behind the attacks?" Stephen stared out the window as the snowy hillside popped into view. He loved the vastness of the countryside, with no forms of civilization to destroy the beauty of God's creation.

"Doubtful."

"What about her assumed half-sibling?" In his books, everyone was a suspect.

"Of course we can't confirm the relation on speculation. But his name is Stuart Price, age eighteen, typical rich kid."

"You'd know about that, huh?" Stephen narrowed his eyes and shot his friend a piercing, steely gaze that seemed to cut through the air. The truck fell silent as the weight of his words hung in the air, creating a tense atmosphere. A faint reminder of Paul's privileged upbringing as the only son of Vanderbilt's top neurosurgeon. Despite the benefits that came with his family's wealth, Paul refused to be swayed. His parents, with their noses held high in disdain, had dismissed his career choice and disapproved of his marriage. Paul had bravely broken free from their suffocating grasp during college, never looking back, except for the occasional call that served as a bitter reminder of their unyielding disappointment.

"I don't deny my arrogant, rich-kid ways, but I'm not that kid anymore. Thank God." Paul gripped the steering wheel, his knuckles turning white.

"You don't think the kid's involved?" Stephen stretched his legs under the seat. "You not taking up for a spoiled rich kid at the expense of my ... Lily?"

"Bro, I'll ignore that comment cause your heart is overpowering your logical brain." Paul pulled the truck to the side of the almost deserted road. The white van with doors open sat in the middle of the road.

"This could get dicey." Stephen slid his gun out, opened his door, and stepped beside Paul.

"Signs of a struggle." Paul pointed to the broken branches and snowy footprints. "Let's go."

God, help this situation not to end in a shootout. Paul prayed as he slipped into the trees.

****

Breathe. Just one breath at a time. Lily glanced into the early morning fog, heart racing, fingers numb. She swatted away the anxiety as she stepped into a clearing. Days, maybe hours, she meandered around the wilderness trying to put distance between herself and the thug, searching for her. Her senses were on high alert; every snapped branch or crunched snow caused her panic to almost destroy her. No doubt the thug after her was following her, even if she couldn't see him. How would she get out of this mess? Stephen. Tears filled her burning eyes, the icy temperatures smacking her in the face. He probably didn't receive medical help in time, and died from his gunshot wound. All her fault.

Why do You hate me so much, God? She wanted to scream the words at the top of her lungs, but decided it would only give her location away. *All I've ever wanted was love. And You've snatched everyone away from me? It's just You and me, God. What's Your defense?* Lily kicked at a pile of snow, causing the white powder to fly into the air. *I'm delusional, talking to a make-believe God.* She balled her fist at her side, trying to soothe the anger. *Why did You take him from me? I-I loved him.* There, she admitted it. A tight smile spread across her face. Her heart swelled with so much love she felt she'd go into cardiac arrest.

She actually loved him. The feeling was new and frightening, but it didn't matter. God cut Stephen's incredible life short because of her. That's why she shielded her heart from him. But now it was too late. If only she had another chance. No more holding onto past disappointments or letting fear control her future. She'd lay it all out, accepting his love as a gift. She was wrong about Stephen. Could her whole mind-set about God be mistaken, too? Did He really hate her? Was she really number one on His hit list? Did God even have a hit list? Stephen tried convincing her that all she thought about God was false. Who was right? Her dad, who cursed God and wasted his life away in a drunken stupor. Or Stephen? Who exhibited faith and strength, plus an unexplainable peace that made no sense in the middle of dodging bullets and escaping hired hit men.

Her heart screamed Stephen's name as her icy tears dropped into the snowy wilderness with a thud. Her whole life and philosophy were false. Vowing to never be like her father, she had built her whole life on top of his lies and deceit. Though dead for many years, he still controlled the reins of her life. He, not God, never thought her worthy of love. First, he separated her from a mother she barely knew. Claiming Lily's hugs and love would corrupt her mother's cancer-ridden body. Naïve. Next, he sent her brother away, destroying their sibling bond before it ever developed. Why did he want her alone and miserable? Of course, her father's notions had kept any potential friends or mates away, never allowing her to see beyond the anger to let others into her heart. All the wasted time. Not only did her wounded spirit keep people away, but it distanced her from God. For twenty-seven years, she thought God was the enemy, but the real enemy was the man she called "father".

Lily fell onto the snow-packed ground, a blast of chilly wind hit her face, causing her to shiver uncontrollably. Her body suddenly felt devoid of any energy, as if all the lies had drained away her strength. It didn't matter an enemy possibly lurked behind the canopy of trees. She had no will to get up and survive. Her whole life was a big lie.

What was the point? She had no one. Not one friend she could call or who would call and check on her. Sure, her boss would call if she missed her shift, but not a welcoming voice of concern, but one of reprimand. She should let the men after her win. All fight gone. She realized that Stephen's protective stance and fierce nature had only rubbed off on her when she could feel his presence. But he was gone, and there was nothing to live for.

She loved her job, but working on the ICU floor would only cement her loneliness. Patients came and went so fast, like the stages of life. Only her stage of loneliness would never go away. She felt a connection with Stephen's family, but what would they think of her once they knew her trouble had stolen Stephen from their lives? Lily sunk her head between her legs, fighting the urge to sleep and never wake up.

Come unto me, all ye that labour and are heavy laden, and I will give you rest. The words popped into her mind as tears streamed down her face. She was utterly alone and without hope. But something inside her heart yearned for the rest that the verse spoke about. Could she finally have rest from fear and anger after twenty-seven years? The burdens were like mounds of snow dumping onto her body, so much so that her lungs refused to work. Her pit was so deep, no one could pull her out. But wait, if God was really all-powerful, couldn't He reach down and yank her out of her grave? Why would He? She had spent her whole life denying Him and spewing anger and bitterness at Him. Why would God forgive her? Help her? Love her? She didn't deserve it. Mercy and grace. She didn't understand it, but through tear-stained eyes, she poured her heart out to God, begging for His redemption.

With a renewed purpose and peace that she couldn't explain, Lily climbed to her feet, brushing off the snow from her pants. *Thank You, God, for loving me and forgiving me and wrapping Your healing touch over my shattered heart, enough to give me something to live for. I don't know how to get out of this wilderness alive. Please, guide my path.*

She turned around, glancing in every direction, trying to find a path out of the freezing cold isolation. Her limbs trembled as a gust of wind yanked the warmth from her body. Every direction looked the same. Snow-covered trees and hilly terrain spread out for miles, or as far as she could see. She had never gone camping and unless you counted walking into the mall from her car, she never went hiking. Lily was out of her element, but she wasn't walking alone anymore. God would guide her steps. She had to believe that.

A piercing, ear-shattering sound abruptly halted Lily's movements, causing her muscles to tense. Her heart pounded in her chest as she desperately scanned her surroundings, trying to identify the source of the noise. Was it the relentless creep lurking in the shadows, closing in on her? Or could it be a long-awaited rescue team, finally arriving to save her from this nightmare? The tantalizing possibility crossed her mind that maybe, just maybe, Stephen hadn't met his tragic end after all. But deep down, she knew it couldn't be true. Stephen couldn't have survived. The bitter chill of the frigid temperature seeped into her bones, reminding her of the imminent danger she faced. With each passing moment, her chances of escaping this frozen abyss and starting a new life, one dedicated to God, seemed to dwindle.

Chapter Thirteen

"Do you see those footprints?" Stephen kneeled down, getting a closer look at the prints. "Gotta be hers. Probably a size six."

"Agreed. But there's two sets of prints." Paul moved a branch out of his way, examining the footprints. "Gotta be the perp."

Stephen heightened to his six-foot frame. "Know what you're thinking. It's written all over your face, and I'm not buying it."

"Ok, I'll play along. Read my mind." Paul's eyes held a bit of humor around the dark hues.

"I'm not in the mood for games." Stephen gazed out into the mid-day snow. Lily could be anywhere. This property rested on the edge of a state park; hundred of miles separated from civilization. "But you don't think we'll find her alive." He winced at the realization of the words. What would he do if she was actually gone? Mourn for the rest of his life? Question God's plan for his life? Rebel against everything he believed in life and run off, never looking back?

He loved her, and he would never get over that love. If she died, he didn't know if he could control the rage forming in his heart. Someone would pay. Even if he had to be the one to do it. Prison didn't bother him.

"Look, man, you have that dangerous glare in your eyes like a predator ready to strike. Take my advice and give your anger to God. We're buds, but don't put me in a situation where I have to arrest you."

Stephen folded his arms over his leather jacket, biting back the words floating in his head. Paul wasn't the enemy. He didn't need to feel the end results of Stephen's wrath. "Answer my question."

"Which is?"

"Do you think she's alive?" Stephen held his breath, waiting for his friend's professional assessment.

"I'm not God."

"But?"

"I've seen cases like this before. The outcome's never good." Paul ran his gloved fingers through his black hair.

"It's déjà vu all over again?"

"Different state park, same story." Paul's eyes trekked ahead, searching for any signs of life.

"Belle made it out of that alive. I'm praying Lily will do the same." Stephen tugged his jacket closer around his neck. The below freezing temperature wasn't playing in Lily's favor. Death by a thug or death by hypothermia?

"Let's not forget Ranger Atlanta lost his life that night." Paul stopped walking and grabbed Stephen's arm. "No matter what, don't play the trigger-happy hero."

Stephen shook his head, frowning. No way would he let his friend and the husband of his sister, and father of his nieces and nephew, take a bullet. If anyone walked out of this wilderness alive, it would be Paul. He'd see to that. Paul's concern touched him, but it didn't matter. This was his battle to fight and as far as he was concerned, Paul was just back up.

"You know my girls wanted a pony for Christmas." Paul's casual change of subject brought a chuckle from Stephen's mouth.

Way to diffuse the situation. Stephen could imagine his nieces' faces when they opened up a life-sized container carrying a horse. "Tell me there's not a pony in the barn at the cabin."

"There's not." Paul moved a branch from in front of his face.

"Losing your touch, old man," Stephen sneered, the words dripping with humor. He could see the faint lines etched on his brother-in-law's weathered face; evidence of a life lived in luxury. Stephen knew that Paul, with his vast inheritance worth millions, hardly even used it.

His parents had disowned him when he married Belle, but fate had a twisted sense of irony. Awaiting their trial for masterminding Belle's attempted murder, they died in a fiery car accident. Suicide? No one knew, but it made sense. No way would the prominent Walkman couple rot in prison if they could help it. Their tragic car accident left Paul with everything - the grand house, sleek cars, and a fortune in stocks. Yet, it all held little meaning for him, burdened by regret and grief. Instead, he channeled his wealth towards fighting social injustices, a noble cause that consumed him. His wife and children never went without, even when one wanted a pony. Stephen knew his brother-in-law wouldn't disappoint his girls on Christmas.

A small smile edged up Paul's face. "I bought two ponies."

"Of course you did." Stephen's face turned stone cold. "Let's make it out of this alive so we can watch our girls on Christmas morning."

"Tomorrow is Christmas. We're missing the gingerbread competition and all the other traditions your parents started." Paul's frown pierced Stephen's heart. Instead of hunting a thug in freezing temperatures, his buddy should be in the warmth of his wife's arms, creating cherished memories and sharing laughter.

"I'm sorry, man." Stephen stepped into the clearing, kneeling down, touching the snowy shoe print.

"Fighting bad guys is my job, even on Christmas." Paul slid his gun out of his waist holster, following the prints. "Shh."

Stephen knew they were so close to Lily and the creep after her. He could feel it in his bones. Although, if they didn't get out of the snowy-deathtrap soon, he wouldn't be feeling anything ever again. Stephen mirrored his friend, yanking his gun out, holding it between his gloved fingers. *Whatever happens, God let Lily and Paul live.*

A scuffling noise, followed by grunts, caught his attention. Without waiting for Paul, he dashed into the wooded canopy, heart almost beating out of his chest. Lily needed him. Nothing else mattered.

He froze for a split second as Lily's emerald-green eyes cut through his heart. The creep had his arm wrapped around her neck, dragging her further into the snowy wilderness. Could he shoot the guy without hitting Lily? Distraction. He needed to create a distraction so Paul could disarm the hit man.

"Let her go." Stephen's voice rumbled out thunderous words.

"Nice try, doc." As the guy laughed with sinister glee, the sound reverberated through the silent woods, infusing the air with a chilling sense of malice.

"Don't tempt me." Stephen steadied his gun at the creep. The guy's fingers trailing over Lily's soft skin sent daggers of warning through his heart.

"You don't have it in you."

Stephen pulled the trigger as the bullet ricocheted off the ground. Distraction completed. The hit man loosened his grip on Lily's neck, curses flowing from his lips. In a split second, Lily dug her teeth into the man's hand, and ran into the protective arms of Stephen.

Paul scowled at Stephen, his brows furrowing as he stared at his friend. He knew there would be consequences for his actions later, but for now, he had to focus on the immediate danger. "Drop the gun," he commanded, his voice unwavering.

"I'm not going down like this," the man responded defiantly, his grip on the gun tightening. With a swift motion, he aimed the weapon at Lily, his finger inching towards the trigger. Fear gripped Stephen's heart, but he refused to let it paralyze him.

Reacting with lightning speed, Paul's finger squeezed the trigger of his own gun. The deafening sound of the gunshot pierced the air, followed by a sickening thud as the bullet found its mark on the man's leg. The force of the impact sent him sprawling into the snow, blood staining the pristine white canvas.

Lily's whimpers filled the air, growing louder with each passing moment. Stephen pulled her closer, his heart aching at the sight of her trembling form. "It's okay, sweetheart. You're safe now," he reassured her, his voice soothing.

Meanwhile, Stephen watched the scene unfold, his eyes darting between Paul apprehending the wounded man and Lily's distress. He knew she couldn't bear to witness any more of the horrifying aftermath. With a determined look, he took her by the hand and guided her towards his car, offering her a refuge from the chaos.

"You're alive!" she exclaimed, her voice filled with relief and disbelief. She came to a stop, her trembling hand reaching out to caress the sides of his cheek. "I thought the bullet earlier had taken you from me." Tears streamed down her face, leaving icy trails in their wake.

Hushing her gently, Stephen enveloped her shivering body in the warmth of his jacket, his heart aching at the faint bluish hue of her skin. He vowed to keep her safe, to protect her from any harm that may come her way.

"God answered my prayers," she whispered, her voice filled with gratitude. Standing on her tiptoes, she brushed her lips against his, a tender and grateful kiss. In that moment, Stephen felt a profound sense of belonging and love. He couldn't ignore the mention of her prayers to God, the peace that now radiated from her face.

They had been through so much, and there was still so much to talk about. But in that moment, Stephen wanted to spend the rest of his life with her. If she would accept his proposal and take away his bachelor status, they could embark on a lifetime of getting to know each other, of building a future together.

****

Lily clung tightly to the warm coffee cup, relishing the comforting sensation as the heat gradually seeped into her body. Shifting her legs on the plush couch, she gazed at

Fleeing from Danger, Jessica West

Stephen, peacefully slumbering beside her. Snuggled beneath layers of cozy blankets, she felt somewhat immobilized. But at this moment, it didn't matter. She felt secure by the watchful eyes of the two men she cherished most; God and Stephen. There was so much she longed to share with Stephen - her newfound faith, her deepening affection for him. When they had brought her back to the cabin, she must have slept for hours, for the encompassing darkness now replaced the once bright daylight. Sensing her need for rest, they must have left her undisturbed on the couch, with Stephen as her ever-vigilant guardian.

Amidst Mrs. Smith's bustling preparations for Christmas, she took a moment to hand Lily a steaming cup of coffee. The rich aroma enveloped the room, filling it with a comforting scent. Mrs. Smith's radiant smile spoke volumes, reflecting her profound gratitude for answered prayers - her family alive and reunited for Christmas. However, Lily knew all too well that the threat to her life was far from over. With yet another hired hit man out of the picture, Cores would undoubtedly send more, his determination unwavering. Yet, for these few precious hours, they could all enjoy a temporary respite.

Lily stared at Stephen as tears swelled up in her eyes. She longed to be in his arms, under the warmth of his embrace. Her past hesitancies about a relationship didn't matter anymore. God didn't have a hit list, and knowing her wouldn't doom Stephen to a life of God's wrath. She didn't understand everything. Like, why couldn't she have had parents who loved her? A distant voice in the back of her mind still questioned why she had lived her whole life alone? What was wrong with her? Having a relationship with God hadn't given her the answers to so many questions. But she had peace in her soul that her whirlwind of emotions and questions couldn't quench.

Stephen shifted on the couch. His long legs grazing the top of her foot, sending electricity bolts through her body. She loved him, but her life was still a mess. She was a mess. He deserved better. As if sensing her stare, he wrapped the covers around his body, plopping next to Lily. His sleepy-eyed look brought warmth seeping out of her heart. She wanted to run her fingers through his disheveled brown hair. But she couldn't. She needed to choose between a love-filled life with him or sacrificing everything for his safety. His family deserved a normal, peaceful life, knowing her had uprooted that from their lives. Was God big enough to stop the hands of the bad guys and protect the Smith family? Yes, but what if He chose not to? Could she live with that?

Stephen scooted so close to her, his Christmas-scented cologne teased her senses. With his big blue eyes fixed on her, he rubbed the side of her cheek with his thumb, causing her heart to melt.

"Hey, beautiful, you're finally awake." His deep voice mingled with the Christmas music playing softly in the kitchen.

Lily took a deep breath, taking in everything about the moment. This moment would be the first interaction with the man she loved, sharing his faith. Meaning, nothing separated them but the bad guys. Before she knew they couldn't be together, but now, she forever could actually be with him.

"Speechless?" He kissed the tip of her nose. "Merry Christmas, sweetheart."

Tears threated to explode from her face as she rested her head on his shoulder. What should she say? *I love you,* but I'm scared. I've never witnessed an actual relationship before. What if I ruin ours? Are you sure you love me? I'm pretty flawed."

Stephen tilted her chin, staring into her eyes. "Your face shows forth all of your thoughts." He leaned in, placing a gentle kiss on her lips. "I hope that answers all of your questions."

How did he know what she was thinking? Did he know her that well? Adverse circumstances, not time, made the heart grow closer. It seemed like she knew him all her life, not weeks.

"Say something." His laughter floated through the air, warming her heart.

"I-I love you." She blurted out the words, not caring about anything but him.

The glow in his eyes blinked his approval. "I like a woman who doesn't beat around the bush."

Lily sat up straighter. She had a lot to say and wanted to do it before an audience of people flocked to the living room. "I have a lot to say, and please don't interrupt."

A huge smile tugged on the corner of his lips as he held his hands in the air in a surrender position. "Ms. Walsh, please continue."

"My whole life, I fed the hatred I had for God. Every circumstance made me bitter and further separated me from God." Lily twisted the blanket around her fingers. "I thought God hated me; even put a hit out on me. None of that was true. I realized, running for my life, that my father had sabotaged my life, and I let him. His influence, though evil, dictated the decisions I made in my life."

Lily took a cleansing breath. She had no one to share her feelings with until now. It wasn't as easy as she thought. But worth it to open up her heart to the man who held the keys to the padlock surrounding her inner core.

"My whole pretense was false; built on lies." Stephen wiped a tear from her cheek. His blue compassionate eyes bore into her heart. "I pushed everyone away; never felt worthy of love. I realized that's what my father's rejection had instilled in me. Lily Walsh, the girl unworthy of anything good in life. And God was to blame. In reality, my father's sick, controlling personality paved the way for my distrust and cynical behavior. But no more."

"What happened in the woods?"

Lily rubbed the sides of her cheeks. This was the part that built a bridge between the two, making a future together possible. "Freezing, on the point of hypothermia, dehydrated, scared, alone…" Her voice trailed off as trembles filled her body.

"Hey, I'm right here." He slipped his arms around her tighter, pulling her to his side.

She could go on; finish her story. His presence gave her courage. "I reached a point of no return. My body tumbled into the icy snow, vowing never to get up. I had nothing to live for, but no peace to die with."

Stephen squeezed her hand in support. His presence meant everything to her. She didn't want to push him away any longer.

"Somehow, my heart cried out to God, not begging for His deliverance, but for His forgiveness. He replaced my anxiety with a peace that I could never describe." A genuine smile covered her olive-tinted face. "I'm new at this Christian thing, and I need someone more experienced to help guide me."

"About that..." Stephen clasped her hands in his, staring into her eyes like he could see every hidden secret and longing.

The lights burst on as chatter and squeals echoed throughout the living room. Christmas morning had begun, and their conversation would have to wait.

He leaned close to her ear, whispering for only her to hear. "Later, we'll finish this conversation."

Lily's eyes watered at the love and peace his presence sent her way. Later, could change her whole life.

****

No! Stephen fell back onto the couch as his family ran into the living room, anticipating the presents under the Christmas tree. A few more seconds and he would have proposed; sealing their bond forever.

Paul stumbled into the room, sleepy-eyed and being dragged by his wife. He nodded to Stephen, grimacing. Stephen chuckled at his friend's dramatics. No way he'd feel sorry for him. Paul had a beautiful, devoted wife and four amazing children. He had everything Stephen prayed God would give him in the future. He was one step closer to that dream until their interruption. Stephen shook off his crabbiness. God had given him another Christmas with his family and had brought the woman he loved back to him safely. He had nothing to complain about. Stephen knew outside the cabin doors lurked evil intent on destroying Lily's life, but today, they'd bask in God's love and protection.

His dad's voice broke through his thoughts. "Sugary, cinnamon rolls, and hot chocolate or loads of presents?"

"I vote we load the kids with so much sugar and let Uncle Stephen watch them." Paul's groggy voice hinted of humor. "And save the presents after a few more hours of sleep."

"You're being a naughty daddy." Kayla slapped the surrounding air. "Everyone knows cousin Kayla is funner that Uncle Stephen."

Stephen rolled his eyes at his cousin's jabs. Kayla was fun to be around. Memories of their childhood pranks rushed through his memories. But the person in front of him wasn't that mischievous, pigtailed girl. When had she grown into a beautiful woman?

"Thinking of a witty comeback?" Kayla playfully punched Stephen on the arm, smiling.

This was how Christmas was supposed to be; surrounded by laughter and family. "No thinking required. My stats are more impressive than yours."

"Yeah, like a doctorate to your name?" Kayla raised her eyebrows and frowned.

"No, silly, my awesome gifts outweigh your sentimental ones." He tucked his arm around Lily's waist. He wanted her to feel at home with his family.

"Let's see which gifts the girls play with more; yours or mine." Kayla never backed down from a challenge. Her spunky, fiery personality always out shined his.

"Children!" His mother held up her hands to silence the adults, acting like children.

"She started it." Stephen stuck his tongue out at his cousin, who busted out laughing.

"You two are impossible." Belle set the twins in a double swing and plopped next to Lily on the couch. "You get a brief glimpse of what you're getting yourself into, if you…" One look from Stephen's crimson face cut Belle's words off.

Stephen's mother swooped into the room, ushering the children into the kitchen. "I think it's time to eat the cinnamon rolls while the icing is hot and gooey."

He mouthed thank you to his mother as everyone crowded into the cinnamon-scented kitchen.

Stephen clasped Lily's hand, pulling her to her feet. "Care to take a walk with me?"

"Is that safe?" Lily bit the bottom of her lip, glancing at the rising sun from the window. The bullet-pierced window looked brand new; no signs of being the recipient of a bullet.

"Probably not, but I never leave home without my trusty friend." He raised his pants, revealing a gun strapped to his ankle holster. "We'll stay on the porch and won't linger long."

"I'll go anywhere with you." She slid her arms inside her jacket, peering at him through love-infused eyes.

"That's what I wanted to hear." Stephen bumped the sides of the little box in his pocket, making sure it was still inside. He was really going to do this.

Stephen opened the door as a chilly burst of air swooped them inside a twister-like vortex. He gripped Lily's hand, steading her as they stepped on the porch. Besides the icy air, the morning looked perfect. The rising sun was peeking over the distant mountain, creating a canvas of pink infiltrating the sky. As breathtaking as the scenery was, he couldn't take his eyes off his exotic beauty snuggled in his arms. A gratitude for God swelled in his heart. God had blessed him with a woman Stephen didn't even know he needed. The thrill of bachelorhood would have died out quickly, leaving him lonely and searching. But God, in His foreknowledge, already knew that and had worked everything out.

Amidst the chill, his hands were sweating with a slight tremor. He cleared his throat, evoking enough courage to bank on a future with her forever. "Before I met you, I convinced myself I'd died an old bachelor. I enjoyed my freedom and lack of responsibilities. Life was good, but something was missing."

Lily gripped his fingers, encouraging him to continue. "You were missing. I never would have thought that night in the ICU would have changed my life, but it did. I'm not talking about being shot at as evil lurking around ready to devour us. That has changed my life too. But God showed me a glimpse of how life could be with a partner."

"A partner?" Hearing her repeat the words made it sound like they had a working, professional relationship. Not the picture he wanted to portray. Time to regroup.

"That came out wrong." Stephen exhaled a breath of air as his misty breath floated into the air. "I'll start over."

Lily shivered under his arms. Her eyes glancing around for any signs of danger. "Stephen, get to the point."

Smart woman. The vast wilderness surrounding them exposed them to whatever hid behind the trees. *Okay. I can do this. If I can stitch up a gunshot wound and treat half the town with an unknown virus, this is a piece of cake.*

"Lily Walsh, I love you. For better or worse, will you be my wife?" He pulled out his grandmother's heirloom; her five-karat white diamond ring.

Her mouth fell open, catching the falling tears. She must be in shock or thinking of a way to decline his offer without breaking his heart. Too late for that.

"Say something." He kissed the back of her hand, praying he didn't jump the gun and destroy whatever he thought they had.

"I..."

Stephen wanted to rewind the clock and undo his proposal. Clearly, she wasn't thinking the same as him. Her hesitation said it all. He was the biggest fool in Tennessee.

A smile spread across her red-cheeked face. "Stephen, I..."

"No, I get it. We haven't known each other that long. I shouldn't have assumed anything. You're running for your life. How insensitive of me to add more pressure to your life. I..."

Her eyes danced with amusement as she stood on her tiptoes, planting a kiss on his lips. "Are you done?"

"What?" He brushed his fingers against the spot her lips had touched. "Maybe we should go inside."

She clung to the side of his sleeve, her delicate fingers gripping with surprising strength, determination etched on her face. "Stephen, let me answer your question," she pleaded.

"I'm listening," he replied, but a sense of dread consumed him. The air felt heavy, as if a storm was brewing within him. He feared her answer would shatter his hopes of a happily ever-after with Lily Walsh.

Her grip tightened, her hands encompassing his own. She locked her gaze with his, her eyes searching for understanding. "You have inner turmoil," she began, her voice soft yet resolute. "So, I'll make this quick." The words hung in the air, mingling with the faint scent of lavender that clung to her.

Her touch sent a jolt of electricity through him, his skin tingling at her closeness. It was a bittersweet sensation, knowing that her actions were driven by a desire to protect him. "I'm sorry," she continued, her voice trembling slightly. "I tried to play god, to shield you from pain. But instead of trusting God, I built a barrier around my heart."

Stephen's heart raced, uncertainty gnawing at him. "Is that your answer?" he questioned, his voice barely a whisper. He held his breath, waiting for her response, the wilderness silent except for the sound of their shallow breaths.

"Yes," she said, her voice filled with a mix of vulnerability and love. The words hung in the air, heavy with meaning. The outside seemed to spin as Stephen grappled with the weight of her answer.

"Yes, you'll marry me, or yes, that was your answer?" His voice wavered, a mixture of hope and shame blending together. He held his gaze on her, his heart pounding in his chest.

"I love you, Stephen," she declared, her words a gentle caress against his soul. A tear escaped her eye, glimmering in the dim light. She leaned forward, pressing a tender kiss on his hand, and a surge of warmth enveloped him. "I'll marry you."

Overwhelmed with emotion, tears streamed down both of their faces, their shared happiness mingling with the saltiness of their tears. With trembling hands, he slid the ring onto her finger, a symbol of their commitment and the beginning of a new chapter in their lives.

****

Thank You, God. Lily wiped a tear from her face as she clung to her fiance's arm. It was so unbelievable that she wasn't alone anymore. The last couple of days, she had experienced God's presence. So, He was enough in her life, but it felt amazing having Stephen in her life. No more playing games by hiding behind fear and never fully opening her heart. God was healing her wounds and changing her from that fearful, cynical person to a joyful, trusting woman.

Lily glanced around at the smiling faces of Stephen's family as they tore into their Christmas gifts. Her new family. She loved the sound of that. She never had a mom, or even a dad, for that matter. God had given her a family to create fresh memories with to replace the bitter ones.

Stephen led her to the couch, never taking his hand from hers. His entire face lit up with a smile, brighter than all the lights on the Christmas tree.

"Okay, what's going on?" Belle set her camera down and stared into her brother's face. "I know it's not the anticipation of what's under the tree, because you have nothing under the tree. You've been a naughty boy." His sister's laughter floated through the living room.

Kayla tossed a piece of her caramel popcorn at Stephen. "Good one."

Stephen leaned over, placing a gentle kiss on Lily's lips. "We…"

"Hey, we have kids in the room," Paul whispered mischievously, his eyes twinkling with mischief. The soft glow of the Christmas lights bathed the room in a warm, cozy ambiance. He couldn't resist the chance to playfully tease his best friend.

"Only we can do that," he added, pulling his wife closer and planting a gentle kiss on her lips. The sound of laughter and chatter filled the air, mingling with the faint scent of freshly baked cookies.

Mr. Smith, a mischievous grin on his face, carefully placed a stack of festively wrapped boxes in front of the beautifully decorated tree. Mr. Smith beside his wife. He playfully nudged her with his elbow.

"Kevin Smith, we are not partaking in our children's immature ways," she scolded, playfully smacking his arm with a dish towel. A sense of joy and anticipation filled the air, tinged with excitement.

"Live a little, baby," Mr. Smith responded, leaning in to give his wife a quick peck on the lips. The room erupted in playful protests and exaggerated gags from Kayla, who leaned over, pretending to be disgusted by the affectionate display.

Amidst the lighthearted banter, Lily held up her hand, the diamond ring on her finger glistening in the soft, dim light of the room. The cheers and hollers from the living room spilled into the space, creating a joyful cacophony. Mrs. Smith pulled Lily into a tight embrace, her love and excitement palpable.

"I have another daughter to love," she exclaimed, her voice filled with genuine happiness. Overwhelmed by emotion, Lily's eyes welled up with tears. She had never known her cancer-stricken mother, but now she would have the motherly love she had longed for all her life.

"I knew you could do it, man." Paul patted Stephen on the back. A huge grin spreading across his tan face. "I'm just surprised she said yes."

Belle punched her husband in the chest, whispering something in his ears.

"I've never seen my son so happy." Mrs. Smith wiped her tears from her face, smiling. "You are what I've prayed for since he was a child."

Lily's heart warmed at the thought. As a little girl, alone and stuck in a loveless home, Mrs. Smith was praying for her. Her childhood hadn't been easy, but without Mrs. Smith's prayers, it could have been so much worse.

"Short engagement?" Kayla nestled one twin, burying her face into his hair.

"I-I." Lily couldn't think of the words to say. With all the attention on her, it was too much. Normally, she blended into the background, being content to be invisible. She would marry now, but that wouldn't be fair to Stephen. Not until the police arrested Mr. Cores.

Stephen wrapped his arm around her shoulder, pulling her closer to his solid frame. "I think what she's trying to say is that we both would love to get married as soon as possible, but the threat to her life isn't over yet. Until it is, we should just enjoy being engaged."

As if on cue, the window exploded glass on the women sitting on the floor. The room, once filled with cheer, now resonated with a tumultuous blend of screams and chaos.

"Mom, take the women and children to the safe room." Paul slid his weapon out of his ankle holster, stepping over broken pieces of glass. The women rushed out of the room, each carrying a child.

Lily gripped the side of Stephen's hand, refusing to let go. "I won't leave you. Not after we finally found our way."

He kissed her on the cheek. "No arguments. Go!"

Lily stood frozen in place. A battle brewing in her soul. She couldn't keep hiding or bringing trouble to her new family. She had to deal with this her way. Whatever that was. She'd sacrifice her amazing future for Stephen's family.

"I love you." She paused in the living room, staring at the most remarkable man she had ever laid eyes on.

"Sweetheart, I love you, too." He stepped to her side, wrapping her in a firm embrace. "Now, go to the safe room. I need to know you'll be here when I get back."

Stephen vanished into the chilly Christmas air with a quick movement, leaving her feeling numb, until the sound of the door shutting snapped her back to reality.

Lily ran down the hallway, planning to seek refuge in the safe room. Her feet had other plans. She stepped into the room, noticing the opened window. A folded card rested against her new Bible. *What in the world?* Lily retrieved the card, taking deep breaths, knowing that whatever was on the card would change her life forever.

Peace lies in your hands. Meet me by the windy trail across the street. Come alone. You come and this family lives in peace. Don't come, and they die. You have one hour.

The card slipped from Lily's trembling fingers, its glossy surface catching the dim light of the room. Panic coursed through her veins, a relentless wave of fear threatening to paralyze her. The smell of fear hung heavy in the air, suffocating her senses. Desperate, she whispered a prayer, her voice barely audible in the stillness.

Standing rooted to the spot or seeking refuge in hiding was not an option. The stakes were too high. She couldn't risk telling Stephen about the new threat, couldn't bear the thought of his family being in danger. The thugs lurking outside grew impatient, their presence a constant menace. Time was running out.

With tear-filled eyes, she removed her engagement ring, the weight of it feeling strangely empty in her palm. Her fingers trembled as she placed it gently beside her new Bible, a symbol of the life she was leaving behind. She knew, deep down, that this was the end. The cozy cabin, the dreams of a future with Stephen, all halted in this moment of truth.

Summoning every ounce of courage, Lily slid one foot through the open window, balancing precariously on the sill. The biting cold air whipped against her face, but it was nothing compared to the ache in her heart. The thought of never feeling Stephen's tender touch again gnawed at her soul.

As she rounded the corner, her heart pounding in her chest, powerful arms seized her wrist, yanking her away from the safety of the cabin. The sound of their rough grip on her flesh echoed in her ears, drowning out any hope of escape.

Chapter Fourteen

Stephen wiped the perspiration popping off his forehead. Hunting crazed thugs was not the way he had planned to spend Christmas. Drinking hot chocolate, eating his mother's famous apple pie, and snuggling with his fiancée, that was his plans for the day. Later. He'd have the opportunity later. But right now, he needed to secure the perimeter and take out any threat to his family. Stephen couldn't wait to trade his gun for a stethoscope and get back to treating an overflowing waiting room with what he did best. His weeks' vacation seemed to last for years. Too much had happened in a couple of days, short of a week. He longed to do normal things with his fiancée, not running for their lives or dodging bullets. She had never even seen his condo. Of course, it was so tiny, it wouldn't work for their first home. No, he'd do repairs and place it on the market. Buying a home where they had plenty of space to grow as a family, adding little ones to their lives. But first, he needed to put an end to these threats for good.

Stephen tightly gripped the cold, metallic gun between his trembling fingers, exchanging a knowing nod with his father. With each step, his boots crunched against the freshly fallen snow, leaving behind a trail of imprints that led to the edge of their property. As he scanned the surroundings, there were no visible signs of an intruder, except for the fading footprints that abruptly vanished near the road.

A surge of thoughts rushed through Stephen's mind, contemplating whether the intruder had fired a single shot into the cabin, abandoning their mission before its completion, or if it was all a clever ruse, designed to lure the men away, leaving the vulnerable women and children exposed. Despite the uncertainty, Stephen's heart remained at ease, knowing they were all safely tucked away in the fortified walls of the secure room.

A warm, contented smile slowly spread across Stephen's face as he envisioned returning to the cozy cabin, relishing in the remaining days of the holiday season, nestled closely beside his beloved future wife. The mere thought of their impending union filled him with overwhelming joy and love, emotions he had never truly comprehended until now, having only observed others experiencing it from a distance. God's praise overflowed from his heart. Life hadn't gone as he had planned it, and for that Stephen could thank God.

Paul motioned for Stephen to follow him to the side of the house. What was going on? By the look on Paul's face, it wasn't any news he wanted to hear.

"What's going on?" Stephen pulled his jacket tighter around his body, the icy air twirling around him like a twister.

"I've tracked one set of footprints around the property."

"Yeah, me too." Nothing that Stephen didn't already know. "But?"

"Look at this footprint. What do you see?" Stephen crouched down next to Paul, getting a closer look at the print.

"It's smaller and fresher than the main print." What did that even mean?

"A grown man's shoe size is normally larger than this one." Paul stood to his feet, dusting snow off his khaki pants.

"So, we're looking at an accomplice?" Stephen's head spun as the realization of what Paul was implying pierced his heart. "A child or..."

"A woman." Paul gestured to the house as Mr. Smith jogged to them.

"Find anything useful?" In the silence, Mr. Smith's deep voice reverberated, filling the air.

"Just a woman's shoe print."

"Notice how there's only one set of prints. Not a kidnapping or the bigger prints would be visible next to the smaller ones." Paul pointed to the snowy prints.

"Someone went willingly."

His father's words hit him like a sharp blow to the gut, leaving him breathless and disoriented. Gasping for air, he stumbled his way back to the cabin, the sound of his own frantic footsteps echoing in his ears. Panic consumed him as he tried to convince himself that it was all just a figment of his imagination, his mind playing cruel tricks on him.

He hoped Lily had sought refuge in the safe room, finding solace within the cold, impenetrable walls of steel. He couldn't bear the thought of her willingly surrendering herself to a hit man, unless ... unless it was the only way to protect his family from danger.

Stephen flung open the front door, the force causing the screen to collide with the door frame, creating a jarring noise that reverberated through the hallway. In a daze, he sprinted down the corridor towards the safe room, his pounding heart drowning out all other sounds. Desperation etched on his face, he pounded on the steel door, the sound echoing in the enclosed space. With a creak, the door swung open, revealing his disheveled and tear-stained mother standing beside it.

His gaze darted past his mother, searching for Lily's captivating green eyes that held the depths of her soul. "Where's Lily?" he pleaded, his voice filled with a mix of fear and urgency.

"She never made it here." His mother's words barely registered as Stephen's mind raced. Without wasting another moment, he sprinted towards the guest room where Lily had been staying. Praying fervently, he barged into the room, hoping to find her peacefully sleeping on the bed.

Silence engulfed him as his eyes swept over the small room, fixating on his grandmother's ring left behind on the dresser. A sinking feeling settled in his chest. Why had Lily taken it off? The answer was obvious—she didn't plan on returning. She sacrificed her own life for the sake of his family's safety.

"Lily, why?" Coarse rage pulsed through his body, causing him to fall to his knees, his fingers tightly clenched into a fist. Frustration boiled inside him, searching for something to punch.

God, I can't lose her. What is going on? His happy engagement turned into a twisted nightmare; one he didn't know if he'd wake up from.

Stephen's trembling hand instinctively swooped a crumpled piece of paper off the cold, hard floor. The weight of the words stared back at him, causing a knot of anguish to tighten in his chest. The room was suffocatingly silent, save for the distant sound of a clock ticking relentlessly, mocking his helplessness. He clenched the note as if it held the secrets of his love's disappearance. Darkness engulfed his soul, shrouding his every thought, as despair flooded his heart like a torrential downpour. Each breath felt labored, as if the very act of living had become an insurmountable challenge.

Paul stood silently in the doorway, his fingers caressing the sides of his face. "We'll find her."

"How?" Stephen mumbled the words, his strength too low to speak.

"God didn't bring you both this far to forsake you now." Paul slid his phone out of his pocket. "I need to make a few phone calls."

Stephen grabbed Lily's pullover off the bed, finding comfort in the lilac-scented fabric. Lily's scent engulfed his nostrils, sending a balm to his troubled heart. He climbed off the floor as a new resolve echoed in his heart. He would find her and when he did, he'd never let her go.

****

"Let go of me." Lily jerked her arms away from the thug with the iron grip. "Not like I didn't come willingly."

The thug, barely taller than her, with balding hair and a potbelly, pushed her into a metal chair in the middle of an empty room.

"Sit. The boss will be here soon." A sly smile spread across his wrinkled face. "Then he can deal with you."

"Let's get this over with." Maybe she could persuade the boss to keep her around. What was worse, death or marrying the head of a crime organization? The worst was marrying a man other than Stephen, knowing she'd never have her happily ever after with him.

Lily straightened her back in the chair. She had made the right decision. Even though it felt like a stabbing pain traveling through her body. She moved the danger away from a family that deserved all the peace and happiness life offered. She could have trusted Paul and Stephen to take down the drug lord and secured her freedom. But could they really take down a man whose reach extended to multiple countries? Doubtful. No, it was better this way. Besides, she didn't even know where they were. Only thing she remembered seeing was a sign for HWY 411 N. From the landscape, they weren't in rural Tennessee anymore. Maybe Knoxville.

The door creaked open, emitting an eerie sound that sent shivers down Lily's spine. A tall, skinny man stepped into the dimly lit room. His dark hair shimmered under the harsh fluorescent light, casting an ominous glow. It was not the image she had expected. Tony Cores, the notorious head of the Cores' drug enterprise, was supposed to be a scarred, wrinkled man in his sixties, not a youthful and baby-faced individual like the one standing before her. Although he couldn't be her age, he appeared disturbingly close.

As he approached her, his presence seemed to slice through her thoughts like a knife. A cloud of overpowering, cheap cologne enveloped her, assaulting her senses and making it difficult to breathe. The scent hung heavy in the air, suffocating and nauseating. "So, we meet again," he said, a smirk spreading across his handsome face.

Lily's heart skipped a beat as the man kneeled down, his gaze locked onto her face. His finger traced along the contour of her lip, sending a wave of revulsion coursing through her. She fought back the urge to vomit, her pulse racing as she stared into the eyes of the man she had once foolishly loved. How could she have been so blind? What was he doing here? Was this some sick joke? Everyone from her past who knew about their relationship was dead, or so she thought.

And then, as if fate was playing a cruel game, Ronald's squeaky voice pierced the air, causing goosebumps to rise on Lily's arms. She couldn't believe her eyes. What were the odds that her old boyfriend was actually a part of the Cores family?

"Surprised to see me?" He leaned closer, planting a kiss on her cheek. "My beautiful Lily. I've planned so meticulously for our reunion. Aren't you glad to see me?"

She had so much she wanted to say, but words refused to escape her lips. *God, what is going on?*

"All my efforts and actions over the years had led up to this very moment. I've successfully eliminated every single hurdle. Nothing stands in our way."

What in the world was he talking about? Eyes that once offered her love, now cold and lifeless. Eleven years. They broke up Eleven years ago, and somehow, he knew all about her and was hoping for a jubilant reunion? Not happening.

"I see the doubt in your eyes. But, baby, we can finally be together. Nothing or no one stands in our way." Lily crossed her arms over her chest. This was not happening.

"Talk to me, baby." He lifted her chin, staring into her eyes.

"What? How? I don't even know where to begin."

"Let's forget the past and start fresh today. I can fly us to a wedding chapel in less than an hour." He reached for her hand as she slapped it away.

Darkness clouded his black eyes as he scooted away from her, falling into a padded chair.

"Tell me everything. Now."

"The abbreviated version." Ronald's chuckle echoed through the steel walls of the warehouse. "I never intended to end our relationship at eighteen. Your father found out about my heritage; mostly the Cores' name. He threatened me, so he had to die. I never intended for you to get trapped in the fire. Miscalculated mistake."

"You killed my father?" With a sudden burst of frustration, she leaped out of her chair, determined to wipe the smug look off his face. Brawny hands yanked her back into her chair so hard her back hit the bottom of the chair, sending pain shooting through her body.

"He never loved you, anyway."

"Maybe, but you didn't have to kill him." She hunched over in the chair, feeling a panic attack trying to form in her stomach.

"Jason…"

"What about my brother?" Lily took a deep, calming breath.

"His love of money signed his death certificate." Ronald wiped at an invisible piece of lint on his black pants. "As a CIA agent investigating my family, he had to die."

"What did you do?" She growled out the words, ready to attack.

"I showed him what actual power was. After getting mixed up in my organization and drug trafficking, his name tarnished. His agency didn't believe him anymore."

"You killed him."

"Like I had a choice. He stole some incriminating information from me, enough to die for. You were the icing on the cake."

"How dare you?" She wanted to jump out of the chair and deck him in the face, but his bodyguard wouldn't let her go. "What happened to Tony?"

"You mean my old-fashioned uncle? He had to die, too." Ronald stepped to her side, but far enough away to avoid her legs and arms. "Don't you see, baby. Everything that's happened has brought us together."

"You're a monster!" She gritted her teeth, struggling with the guard for the freedom of her arms.

"Only thing that stood in our way was that lousy boyfriend. I'm disappointed. I thought what we had was real." He ran his calloused finger along her cheek.

"If you touch him or his family…"

"You'll what? Kill me? Then you'll be no better than me." He stepped away from Lily and leaned into his chair. "I'm not worried about your boyfriend. I'm a real man, and he could never compete. Besides, his wellbeing is up to you."

Fire raged in Lily's eyes. How could this be happening? After all these years, Ronald was keeping tabs on her. She felt violated.

"Baby, where should be tie the knot at? The Bahamas? Las Vegas? You name it, and I'll make it happen." He rubbed his palms together, smiling.

"I'll never marry you!"

"Oh, but you will." He jumped up from his chair, circling around her. "If you refuse, I'll kill off your boyfriend's family, one person at a time. The best part, you'll have a front-row seat."

"Never! You monster." Lily broke free from the guard and gripped the front of Ronald's jacket. Fighting the urge to take him down.

"Guard, take her away." He motioned to his guard and pointed to a room on the side. "Two hours. Afterwards, you either marry me or watch your boyfriend die."

Lily's body trembled under the weight of the guard. *God, I can't fight this evil.*

"And, baby, your fiery spirit will come in handy as the wife of the biggest drug lord in the US."

The guard tossed her in a room no bigger than a closet, sealing her doom. Tears poured down her pale face. All hope fleeing her body.

****

Stephen smashed the paper cup between his fingers as he stared at the white wall. Too much caffeine and his insides were about to explode. He felt like a caged animal, ready to pounce on his prey. He had spent the rest of Christmas day searching the Internet for any clues of the Cores family's hideout. Of course, Paul didn't actually need his help with his partner back in town, but Stephen needed to stay busy or he'd go insane.

After a round of phone calls, Paul met his partner at the Knoxville police station. He wanted Stephen to stand down and wait with their family until they had rescued Lily. Fat chance of that happening. Besides, someone might need a doctor. And Paul couldn't even wrap a bandage on right. The waiting game was never something he did well. Too much energy and built up nerves to relax in an uncomfortable chair, sipping stale coffee.

What he wouldn't give for a Christmas do-over. Rejoicing in the amazing company of his fiancée, while watching his nieces tear into their gifts. He hadn't seen the look on their faces as they unwrapped their ponies. He could imagine their gleeful squeals at the sight of their long-haired pets. But none of that mattered now. His family was safe at the cabin with his combat-skilled dad as their bodyguard.

He couldn't relax until Lily, his exotic princess, rested safely in his arms. Stephen tried to pray, but his mind wouldn't focus past a few jumbled sentences. The scent of coffee filled the air, making his stomach churn. God knew his heart and the words he needed to pray, but couldn't. That had to be enough, because Stephen counted on God to bring his fiancée home.

"I think we got something." Paul set a laptop down in front of Stephen's chair. His suit coat had come off an hour ago, replaced by a Christmas-themed dress shirt with rolled-up sleeves.

Stephen leaned toward the desk, staring at a list of addresses. The flickering fluorescent lights above him cast a pale glow on the room. "What am I looking at?"

"Properties listed under the Cores' Enterprise." Paul leaned against the edge of the desk. His buddy, the Knoxville police chief, let him take up station at the department as well as using their resources. Granted, his officers would get a piece of the action, being in their jurisdiction and all.

"It's an extensive list," Stephen frowned. The faint hum of computers filled the room, accompanied by the occasional ringing of phones. No way would they rescue Lily in time.

"Officers are doing a drive by, seeing if any of the properties are leaking with activity." Paul glanced at the clock on the wall. The ticking of the second hand seemed to echo in the silence. "Should hear from them soon."

"I have some disturbing news." A man equal in height to Stephen, yet baby-faced and barely old enough to hold a gun, stepped to the desk.

"Stephen, this is Detective Zach Rivers, my new partner." Paul took the file from Detective Rivers' extended hand. The scent of freshly brewed coffee wafted through the room, mixing with the faint smell of ink from the printed documents.

"The department is recruiting them young these days. You know how to use that gun?" A playful smirk spread across Stephen's sleep-deprived face.

"Don't knock my youthfulness cause you don't have any." Zach's southern drawl slurred out the words.

Stephen raised his hands in surrender, smiling. "Detective, it'll take your grit to stay alive in our potted-plant-stealing community."

"Doctor, don't act all innocent. My partner informed me how trouble gravitates toward you."

Stephen choked back a chuckle. The weight of the room seemed to lighten, filled with a sense of camaraderie. "Okay, men, back to the case."

"Unbelievable." Paul flipped through the file, letting out a low whistle.

"What?"

"Tony Cores' body washed up on the Mississippi River bank three days ago." Paul tossed the folder on the desk, a hard look glazed over his dark eyes. "He's not running the show anymore."

"Question is, who is?" Detective Rivers sank into the worn leather chair, its creak echoing in the dimly lit room. "Who would dare to eliminate the most feared drug lord in

North America and emerge unscathed, ready to seize control?" he mused aloud.

Paul glanced up from his phone screen, the glow casting a soft blue light on his face, before swiftly snatching his jacket from the chair's back. The fabric whispered against his fingertips as he hastily tugged it on. "Officers discovered two buildings teeming with activity," he informed, his voice tinged with urgency. "A witness reported seeing a woman who matched Lily's description enter nearly two hours ago. Though it's quieter now, it might be worth a drive by."

Stephen, his heart pounding with determination, gripped the edges of his jacket and pulled it up, revealing the glint of a holstered gun. The metal clasps clicked softly as he secured it in place. "Count me in," he declared, his voice brimming with unwavering resolve. Even if they cuffed him to a chair, he'd break free. With purposeful strides, he followed the detectives, the sound of his footsteps echoing through the corridor.

"You have a permit for that gun? Do you even know how to use it?" Detective River's voice drawled with humor.

"Don't worry about me. I'm just back up."

As they reached the unmarked SUV, Stephen's breath mingled with the crisp evening air, forming faint puffs of vapor. He slid into the backseat, the worn leather sticking slightly to his palms. The scent of aged leather and faint traces of cologne filled his nostrils, mingling with the anticipation that hung heavy in the air.

With a quick flick of the wrist, Paul shifted the gear into Drive and sped down the road, the tires screeching. "Remember, no heroics," he warned, emphasizing the importance of caution.

Like he would really stay in the background if his fiancée needed him. Stephen would do whatever it took to see she got out of this situation alive. Being bullheaded wasn't part of the plan or going rogue. But he'd step in where needed.

Paul eased the SUV into an abandoned-looking building in the middle of downtown Knoxville. No cars parked in the lot or visible signs of occupancy.

"Is this the place?" Detective Rivers fidgeted with the gun in the holster. Apparently, nerves shot through his veins.

"Yeah, something about the eerie silence doesn't sit right with me." Paul checked his gun chamber before sliding it back into his shoulder holster.

"You okay, rookie?" Stephen gripped the door, ready to jump out of the backseat and into action.

"Haven't been a rookie in more than a year." Zach gritted his teeth together, clearly uncomfortable with his status as a law enforcement officer.

"No time for this," Paul muttered under his breath as he gripped the handle of his car door. The metal latch clicked as he pulled it open, and a rush of cool evening air filled the vehicle. Stepping out onto the pavement, he moved with silent precision, his footsteps barely making a sound.

"Stephen, stand back," Paul whispered, his voice barely audible. "And do nothing stupid."

Stephen nodded, his heart pounding in his chest. He could feel the tension in the air as they approached the building. It was a mix of excitement and fear, a cocktail of adrenaline that surged through his veins. The scent of damp earth mingled with the faint aroma of exhaust fumes, a reminder of the world outside their mission.

As they neared the entrance, Stephen took a slow, calming breath. His senses heightened. He could hear the distant hum of traffic in the background, a symphony of city sounds. The building loomed before them, its darkened windows a mystery waiting to be unraveled.

He fought the urge to charge in, to unleash his inner Rambo, knowing that there was no room for mistakes. Instead, he relied on his faith, praying silently that God would guide their every step, granting them victory in the unknown.

****

"What's your decision?" Ronald folded his arms over his chest, revealing his family crest tattooed on his upper arm.

Lily stared wildly at him. She had spent an hour locked in a smelly, damp closet. She still didn't know what to do. Lily had begged God for deliverance, but none came. Her old self would blame God, and being at the top of His hit list. She didn't believe that anymore. God's plans were not her own. Even though she didn't understand it, she'd trust Him until her dying breath. She owed Him that much. Unexplainable peace had flooded her soul, and she knew everything would be fine. Whether that meant deliverance or death, she was ready for both.

"Are you ready to be Mrs. Cores, or ready to watch your new family die?" His sharp words cut through the tension in the room. Lily wasn't ready for either. She gazed into the face of the guy she thought she was in love with twelve years ago. Against her father's warnings, she would sneak out of the house, dashing off with her eighteen-year-old boyfriend. Only being fifteen, that probably wasn't the smartest thing she did, but she thought he loved her. Her sixteen-year-old heart couldn't take his rejection when he broke up with her once she moved to foster care. Knowing he had set the fire, killing her father, which ultimately sent her to foster care, lit a fire in her heart.

Lily wanted to smack him in the face. His arrogant attitude hadn't changed. But how did she not know back then that he was Ronald Cores, a part of the largest criminal family in North America? He must have used his mother's maiden name, Fisher, to weasel his way into her heart. She was a fool. If she accepted his proposal, she was still a fool. But Stephen and his family would be safe, if she believed a low-down criminal. Ronald would probably treat her well, besides holding her against her will, making sure she never left him. They'd raise a family of lawless children, bent on taking their roles in the drug trade. Forget about God and church. No way would He approve of lying, stealing, drug trafficking and everything else that entails a life of crime.

For Stephen's safety, she'd do anything. Sucking in a deep breath, she muttered, "I'll marry you." All life seeped out of her body at the words.

A sly smile spread across Ronald's semi-handsome face. "Good choice." He nodded to his bodyguard. "Find Stephen Smith, and make sure he's disposed of. I'd hate for my wife to run off with him one day."

"No!" Lily jumped in Ronald's face, clutching his shirt with her fingers. "You promised his safety for marriage."

"Guess I'm not trustworthy." He shrugged his shoulders, prying her fingers off his shirt.

"You liar!" Lily spit the words out. No way would she marry him now.

Ronald's bodyguard grabbed Lily's arm, twisting it behind her back as pain pierced through her body. "Call off your bodyguard, and fight like a man."

"Oh, baby, there'll never be a dull moment in our marriage with your fiery personality." Ronald rubbed his finger over her top lip, smiling.

"Don't touch me." She spewed out the words like fire as she chomped her teeth like a dog ready to bite off the enemy.

"This whole warrior persona is attractive." He took a step away from her, motioning to his guard. "Leave us alone. I need to get reacquainted with my soon-to-be bride."

The guard unhooked Lily's arms as the blood started flowing again. With a sigh of relief, she whispered a quick prayer for God's deliverance.

"Baby, we're leaving in thirty minutes for our destination wedding." He slid a plastic rope out of his pocket. "Until then, I need to make sure you don't escape." He secured her arms in the rope, pulling to tighten it around her wrist.

"I refuse to go with you." Fire burned in her eyes as she tried wiggling her hands. Pointless. The rope was too tight. Who taught him how to tie a rope? A Boy Scout?

"Then I'll kill each member of your boyfriend's family, making it long and painful. And I still won't let you escape." He winked his eyes at her like he had just spoken of something charming instead of evil.

If she had a slight hope of Stephen rescuing her, she'd hold Ronald off, but no way could he find her. But it couldn't hurt stalling him. Once she got on the plane, there would be no turning back.

"Why me?" Lily wiggled her bound hands, hoping to get some feeling into her fingers.

"You were impossible to forget." His voice held no emotions at all.

"It's been eleven years." She plopped down in the metal chair, staring at Ronald's profile. The years had not been kind to him. His blue eyes were icy like stone, and his once baby-face had visible scars and fine lines.

"At eighteen, I would have married you, if not for your insane father. He didn't know what was best for you. He barely knew you." Ronald pounded his fist in his hand, cursing under his breath.

"I wasn't even sixteen when we met. You used my grief and loveless life to take advantage of me. I thought you loved me until you left." Why was she so naïve? How could a guy like him love anyone but himself?

"Love, lust, what's the difference? All I know is I had to climb up the ladder of my father's business. Once I did, I planned to find you and marry you." He shot her an uneasy look. "It didn't happen that way. You disappeared from the face of the planet. Until I ran into Jason. Then everything fell into place."

"You turned me away from love and destroyed me." She couldn't stand casually sitting around talking to this jerk like they were friends. They would be nothing. If he forced her to marry him, she would escape. Maybe not right away, but when he least expected it.

"Works for me. Now I can have you all to myself." A smile spread across his face. "Speaking of which, it's almost time to get hitched."

Nausea rolled through her stomach. This must be a nightmare. She could not be marrying a ghost from her past. *God, intervene.*

The metal front door swung open as the guard kicked a figure inside the warehouse. Unease covered Lily's body as she stared at the man she longed to spend forever with.

"Look who we have here." Ronald stepped to Stephen's side as he threw his arm back, landing a blow to Stephen's stomach.

All hope of rescue disappeared as Lily stared in unbelief at Stephen's hunched over, bloody body. Her future was over. Stephen's future was over. Lost to the hands of the Cores family and their evil grip.

****

Well, that didn't go quite as planned. Stephen held his ribcage as pain shot through his body. So, he went rogue and approached the building once he heard Lily's high-pitched voice. No backup or solid plan. He was going Rambo style, expect guns weren't blazing, and the enemy had captured him. If he made it out of this alive, Paul would give him a piece of his mind. No matter, he knew how foolish his actions were. But he couldn't stand the idea of some thug hurting his woman. Gun in hand, he slid around the building, hoping to sneak in undetected. He didn't know that a guard would exit the building at the exact time. Knocking Stephen off balance, the creep got the upper hand. Thus, why he was beat up and bloody. It didn't hurt as bad as it looked. He could still fight, even if the guy frisked him and stole his guns away. His dad taught him how to fight with only his hands as weapons. He just needed to fake his injuries enough for them to think his defenses were gone. Then, he'd strike at the right time. Pain didn't matter as he laid eyes on his love. Lily, the definition of beauty, seemed unharmed, besides a fire burning in her green eyes.

"I'm so glad you could drop in." Ronald's voice held a hint of amusement. "Stephen Smith, ER doctor, age twenty-eight. Son of Ken and Lea Smith."

How did this guy know everything about him? He knew nothing about him, only he wasn't Tony Cores. Who was this joke? And how did he know Lily?

"I see the hint of confusions in your eyes, doctor." Ronald circled around him, standing next to Lily, arms circled around her waist. "Lily and I go way back, first love and all."

What? That didn't even make sense. Who was he? Stephen glanced at Lily. Her breathing was rapid and her face pale. Not another panic attack.

"Ronald, the new head of the Cores legacy." Ronald extended his hand, then retracted it fast. "You can call me Lily's fiancé."

Seriously? I don't think so. Stephen stood all the way to his feet, feeling blood dripping from his face. He just wanted five minutes to teach this thug a lesson on respect. And not to put his hands on his fiancé.

"Stephen…" Lily spoke, but Ronald tugged her closer to his side, cutting off her words.

"You don't owe him any explanation. The better man got the girl. End of the story." Ronald ran his lips over Lily's cheek.

Steam boiled in his heart at the sight of this creep grazing his lips over *his* fiancé. Before Stephen could react, Lily had rammed her elbow into Ronald's side, causing him to bend over breathless.

That's my girl. Pride swelled in his heart at the twinkle in her luscious eyes. Without waiting for Ronald to recover, Stephen planted an uppercut on Ronald's chin, sending him splattered to the concrete floor.

Lily gasped as she ran into Stephen's arms, hiding her face from the sight of Ronald. Blood trickled onto the concrete floor.

"He can't hurt you anymore." Stephen stroked the top of her head with his hand. She was safe. Maybe his rejoicing was premature. The bodyguard swooped into position and knocked Stephen to the ground. His vision blurred as he banged his head on the concrete ground.

"Let go of me," Lily's voice screamed as Stephen fought to stay conscious.

With Ronald down, he only needed to take out one more person to secure Lily's freedom. What happened to Paul and Zach? He could use some backup.

Stephen climbed off the cold floor, stumbling to stay on his feet. "Get your hands off her."

"You gonna stop me?" The guard tightened his grip on Lily's arm.

"Not this time." Stephen's vision blurred as he saw Paul and Zach creep into the building.

"Police, let go of Belle." Paul pointed his gun at the thug as Zach cuffed Ronald. "There's no way out. Let her go."

The thug dropped Lily's arm, grabbing his gun, trying to fire a round as Stephen tackled him to the ground. Paul ran to his friend's side, slapping cuffs on the guard's wrists.

Three Knoxville police officers ran into the building, guns raised.

"Take them away." Paul motioned to the two guys in cuffs. He turned to Stephen, helping him off the ground. "Stupid move, Smith."

"But?" Stephen wrapped his arms around Lily's waist, basking in her closeness. He never wanted to let go.

"Thanks for having my back." Paul grunted the words as his partner stopped in front of Stephen, shaking his head.

"Took you long enough to get in the building," Stephen said.

"Someone ambushed us. It took us a few minutes to break through the thugs to step inside." A smirk spread across Zach's face. "You handled yourself well. If you ever tire of being a doctor, we could use more men like you on the force."

"No thanks, Rivers." Stephen wrapped his arms around Lily as he led her to the metal door. "I'll stick to my calling and appreciate yours even more now."

"Don't leave. I need both of your statements."

"We'll be outside. We need a minute alone." Stephen opened the door and led Lily outside into the chilly evening air. It was still Christmas day. And God had performed a Christmas miracle.

Lily clung to his arm. Through teary eyes, she gazed into his face. "You saved me, again. And God knows I did not want to marry him."

Peace flooded Stephen's soul as he leaned over, brushing a kiss over her lips. "Who would you rather marry?"

"There's this insanely brave man who is both charming and incredibly smart. I'm not sure if he still wants me and all of my trouble, but I'm in love with him."

Stephen reached into his pocket, feeling the smooth texture of the ring between his fingers. "I love you so much," he whispered, his voice filled with tenderness. "I'll ask you again. Will you marry me?"

"Yes. Forever and ever." Stephen slid the ring on her finger, knowing that nothing would tear them apart again.

Epilogue

"What do you think, Mrs. Smith?" Stephen clasped his hands in Lily's as they walked around a partly constructed build.

A giant smile spread across her olive-tinted face. "I love it. It's way better than the farmhouse here before."

So much had happened since Ronald Cores and his thugs had attacked Lily and Stephen. They finished Christmas day, praising God as they surrounded themselves with their family. Not wanting to spend any more time apart, they enjoyed a small wedding ceremony on New Year's Day. Lily had never felt so loved or cherished before. Starting the new year as a married couple felt so right. He was the other half that she never knew she needed. Everything about his perfectly flawed personality suited her. She didn't even mind when he threw his clothes on the floor or left his dirty dishes in the sink. Though he was trying harder, just to his mother's delight. The domesticated life suited Lily. She'd never stop praising God for the new life He had given her.

"Pinch me." Stephen's blue eyes glistened in the morning light.

"Happy to oblige." Lily squeezed Stephen's arm hair, giving him a little pinch. "You know, all of this is real."

"I have to keep reminding myself that. Not sure how I ever wanted to live the bachelor's life permanently." He stepped past a row of lilies, basking in the morning light in the garden.

"How long have we been married?" She pulled at the bottom of her shirt, as butterflies danced in her stomach. How would Stephen take her news? He enjoyed married life, but life moved fast and they didn't plan everything.

"Seven glorious months."

"What do you think the next step in our lives are?" Lily guided him to the swing behind the house. She hoped she liked the answer he'd give her.

"I've been praying about us working with Doctor's Without Borders. A team is going to Africa in two months." Stephen gently pulled Lily down next to him, wrapping his arms around her waist. "I know it's sudden, but we need to travel before we start a family. What to you say?"

Sure, she could go, but she didn't want to take the chance of catching anything in her vulnerable state. Time to break the news to her husband. "It's a great idea."

"Awesome. I'll go contact the director and get everything started." Stephen jumped up from the swing, but not letting go of Lily's hand.

"Sit down, honey. We need to talk."

Stephen's smile faded as he edged himself into the swing. She stared into his ocean-blue eyes, never getting over the love she saw reflected there.

"Don't worry, you're not in trouble," she smiled, hoping he'd relax.

"I was hoping you, Mom, and Belle weren't setting up an intervention for my messy ways." He squeezed her hand as a glint of humor flashed in his eyes. "I picked up my laundry off the floor today and washed a load."

"And turned my whites pink, but that's a talk for another day."

"I'm a work in progress, sweetie." He leaned over and planted a kiss on her cheek. "Seriously, what do you want to talk about?"

"The floor plan." Why couldn't she just blurt it out?

"Okay."

"I think we need to add a bedroom next to the master bedroom." Lily gestured with her hands.

"Not in the original plans, but we can make it work." He raised his eyebrows and looked at her comically. "What does that have to do with postponing the mission trip? Just spit it out?"

"I'd like to be cautious. Considering I've never experienced this before." She touched her stomach, smiling.

"Are we dancing around the topic?" Stephen's mouth fell open as he grabbed her fingers in his. "Are you pregnant?"

A dazzling smile covered her face. "I thought you'd never guess. Tell me you're not upset."

"Are you kidding? I'm gonna be a daddy." Stephen jumped up from the swing, hollering in excitement. "I've never been happier."

He picked her up, squeezing her in his arms, thanking God for answering prayers that he never prayed and rejecting prayers that weren't God's plan for his life. The future looked amazing, and with God in the front, they'd never go wrong.

THE END

Fleeing from Danger, Jessica West

Deadly Stalker

An East Tennessee Mystery Series

Book 3

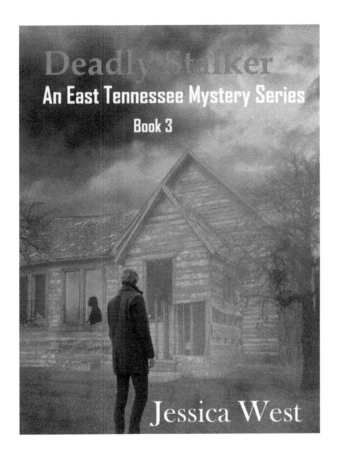

Deadly Stalker Preview:

"Pretty flowers, Ms. Smith," a student called over her shoulders as she yanked her book bag off the peg and raced into the hall.

Kayla stared at the bouquet of white roses. When was the last time anyone had sent her flowers? She stuffed a folder of papers into her bag, hoping to grade them later, when her mind could focus. Her pulse quickened as she stared at the harmless roses. To a bystander, the roses looked like a thoughtful gift, but to her, the contents of the vase sent goosebumps crawling over her arms.

Get a grip, Kayla. Nothing nefarious is happening. One of your students sent flowers. End of the story. Except she had been a teacher for a year, and the only thing her sixth-grade students sent her was a hard time. At twenty-three, and a recent college graduate, Kayla didn't have her pick of schools. She had a lot to prove and the McMinn County Schools were the only school system willing to take a risk on her non-experienced-self. The old sixth-grade English teacher retired suddenly, putting the school in a bind. Thus, why they hired her. Moving to East Tennessee after attending NC State was a big decision, but she didn't regret being closer to family.

The roaring bell knocked her out of her thoughts as an attractive man in his late-twenties sauntered into the classroom. "Secret admirer?"

"What?" Kayla shook her head, causing her bangs to fall over her eyes. "No." Why was he in her room again? The man never gave up.

"I thought you didn't date? Someone thinks otherwise." He leaned against her desk, staring at her with a predatory stare. Something about Thomas Holmes made her uncomfortable. He had worked for the public school system as a substitute math teacher for three years before transferring to Athens City Middle School full time.

"A sweet gesture from a parent." Kayla's fingers trembled as she stuffed the rest of the papers in her bag. She wanted to get far away from Thomas and school for a few days. Good thing it was past three o'clock on a Friday.

"Not buying it." He trailed his fingers over the white envelope as Kayla snatched the card from his grip. "Who's my competition?"

"Please, Thomas, I'm not in the mood." Why didn't he take no for an answer?

"How about dinner at my place?" Thomas Holmes asked, his tan face illuminated by a bright smile. His brown eyes twinkled with anticipation. Kayla couldn't deny that he was attractive, but his persistence was overwhelming. She knew she couldn't date, not after that unforgettable night five years ago. The memory still haunted her, a constant reminder of her past weakness.

"No," Kayla replied firmly, her wavy blond hair swaying as she tossed it to the side. She adjusted her strap on her shoulder, feeling the weight of it. All she wanted was to retreat to the comfort of her home and indulge in a relaxing bubble bath, hoping to wash away the tension that had built up. But first, she had to dismiss Thomas so she could finally escape.

"You're no fun." He touched the top of her arm as warnings flared up her body.

"It's been a stressful day. I just want to drown my sorrows in a carton of mint chocolate chip ice cream while watching horrible reality television."

"Bobby White, again?" He pounded his fist in his open palm. "Someone needs to teach that kid a lesson."

"I'll settle on teaching him how to diagram a sentence." Kayla gripped the card between her sweaty fingers. If not for the phone calls and eerie feeling of being watched, she'd assume the flowers were an innocent gesture, but nothing was that simple.

"Read the card already." He snatched the envelope out of her fingers, smirking at her astonished look. "Soon, my sweet Care Bear, we'll meet, and no one will separate us again." His voice trailed off at the words.

"Give me the card." Her pulse quickened as the words attacked her common sense. She was tired of this silly mind game. Who was stalking her? No, not stalking, sending unwanted extra attention. Maybe it was Thomas, but his forward ways would never hide behind a mystery admirer.

"Kind of creepy, if you want my opinion." He ran his fingers through his tad-bit-too-long brown hair. "Need me to follow you home? I have a black belt in karate."

"Generous offer, but Sarah and Rachel should be home by now." Kayla glanced at the wall clock as the second hand quickened around the clock.

"Oh, yes, your infamous sisters that I have yet to meet." He flashed her his million-dollar smile. The kind that caused half the female teachers at Athens Middle School to swoon over his charm. Not her. She dealt with too many good-looking-I-always-get-what-I want types to last a lifetime.

"I can be a true Southern gentleman. Let me escort you to your car." He slid her bag off her shoulders, clenching the strap between his large fingers.

"You're too persistent," Kayla huffed in exasperation. "Go pick on another female teacher." She grabbed her bag from his fingers, frowning.

"Fine, but you won't get rid of me that easily." He saluted, then stepped into the hall. His shoes echoing down the tiled-hall.

"Finally." Kayla tossed the roses into the trashcan, flipping off the lights.

She stepped into the empty, darkened hall as the silence sent a wave of panic coursing through her body. Heavy footsteps sounded down the long corridor of the first floor of the school. Thomas? No, his footsteps had a musical swag to them. Besides, he probably slipped out after her rejection.

"Hello?" Her voice bounced off the lockers.

Silence.

Why did Kayla insist on parking in the farthest lot from her classroom? Probably because she was at the bottom of the totem pole and Principal Langley had designated the suitable spots for his favorite staff. Which she would never be.

A low-pitched growl reverberated through the dimly lit hall, echoing ominously as the heavy footsteps drew nearer. *Stop being paranoid,* she chastised herself, her heart pounding in her chest. The faint scent of fear hung in the air, mingling with the faint aroma of musty books.

In her haste, her feet tangled together, causing her to stumble and crash onto the cold, unforgiving floor. Agonizing pain shot through her legs, intensifying the panic that surged within her. Frantically, she gathered her scattered papers, the crisp sound of rustling documents filling the tense silence.

Suddenly, a gloved hand clamped tightly over her mouth, stifling her desperate cries. Panic flooded her senses, suffocating her in its grip. No! Kayla pleaded silently, her muffled screams falling on deaf ears. The metallic tang of fear coated her tongue, her mind racing with a primal instinct to survive.

A deep, foreboding voice whispered into her ear, its chilling words causing goosebumps to erupt across her flesh. "Soon, Care Bear, we'll be together." The air turned heavy with an unsettling aura, thick with menace. Trembling, she felt a surge of adrenaline coursing through her veins, heightening her senses.

In a desperate bid for escape, Kayla's hand instinctively reached for a fallen pencil, its familiar weight giving her a sense of fleeting empowerment. With a swift, determined motion, she drove it into her assailant's shoulder, eliciting a startled grunt of pain. Without daring to look back, she sprinted towards the exit, her heart pounding in her ears.

Outside, the cool evening air washed over her, offering a momentary respite from the suffocating fear that had consumed her. She hurriedly made her way to her small Dodge Journey, her trembling hands fumbling with the keys. One glance at her flattened tire made her think things she shouldn't. She jumped into her car, locking the door behind her.

She punched in a number on her phone as she looked around for her assailant.

"What's up, Kayla?" The deep voice sounded over the phone.

"Someone attacked me at school, and my tire's flat." Her voice rose an octave as her fear tried to choke her.

"Where are you?"

"In the parking lot. Locked in my car." She checked her mirrors out of nervous habit.

"Stay put. My partner, Zach Rivers and I will be there soon."

"Zach Rivers?" It couldn't be. The universe wasn't that small.

"Yeah, we've worked together for two years."

He'd been in the same town as her for two years? Kayla leaned over as the phone slipped from her fingers. *I'm gonna be sick.*

"Kayla?" Ignoring his call, she opened the door and puked into the parking lot.

Milton Keynes UK
Ingram Content Group UK Ltd.
UKHW050500310724
446264UK00008B/96